I0667082

A Cowboy's Love

Books by J. M. Bronston

A PURRFECT ROMANCE

HER WINNING WAYS

SUMMER ON THE CAPE

A COWBOY'S LOVE

Published by Kensington Publishing Corporation

A Cowboy's Love

J. M. Bronston

LYRICAL SHINE
Kensington Publishing Corp.
www.kensingtonbook.com

To the extent that the image or images on the cover of this book depict a person or persons, such person or persons are merely models, and are not intended to portray any character or characters featured in the book.

LYRICAL SHINE BOOKS are published by

Kensington Publishing Corp.
119 West 40th Street
New York, NY 10018

Copyright © 2016 by J. M. Bronston

All rights reserved. No part of this book may be reproduced in any form or by any means without the prior written consent of the Publisher, excepting brief quotes used in reviews.

This book is a work of fiction. Names, characters, places, and incidents either are products of the author's imagination or are used fictitiously. Any resemblance to actual events or locales or persons living or dead is entirely coincidental.

All Kensington titles, imprints, and distributed lines are available at special quantity discounts for bulk purchases for sales promotion, premiums, fund-raising, educational, or institutional use.

Special book excerpts or customized printings can also be created to fit specific needs. For details, write or phone the office of the Kensington Sales Manager: Kensington Publishing Corp., 119 West 40th Street, New York, NY 10018. Attn. Sales Department. Phone: 1-800-221-2647.

Lyrical Shine and Lyrical Shine logo Reg. U.S. Pat. & TM Off.

First Electronic Edition: December 2016
eISBN-13: 978-1-60183-623-6
eISBN-10: 1-60183-623-6

First Print Edition: December 2016
ISBN-13: 978-1-60183-624-3
ISBN-10: 1-60183-624-4

Printed in the United States of America

ACKNOWLEDGMENTS

I am pleased to express my thanks to Liza Fleissig and Ginger Harris-Dontzin. They pack a ton of energy, enthusiasm, and effectiveness into their Liza Royce Literary Agency, and I am profoundly thankful for their encouragement and their hard work. I am also thankful for the unfailing care and attention I have received from John Scognamiglio, Rebecca Cremonese, Michelle Forde, Lauren Jernigan, and so many others at Kensington Books. They are an invaluable team and every writer should be so lucky.

My appreciation also goes to Sandra Kitt, a dear friend and reliable cheerleader who has held my hand and guided me through many steps of my literary journey. You blazed a trail, Sandi, and I am a fervent admirer.

Michael Anderson, Esq., a Utah attorney, gave me good information when I most needed it. And Google answered a thousand questions—at least a thousand—that were well outside my personal databank. Friends and relatives were sympathetic when I couldn't come out to play, and neighbors smiled and said, "We didn't want to bother you. We knew you were working."

I acknowledge also, in fond memory, Jim Brady, cowboy, horse whisperer and, in World War II, Navy frogman. This book owes so much to him.

And then there are my daughters. My dear, perfect three girls, Annie, Mary, and Margaret. To you I owe the most. Thank you.

Chapter One

A cloud of gritty, coppery dust swirled above the twisting back-hoe. It caught the sunset's light out of the big western sky, diffused it into sandy red and gold vapors, and drifted back to the desert floor where the big earth-moving machine was cutting a new interstate highway through the ragged sage and rabbit grasses of the wide-open range.

It often got to well over a hundred degrees out there in the desert, and the girl at the center of the cloud, sitting high up in the backhoe's swivel seat, wore only a tank top beneath her Day-Glo orange construction vest. Her arms, deeply tanned, shone with sweat despite the dry desert air and her pale blonde hair, hanging straight to her shoulders, was damp beneath the white hard hat. She lifted her work-gloved hand to brush the clinging strands away from her forehead.

With the big plastic pads protecting her ears from the noise of the racketing engine, she wouldn't have been able to hear the foreman's signal, but she knew, from the angle of the light as the sun moved toward the rim of the distant mountains, that it must be close to quitting time. She moved the boom to make the big bucket take one last bite of the sandy, red-gold earth, swung it to the side to drop its mouthful into the trench, and then pulled back the cuff of her glove to check her watch. Even as she did, Gordon Callister came up beside the rig and tapped the doorframe to catch her glance.

"Okay, Jamie," he said. "Time to knock off."

The girl lifted her hand, nodded her head in response, and Gordon moved on to signal the next man.

One by one, all along the construction site, the earth-moving machines stopped where they were and the operators dropped off them, leaving the machines scattered and still, under the slow-settling dust, where they would wait like yellow monsters until Monday morning, when they would be roused again to their slow, powerful work.

Jamie set the backhoe's big pod stabilizers and dropped the front loader to the ground. Then she switched off the engine and the cloud of dust that shimmered around her began its final slow descent. She climbed down from her high perch, peeled off her gloves and ear protectors, dropped them onto the shoulder-high fender, and headed to the construction shed to log out and pick up her paycheck.

"Hey, Jamie." The men were walking to their trucks and cars parked near the shed. "How about a couple of beers?"

Sounded good. A shower would be nice, too. And a change out of the dirty jeans and the heavy work boots. She undid the yellow bandana tied loosely around her throat, and wiped the back of her neck.

"Okay. Just a quick one. Where you guys headed?"

"We're going into town, to the Canyon Rim. Right off the interstate, just past the Chevron station. Know where it is?"

She forced a casual smile. "I know where it is."

I know where everything in this town is.

"Catch up with you there soon as I log out."

And these guys don't need to hear my life story.

She climbed the steps to the shed and went in to get her check.

One good thing about these big government contracts. Beside the good pay. Gordie's crews come from everywhere, and they don't stay around long enough to pick up the local gossip. Best to leave it that way.

When she reached her battered little green Civic, she tossed her hard hat onto the front seat and climbed in. She glanced into the rearview mirror and frowned at the reflection; she saw what fatigue and too much anger were doing to her. She raked her hands impatiently through her fine hair.

Twenty-four years old, and I'm already beginning to look like a mean old lady. The way things are going, I'm going to wind up tough and dry before I'm thirty. Like some old pinyon pine out in the desert.

She adjusted her sunglasses in the mirror.

But as long as Mandy is here in Sharperville, and the Nixons have her . . .

She couldn't help the anger and frustration that every day were etching their marks on her face. Two years since the divorce, and that judge gave custody to Ray. Not that Ray had ever wanted to be bothered with a two-year-old. He'd handed her right over to his parents, and Edna and Ervil Nixon just couldn't wait to grab their little grand-daughter away from Jamie. They'd never forgiven her for marrying their precious boy and they had jumped at the chance to bring up the child in what they called "the ways of righteousness."

God! How Jamie hated the Nixons and their smug show of self-important religious superiority. If they really were so full of piety, she thought, they couldn't possibly have been so cruel.

The anger and frustration were hard enough to live with, but just as painful was the humiliation. She looked again into the mirror and tried to smooth out her expression. Only she knew how ashamed she was. Ashamed of how they'd all outfoxed her. Ashamed of the way they'd done it, setting her up the way they did. Ray and that bitch, Tina, and the Nixons, too. And that other one . . .

She'd been so damned young, just a kid herself, with no one to help her, no one to advise her, and she hadn't known how to handle the whole thing. She'd been dumb and she'd made mistakes, and now, all she had left was a precious half day every other Saturday—one delicious afternoon every fourteen days. Followed always—*oh, God!*—by those awful long bouts of tears and sleepless nights.

She turned the key in the ignition and, for the thousandth time, the old Honda struggled to get going, and for the thousandth time she hoped she'd be able to keep her battered old wreck of a car running a couple of months longer. Maybe she could get one of the guys down at the service station to look it over for her, maybe patch it up again. The last thing she needed was to pour more nickels and dimes into her car. Every penny had to be saved so she could get herself a de-cent lawyer. This time, she was determined she'd get that custody award turned around.

But right now it would do her good to just kick back for a while, have a couple of beers with the guys. She switched the car's radio to the country setting out of Kanab, and let the easy music work its magic, smoothing away the angry tension at the back of her neck. With her paycheck in her pocket and the prospect of a visit with Mandy tomorrow, she felt a little better. She turned the old car south onto the empty highway and, humming along at last with the radio and squinting away from the big sun that was blazing its way west, down into the mountains that were still snow-tipped, even at this time of the year, Jamie headed toward town and a little relaxation.

*   *   *

The Canyon Rim got noisy on Friday evenings when construction crews and cowhands began to drift in, looking to spend their paychecks. Weekdays, it was a quiet place; just a few locals hanging out and maybe the sheriff stopping in for a cup of coffee, or the hunters, during deer season, finishing off their day in the mountains with a steak and some fries. But on Friday night, the dirt parking lot filled up early with pickup trucks and Yamaha bikes and Kawasakis. And a country band, well amplified, started up at six o'clock. By seven, the tiny dance floor was jammed.

This Friday night, when Jamie got there, the Canyon Rim was already loud with the throbbing music, the air was sharp with the smell of beer, and the air-conditioning was cool on her bare shoulders. She hiked her small frame up onto the empty barstool next to her foreman, Gordie, who always stopped in for one quick one on Friday nights—with a mental wink at his church's elders—before he went home to LaRaine and the seven kids. His orange hard hat was bright on the bar stool next to him; his summer straw Stetson was on his head. Milt, behind the bar, wiped off the space in front of her.

"What can I get for you, Jamie?"

"Let me have a Coors, Milt." She picked some tortilla chips out of the bowl in front of Gordon. "And can I get some salsa?"

"You betcha." Milt brought her the beer, setting it on the bar in front of her.

She turned on the stool and scanned the room quickly, looking for Harry Marsh and Hutch, and the other men from the crew.

"Where are the guys?" She swiveled on the stool to face Gordon. "They said they were coming down for a beer."

"They won't be in till later. Couple of days ago, Al Wideman spotted a big cougar up by his place—damned thing came right down into his alfalfa field, not a hundred yards behind his house, and today one of his calves turned up missing. Some of the guys went along to help him look. They'll be in later, soon's it gets dark." He scooped some salsa up on a chip and swallowed it all in one big bite. "But I'm staying only a minute, Jamie." He leaned his balding head closer to her as the music's volume was suddenly increased. "LaRaine and I have to be over at the school tonight. Coach says he's ready to put young Gordie into the game and we want to be there to cheer the kid."

"Sure thing, Gordie. I'm just going to listen to the music for a while. Then I'm headed home for a shower and a good night's sleep."

She swiveled around again and leaned her elbows back on the bar behind her. She let her gaze wander casually over the crowd on the floor, boisterous and boozy in the hazy light. It was just what she needed, just to hang out and enjoy the band and the good end-of-the-week intensity of the noisy dancers.

She was not aware that while she watched the couples on the dance floor there were other eyes on her. At least one person had been interested ever since she'd come through the door.

Orrin Dwayne Fletcher leaned against the far wall, nursing his third tequila. His buddies had already picked up a couple of girls and were out on the floor dancing, but O.D. was looking. Then Jamie walked in and he figured he'd found the action he'd been looking for. He was amused by the possibilities Jamie's arrival presented, and he watched for an opportunity to move in on her. He didn't need to wait more than a couple of minutes.

At the bar, Gordon finished his beer, resettled the Stetson in place over the remaining fringe of sparse, graying hair, and stood up from the stool.

"Okay, Jamie. I gotta go now." He dropped some bills next to his glass and picked up his hard hat. "See you on Monday morning. Have a good weekend."

"You, too, Gordie. And you tell that boy of yours to score at least one run for me." She waved after Gordon's disappearing figure as he made his way through the haze.

The stool next to Jamie wasn't empty for more than a moment. As soon as Gordon left the bar, Fletcher slipped into the vacant seat, setting his glass down roughly, letting his drink splash over his hand and wet the bar top.

"Well, well, well," he said. His speech was already thick and slurred. "Look at who's here."

Jamie's stomach clutched as she recognized the voice. Two years, but that was one voice she wasn't going to forget. She turned and saw him, an ugly part of her past, the same pale eyes, now tequila-clouded and mean, the same hollow face, the same thin-lipped, cold smile.

I'm in trouble.

Maybe if he hadn't surprised her, coming at her out of nowhere like that, maybe if she'd had a chance to prepare herself, she wouldn't have felt so frightened. Maybe she should have been able to handle him more calmly, but he was such a slimy little bastard, and he'd already done her so much harm . . .

"What are you doing in Sharperville, Orrin? I thought they had you locked up." She tried to keep her voice steady.

"Well, they did, Jamie. So they did." He circled his damp glass around and around in the little puddle he'd made on the bar top. "But not forever, y'know. Not forever. And now I'm out of there"—there was a sly edge to his voice—"and I just thought I'd check out Sharperville, see what's doing around here, look up some old friends. Maybe get a job or something, y'know?"

"That'll be the day," Jamie said. She pulled some dollars out of her pocket and laid them on the bar for Milt, but as she did, Fletcher reached toward her bare arm and, with one wet fingertip, lazily stroked the smooth skin. His touch disgusted her.

"Hey, Jamie, don't leave now, honey. I was thinking you and me could maybe pick up where we left off. I mean, shit, I never did forget that last, wonderful night we spent together."

The sonofabitch was having a good time. His eyebrows lifted in mock sincerity, as though he really, truly, expected her to believe him.

Jamie stood up abruptly. "I'm getting out of here, Orrin."

Drunk as he was, Orrin still responded quickly. One strong hand closed roughly over her wrist, pulling her back against the stool. "Hey, where you going, Jamie-girl? The evening's young and I just got here."

"Leave me alone, Orrin. Just leave me alone." Jamie twisted in his grip, but he wasn't letting her go.

"Hey, darlin' "—his eyes glittered—"is that any way to talk to an old drinking buddy?"

"Don't be stupid, Orrin. We sure as hell were never any kind of buddies."

She pulled helplessly against his grip as tears rose in her eyes.

Don't let me cry, not now, not here, not in front of him!

"Well, that's not the way I remember it. Seems to me the last night me and you spent together, we had some real fun." Orrin rubbed his free hand over his mouth, his fingers caressing the stubble on his cheek, as though he was enjoying the memory. His smile grew meaner, his eyes colder.

"You know it wasn't like that!"

She tried to pry his fingers loose but they only tightened on her wrist, hurting her. Panic filled her chest and she tried desperately to control it. "Please, Orrin!"

She could hear herself pleading and she tried to get the helplessness out of her voice. "Orrin, just leave me alone!"

This was the kind of thing Orrin Fletcher enjoyed. He knew he was scaring her.

"Well, now. Maybe you're right, Jamie. Maybe I have misremembered how it was that last time. It's been a couple of years, and a man forgets, sometimes, when he has more important things on his mind." He lifted his glass and swallowed the last of his drink, wiping his mouth with the back of his hand. "Of course, up at Bluffdale, I had other things to think about, but I'm out now, and I'm just visiting old friends here in town. Reestablishing old connections, you might say."

She tried to keep the fear out of her voice. "Orrin, I don't want any trouble. Just let go of my arm and I'll get out of here." She couldn't bear the feeling of his hand on her wrist, gripping her so casually, so easily. "I don't want to have to make a scene here." She sure didn't, not in front of all these people. "I just want to get home. Let me go, Orrin!"

"Sure, honey. No problem." Orrin was having a good time. "And I'll tell you what." He leaned close to her, his breath heavy against her face, his words slurred, only a bit above a whisper, almost drowned out by the raucous music and laughter that filled the air around them. "Just to be sure you get home safe, why don't I go along with you? Give us a chance to renew old memories. We can just walk out of here quiet-like, no one will ever know."

"No, Orrin, no!" Her fingers were frantic now, the tears imminent.

"Hey, Jamie. Take it easy, honey. We're just going to have a little fun."

Across the dance floor, Harvey Jackman set the pitcher of beer onto the table and dropped his big frame into his chair.

"What you staring at, Cal?" Harvey had picked his way, with considerable difficulty, through the noisy crowd of couples that filled the little patch of wooden floor, and his buddy seemed hardly aware that he'd arrived at their table.

Cal Cameron was leaning way back in his chair, resting it casually, just balanced, against the wall behind him, his thumbs hooked into the belt loops of his jeans, his long legs stretched out to brace the heels of his boots against the floor. His buff-colored Stetson was pushed to the back of his head, exposing black hair that curled above a deeply tanned face. A frown had drawn his black brows down, and his eyes, coal-black and narrowed slightly, were focused intently across the noisy room.

"Hey, Harvey. Who's the pretty little lady over at the bar?" He lifted his chin, gesturing toward Jamie. He hadn't taken his eyes off her since she'd walked in. "The little blonde in the orange vest." The little blonde, he was thinking, with the slim, trim shape that looked especially interesting in jeans and work boots and a Day-Glo construction vest. A small girl in what looked maybe to be in some big trouble.

Harvey was filling their glasses from the pitcher. He looked up and followed the line of Cal's gaze.

"Oh," he said after a quick glance. "That's Jamie Sundstrom." He finished pouring the beer and set the pitcher back onto the tabletop. A dismissive air passed over his good-natured face. "Only I'm not so sure you could call Jamie Sundstrom a lady." Immediately, as though in self-reproach, his smile became self-conscious and awkward; Harvey didn't like to speak unkindly of anyone.

Cal's eyebrows lifted questioningly, but he didn't take his eyes off Jamie. "She sure looks like a lady to me, Harv."

"Yeah, well, maybe so. All I know is I've heard talk that her family's no good, her dad's a drunk, her husband kicked her out, and the judge took her kid away from her. Couple of years ago."

"That's tough." Cal's frown was deepening as he continued to watch what was happening at the bar. "Still, Harvey, lady or not, she's just a little bit of a thing, and I don't like to see any man push a woman around the way that drunk sonofabitch is doing."

With a deliberate motion, he moved his hat forward, settling it down firmly on his forehead.

"Shoot, Cal. You going to start a fuss?"

"Don't worry, Harv. No fuss, no muss." Cal braced his hands on the table, letting his chair steady itself on its four legs, and he raised himself slowly from it. "This'll just take a minute."

Harvey sighed as Cal started across the room.

"Shoot," Harvey said, his words lost in the din that filled the place. "I thought we'd just stop in for a nice quiet drink before heading back to the ranch."

At the bar, Jamie was trying desperately to get out of Orrin's grip. He was hurting her arm and she was going to have to start yelling for help. But a scene, here in the bar, was the last thing she wanted. Waves of panic flooded through her as she cast her eyes helplessly around the smoke-filled, crowded room. That's when she saw the cowboy, his eyes fixed on Orrin, moving slowly toward them. She wasn't noticing much about him, scared as she was, except for that steady gaze and the solid build—that, and a slight limp, as though he'd hurt his knee.

The man came up close to them and his quiet voice reached her clearly through the boisterous racket of the music and the laughter.

"This fellow giving you any trouble, ma'am?" His dark eyes, cool and genial, smiled at her and relief beyond words flooded over her. Clearly he'd read the situation right and had come to rescue her.

Orrin's hand didn't move from Jamie's arm and his eyes glittered meanly.

"Shove off, cowboy." There was no smile on his face now. "We're just having a good time here."

"Is that right, ma'am?" The man's eyes held hers steadily. He seemed to be ignoring O.D. "You having a good time?" Jamie didn't need to answer. He could read the call for help that flashed from her eyes.

"Well, then," he said, making a move that was much too quick for Jamie to follow. His left hand closed over Fletcher's fingers, breaking his grip on Jamie and pulling the man's arm back, spinning him on the stool, to face the bar. In the same moment, the cowboy brought his right hand up under Fletcher's free arm, locking his fist against the back of O.D.'s neck. Holding Fetcher immobile in a powerful grip, he leaned his face down close to the back of Fletcher's head, speaking softly, directly into his ear.

"Now, buddy, I think maybe you had just a mite too much to drink tonight. So I'm going to ask your friends over there to do us all a big favor and take you on home." He tightened his grip on Fletcher, who winced painfully. "You hear me, buddy?"

"Yeah. Yeah! Jeez, cut it out! You're breaking my arm!"

"Not yet, I'm not."

Keeping Fletcher's arm pinned behind him, Cal pulled him off the stool and stood him up. He could feel the man's wobble and knew he was too drunk to cause any more real trouble tonight. Fletcher's pals were looking for him and Cal signaled them with a lift of his head. They sized up the situation right away and came over to the bar, laughing.

"Hey, O.D.," said the taller man, bow-legged and bearded, in faded jeans, "looks like you found yourself a little action after all."

"Whyn't you guys just get lost." Fletcher was muttering, suddenly resentful, his speech thickening. "I'm doing just fine without any of your help." The liquor had him now and between that and Cal's powerful grip, he was completely muddled.

"I think your friend here needs a ride home," Cal said, still holding on to Fletcher. "Think you guys can take care of that?'

"You betcha, cowboy." We'll get him out of here. No problem." Cal released Fletcher, and his friends each grabbed an arm, laughing as they walked him, staggering, through the crowd and out of the bar. "A little fresh air's all he needs," the taller one was saying. "No harm done. Just get him out in the fresh air—" and they were gone.

Cal turned to Jamie, who'd sat frozen through the few moments it had taken him to rescue her. He saw the tears, still shining in her eyes, and wondered how any eyes could be as blue as hers. Bright blue, they were, bright, as though the sun was shining out of them, right through those tears. That bastard had really scared her. And hurt her. Cal's glance caught the red welts forming on her arm.

"You going to be all right, ma'am?" He saw her quick gesture, trying to wipe at the tears so he wouldn't see them.

"Yes. Thanks. I'll be okay." Her heart was clattering against her ribs and her hands were shaking. "I just need a minute. I'll be okay," she repeated.

His eyes are so dark. So dark, they're almost black.

She realized she was staring and she was embarrassed. She turned on the stool to face the bar.

"You sure?"

"I'm sure. I just need to get out of here. My car's outside." She pushed another five for Milt across the top of the bar. "I just want to go home."

"I'll be glad to drive you, ma'am—"

"No!" Jamie's sharp response was involuntary and she realized she'd startled him. More calmly, she said, "No, it's all right. I'd rather go by myself. Really."

The dark eyes grew blacker still, and the barest shade of a frown passed over Cal's face. He straightened a bit and resettled his Stetson toward the back of his head, letting the unruly black curls fall forward

"Well, then, ma'am. If you're sure, then I'll just say good night." For a moment, he seemed uncertain. Then he smiled. "And if that fellow bothers you again, you just yell in my direction, you hear? The name's Cameron. Cal Cameron."

He turned and walked back to the table where Harvey, grinning now, had been watching the whole thing, ready to join in if he was needed. And as he watched, Harvey could see something else that Cal couldn't see. Harvey could see that Jamie had turned and her gaze was following Cal's retreating figure. It was Harvey's guess that she was interested in what she saw.

Harvey was right. Jamie couldn't resist one long, appraising look as Cal walked away, taking in the long legs in the dark blue Wranglers, the slow and east stride—easy except for that slight limp—a stride that matched his patient, soft-spoken manner. Then she turned away, back to the bar, took a couple deep breaths, as she gradually steadied down. In a couple of minutes, she'd be able to walk out. As soon as her knees stopped shaking.

And as she calmed down, her thoughts focused on what had just happened. On Orrin Fletcher, turning up like real bad news.

What is he doing in town?

She knew it couldn't mean anything but trouble. And he'd for sure be hooking up with Ray again. Now she really needed that hot shower. She had to scrub off the slimy feeling of Orrin's fingers on her sore arm.

I need to get out of here.

She got off the stool and headed for the door. The image of the gallant young cowboy flashed through her head, but she didn't allow herself to turn and look at him again.

Just more trouble.

A fresh wave of anger gripped her as she went out into the dark parking lot.

Just forget about him. Just another cowboy. You can take care of yourself, Jamie. You've done just fine till now. Best to keep it that way.

Only minutes had passed since Orrin had scared the hell out of her, and here she was already sticking her chin out again, putting on a tough face, convincing herself she'd be okay, that she could handle everything without help from anyone.

Just forget about him!

Cal leaned his chair precariously back against the wall again and locked his hands behind his head, tipping his hat forward over the black curls. He'd continued to stare at Jamie from across the room, watching her thoughtfully as she walked out of the place. He couldn't take his eyes off her and he couldn't forget what he'd seen in those blue eyes, the desperate fear and an almost violent flash of pride.

"Well, you were right, Cal," Harvey was saying. "Didn't take but a couple of minutes." He pushed Cal's glass toward him. "You want your beer?"

"Sure thing, Harv."

Cal, preoccupied with his thoughts, didn't touch the drink and didn't seem to realize it was there. He was silent for a long minute.

"Harv," he said, finally, "that girl was really scared."

He was wondering what he'd seen, deep inside those lovely eyes. Whatever it was that was frightening her, it had made her want to get rid of him, too, and fast.

"Well, I'm not surprised," Harvey said. "That was Orrin Fletcher with her." He pulled a pack of Camels out of his shirt pocket and lit one up. He offered one to Cal who waved it away, his eyes still fixed on the door.

"What about him?"

"Fletcher? He's just a two-bit trouble maker. They got him on a robbery or something, and he spent some time up in the state prison. He must have just got out." He paused, studying Cal's face. "I wouldn't worry about either one of them. Way I hear it, Jamie Sundstrom is one tough cookie. She can take care of herself. And Orrin Fletcher's just real small-time." Harvey's short laugh was derisive. "Only bothers little bitty girls like Jamie."

"Hmmm." Cal was silent for a few moments, thinking. "Yeah. That's what I figured. Well," he said, straightening up his chair, "I think I'm just going to head on back to the ranch now." He stood up. His eyes had never left that door. "I'll see you in the morning, Harv."

"Hey, Cal." Harvey called after him. "You never even drank your beer."

But Cal didn't answer him. He had already reached the door.

Chapter Two

Every shadow in the parking lot spooked her, and she wished she hadn't parked so far from the Canyon Rim's bright entrance. Orrin's buddies had had plenty of time to get him away, so she ought to be safe from him, but as the music and laughter in the bar grew fainter behind her, leaving only the nighttime whirring of the crickets to keep her company, she realized she hadn't really gotten over the scare he'd given her. When she reached her car, she checked the back seat before she opened the door, almost surprised to see that it was empty. She got in and slammed the door hard, as though hoping the noise would scare away any danger.

It was bad enough that Orrin had made such an ugly scene, but he'd also made her mask of self-assurance slip away and that cowboy had seen it happen. He'd seen her without her brave face. She was lucky, of course, that he'd showed up when he did, but she hated to have anyone see her so scared.

She needed to pull her pride back together and get her self-control firmly in place.

I refuse to worry about every cowhand that drifts into Sharperville and then out again. I thanked him—I think I thanked him—and now that's that. Just forget about it.

She replayed the whole thing in her head—and realized she hadn't really thanked him. Which told her just how scared she'd really been.

Couldn't be helped.

A hot shower and a good night's sleep. That's all I need. Put it all behind me—a bad dream.

But Jamie's troubles weren't over yet. As soon as she turned the key in the ignition of the old Honda, she heard a brief sputtering sound from under the hood and then there was nothing. Nothing. Not even a brief whimper came out of the engine, and she knew what it was right away. That fuel line had finally given out.

The already exhausted shell of her self-control was beginning to break up into helpless slivers, crumbling, crumpling, giving up. She dropped her head onto her fist, clasped miserably at the top of the steering wheel. It was hard enough, just getting along from one day to the next, working so hard, always worrying about money, always trying to figure out what to do about Mandy, how to get her away from Ray and his family without doing something illegal, or something stupid, without making everything much worse. Every day seemed to be such a struggle. And then tonight, just going out for a beer and who turns up but that slimeball, Orrin Fletcher. Getting hassled by him, feeling his cold hands on her arm, his fingers grabbing her wrist, his rotten breath on her, scaring her practically mindless.

"And now, on top of everything, this old car has to pick this night to die," she whispered into the silence that surrounded her.

She knew that crying never helped, but now, alone in the dark, the tears came anyway and she let herself give in to the piled-up frustrations.

"It's too much," she repeated miserably. "It's just too much!"

There'd be no one at the service station this late and Gordie Callister had already left the bar. Hutch and other guys hadn't showed up yet and she sure didn't want to walk all the way home, especially with Orrin Fletcher out and about, and anyway, it was more than seven miles beyond the other side of town to the house where she lived with her father. And there was no use calling him to come and get her. Lee Sundstrom was rarely sober any time of the day or night and chances were he was already passed out on the couch in front of the television. In any case, drunk or sober, he'd be no help to her.

Minutes passed before the tightness in her chest eased up. She lifted her head from where she had buried it in her arms and, with a last sob or two and a snuffle, she dried her face with the yellow bandana.

Okay, Jamie. Enough of this. Let's just pull it together, one more time. You'll figure out something.

She allowed herself one more shivery sob.

Then, clamping her teeth together resolutely, she made one last effort to start the car, even as she knew it was useless. There was no response at all and she had just slammed her hand angrily on the top of the steering wheel when she realized someone was standing next to the car, looking into the window at her side. The panic jumped right up again.

Orrin's back!

But it wasn't Orrin.

It was the dark-eyed cowboy.

He was resting his arm on the door's top, above the door frame, and he was leaning his head down to the open window. "You having some trouble with your car, ma'am? Anything I can do?"

Oh, God! Did he see me crying?

And all in a rush her emotional turmoil was made more complicated as she registered the broad chest and the dark hair showing where his shirt was open at the throat, the genial, reassuring smile, and the utterly useless thought as she realized how good-looking he was. For an instant—or maybe it was more than an instant—she was in a muddle of sweet confusion and unfamiliar emotions. It was the second time tonight that this dark-eyed, handsome stranger showed up just when she really needed help.

Had he seen her crying? She saw only genuine concern in those black eyes, blacker than the dark night shadows.

But yes, Cal *had* seen her crying. He'd been crossing the parking lot, looking for her, when he'd heard the sputtering engine and he'd seen Jamie's head drop forward to the wheel. He'd heard her helpless sobs, and he'd chosen to stay in the shadows and wait until she'd recovered before he'd let her know he was there. And now, again, he waited.

For her part, Jamie managed to sound as though her car was the only thing on her mind.

"It's probably the fuel line." She lifted her hands from the wheel in a gesture of frustration. "The guys down at the service station told me it wasn't going to hold."

"I can take a look, if you like. Have you got a flashlight?"

She dug a light out of the glove compartment and handed it to him. Cal dropped to one knee and flashed the light under the car. Then he reached forward and felt what looked like a wet patch in the dirt. He stood up and sniffed at his fingers.

"You're probably right." He brushed the dirt from his pants. "Smells like gas. I'll take a look under the hood."

He walked to the front of the car, released the latch, and lifted the hood, flashing the light over the engine. She could see him reach in and then lift his hand again.

"It's your fuel line, all right. The connector's all rotted, broken clean away from the carburetor."

He closed the hood and brought the flashlight back to her, and handed it in through the window. Then he pulled a bandana from his pocket and wiped the gasoline off his hand. He rested his arms against the car top again, pushed his hat back on his head.

"I'm real sorry, ma'am, but this car isn't going anywhere tonight." He saw her set her small jaw and press her lips together. Before she could say anything, he added, "Would you like to call someone to come pick you up?" He pointed at the hard hat on the seat next to her. "Your boyfriend, maybe?"

She looked where he was pointing.

"The hat's mine." She saw the slight lift of his eyebrows and was momentarily amused, knowing she'd surprised him. "And there's no boyfriend. There isn't anybody to call."

A big smile spread over Cal's face.

"Well, then, ma'am. I'd be real pleased to give you a ride home. My truck's right over there." He pointed to a big Ford pickup parked nearby.

Jamie knew enough to stay out of a stranger's car—especially with Orrin there tonight to remind her. And yet, as she looked into Cal's open, genial face, she also knew that this cowboy was no Orrin Fletcher. Despite his easygoing style, despite the quick grin and the black curls spilling out from under the white hat, despite his youth— Jamie judged him to be no more than twenty-six, twenty-seven at the most—there was a steadiness in those dark eyes. She saw a serious- ness in the creases that were already beginning to form alongside his mouth that made her think this handsome cowboy could be trusted. And after all, hadn't he known how to get rid of Orrin?

I guess it's a judgment call. And I guess I'm making a judgment in his favor.

Also in his favor, although Jamie was very far from admitting it, even to herself, were his long legs, lean and hard in the dark jeans, and the strong arms, and the big, work-hardened hands. She really liked those hands; they seemed somehow competent, reliable, strong . . .

She picked up her hard hat, slipped the car keys well in below the front seat, and opened the door.

"Well," she said as she got out, "I guess I don't have much of a choice."

Cal held the door for her and kept his eyes on her pretty shape as she walked away from him toward his truck, intrigued all over again by the form that was hidden by the orange construction vest. For such a slim little thing, he was thinking, she surely has a nice, strong way about her. Strong but not as tough as she's trying to be. He'd heard those tears only minutes earlier and he'd also seen how she'd tried to conceal them, too proud to play the frail maiden in distress. He liked that.

He recalled Harvey's brief account of her, and repeated to himself the words he had spoken earlier, whispering into the darkness.

"I don't care what anyone says. She sure looks like a lady to me!"

Then he lifted his eyes upwards and smiled broadly at the vast, star-filled sky. He almost laughed aloud as he raised his hat from his head, as though in a modest salute.

"Lord," he whispered up to the stars, "I sure do want to thank you for finishing off that fuel line just when you did!"

Then he put the hat back on his head and ran after Jamie to help her into the big truck.

The town of Sharperville was not much more than a ragged cluster of little streets surrounded by a hundred miles of open ranch country that stretched empty in all directions away from the town. The vast plateau was further isolated by twelve-thousand foot mountains that rose up like a natural fortress around the high, windswept desert. The interstate highway ran right through the center of town, along Main Street, where a few stores and a couple of motels slowed down the occasional traffic. There were no sidewalks on the dusty streets and only the hardier varieties of trees grew there, tall cottonwoods, pinyon pine, and juniper. Sometimes some wild plum grew up around the tidy houses. There was a church and a service station, but no school, so the children were bused to the elementary school over in Butcher's Fork, more than thirty miles away over Boulder Pass. The nearest movie theater was in Summersby, about a two-hour drive. Years ago high school kids had boarded away from home, coming back to town only on weekends and again in the summer, when school was out and they were needed on the ranch. Everyone learned to drive early and there wasn't anyone who couldn't handle a horse. Close to town there were still a few small farms—sugar beets and grain, mostly—started more than a century ago by Scandinavian settlers. It was hard country, dry and unforgiving.

On this night, as Cal drove Jamie away from the Canyon Rim, the moon was just rising, half-full, but even at that, it lit up the clear night and put a sheen over the desert floor that made the sage and the juniper silvery. Every now and then, off to the side, a curious gopher peered at them, momentarily rigid in the truck's headlights, but it would always whisk away before they reached it. Sometimes a cow, her calf nearby, would lift her head from her constant grazing. But mostly, the valley was nighttime quiet.

Jamie and Cal were both quiet, too, maybe a little shy, being strangers to each other, and Jamie did a quick inventory of the interior of Cal's truck. It was pretty much like any other ranch vehicle. A pair of heavy buckskin work gloves and a wrench had been tossed onto the dashboard, and there were several lengths of rope on the floor. Three rifles were stacked in the gun rack behind her and on the seat between them there were veterinary syringes for doctoring cattle, a cell phone, and an opened box of Oreos. She hadn't eaten since breakfast, but even as she realized the emptiness in her stomach, she knew there were other hungers—unwelcome hungers—that were stirring in her, had been stirring ever since this cowboy had shown up, ever since she'd first seen him coming across the dance floor, back at the bar. She didn't dare turn to examine his face directly, but she did manage a sideways glance.

The glow of the dashboard lights that lit up the underside of the brim of his Stetson, the clear lines of his strong young profile. And those nice hands, the right one at the top of the steering wheel and the fingertips of the left just barely touching the side of the wheel, with his arm resting on the open window frame. She smiled to herself, noticing he needed a shave, and in that moment, as though he'd read her mind, he took one hand from the wheel and rubbed his fingers across his cheek. He seemed irritated to feel the late-day stubble there.

Again, a confusion of feelings—attracted and frightened—swept over her and she was becoming uncomfortable in the silence. She forced herself into a pose of nonchalance; she grasped at small talk.

"What brought you here to Sharperville?" Her voice sounded okay, she decided—not ill at ease. "Not many people find their way to this part of the state."

"It's a long story." She saw his left hand drop down involuntarily to his knee, massaging it gently, and his gaze, concentrated on the road ahead of them, seemed to focus somewhere miles away. "I grew up in Nevada, up by Bennion. Now I'm working on Harvey Jackman's ranch. Harvey's married to my sister Ellie." Before she could say anything, he switched the subject, turning to her and pointing to the hard hat that was resting in her lap. "I couldn't help noticing the hat. What kind of work do you do, ma'am?"

She let him deflect her question. She got that he didn't want to talk about himself.

"I do road construction, mostly. I work a backhoe."

"No kidding? That's funny work for a woman to be doing, and you such a little bit of a thing—"

"No," she said sharply, interrupting him. "It isn't funny work. It isn't funny at all. It's good work."

"Well, sure it is, ma'am. Sure it's good work." He'd caught the edge of irritation in her voice and realized he'd offended her—the very last thing in the world he'd wanted to do. "I didn't mean any harm. I realize there's plenty of women running heavy equipment nowadays. I just don't meet too many of them, so I was surprised is all. I surely didn't mean to offend you, ma'am." His eyes left the road long enough to look at her. "Do you like doing road construction?"

"Well, it's a job and I have to support myself." He said nothing and Jamie realized she hadn't answered his question. "I guess I like it well enough," she added with some curtness.

You hardly know the man. You don't need to trade the story of your life just for a ride home!

"Isn't it hard for a woman to break into that line of work?"

"Not anymore. The big construction companies can't get federal contracts if they don't hire women. A couple of years ago, when the economy was getting tight around here and I got laid off from my other job, Gordon Callister offered to train me so I could get a job with his company." She felt her feistiness simmering down, soothed by Cal's easy tone. "Gordon's the foreman on this job." *He's also one of the few decent people in this town.* "I owe a lot to Gordie. I was working in the office at the Feed and Grain store, over in Butcher's Fork." Jamie paused. She was already telling him more than she meant to, but she found herself going on anyway. "Happens it was a tough time for me. I needed a job really bad and just then Gordon's construction company was looking for women to train."

She hesitated, remembering how rough it had been—when her marriage broke up and Mandy was taken from her—when her whole world had come apart. Not something she'd share with this cowboy, so she did a little deflecting of her own.

"It's mostly seasonal work, of course, but the pay is good, and I like being outdoors all day. I like it better than working inside, in an office, that's for sure."

"I do know what you mean."

She'd touched some nerve, she could tell; he said nothing more and they drove on silently. The moon was high over the ridge of the mountains to the east, lighting up the valley, turning the sparse growth into spiky shadows and the road ahead of them into a bright ribbon that ran flat out along the valley floor. Cal was absorbed in his own thoughts and it was a long time before he spoke.

"I've worked out under the open sky all my life," he said at last. "I wouldn't like to get roped in real close." Jamie noticed that his hand went to his knee again, as though it was hurting him, and the muscle in his jaw was working. "I guess there's some kinds of creatures just naturally die if they're corralled in too tight."

We hardly know each other. Guess he has his story, too. And isn't talking.

She said nothing more and they drove on quietly for a couple of miles until she raised an arm, pointing a finger ahead of them.

"It's that dirt road up there, to the right. Just beyond the big cedars."

Cal turned off the highway and drove until they reached an old farmhouse that stood isolated in the great, empty moonlit space, a shabby old place with a few ramshackle outbuildings around it. A rusted pickup was parked carelessly at the side and some decrepit farm equipment, too worn and broken to be of any use, obviously abandoned long ago, was lying about. Cal pulled the truck into the unkempt, rutted driveway and stopped in front of the house.

Since she'd moved back here to live with her father—just after the divorce—no one she knew ever came to this place, and she'd long ago learned to look past the disrepair. But now she saw the place through Cal's eyes and she was ashamed. She wished she didn't have to acknowledge it as her home. She wished she had some excuse to go anywhere but into that house. She wished she didn't have to leave the truck.

"Well, I guess you're home." Cal had let himself out on his side and come around to open the door for her.

She made no move to get out and Cal, puzzled by her expressionless face, rested one arm across the top of the open door and waited to figure out what was going on. He followed the line of her gaze and turned to look over his shoulder.

He had seen the condition of the house as he'd pulled into its weedy driveway and knew that it needed a lot more than new paint. Cal would have been ashamed to let any place he lived in get so run down. Even in the dark he could see that everything about it, from missing roof shingles to the broken steps and the sagging porch, needed repair. The land that stretched far beyond the house was not being worked, and he'd have been willing to bet there wasn't even a kitchen garden out back. Through the front window, he saw the flickering light of a television, and he realized there was someone living in the house beside Jamie. Someone Jamie didn't want to see. He remembered what Harvey had told him, ". . . heard talk her family was no good."

"Would you just as soon not go in right now?" He spoke gently.

Startled, her eyes rose to his. It seemed he really was reading her thoughts.

"I guess . . ." She was surprised to hear her own hesitation.

"Well then, ma'am, I'll tell you what. Why don't you and me just take a drive. It's a nice night. We could ride up into the canyon, take a look down at the valley in the moonlight. It'll be real pretty. Come back any time you say." A nice night, he was thinking. Hell, it's a *beautiful* night! He wanted to say that the moon was lighting up the big valley like an enormous dance floor and reaching silvery into the canyons, slipping around the spiky scrub oak and the great, red rock boulders, making the stillness come alive. It was so breathtakingly beautiful, it could make your heart crack right into two pieces.

But he stayed quiet, leaning on the truck door. He'd already figured this girl would spook easy, so he took his time, letting her come slowly to her own decision.

Jamie looked again at the television light flickering through the window of the front room where her father would have been sprawled on the couch for a couple of hours by now.

He's probably already passed out. Or maybe he's still working on his nightly six-pack, just waiting for me to come in, just waiting to pick a fight.

That's what usually happened. She'd come in and he'd snarl something stupid at her, some kind of accusation or reproach that didn't make any sense, and she'd just ignore him, maybe get something to eat out of the kitchen and take it upstairs to her room, and he'd go on muttering to himself till he fell asleep right there in the front room.

At least he's not a dangerous drunk. Just mean-mouthed and sloppy. The only way he'd damage anything would be if he fell on it.

It had been this way since she'd been a kid and by now she knew how to handle him. Mostly she just stayed out of his way.

How sweet it would be to have an excuse—any excuse—not to have to go in just yet.

Just a drive up in the canyon—and it really is such a pretty night . . .

Young as she was, life had taught her plenty and she knew enough to be wary. She had no illusions about men's intentions.

And yet, there was something about this man, this stranger who'd just drifted into town, something that was the damnedest combination of exciting and comfortable, all at the same time.

Which was more surprising—that odd feeling of being so easily comfortable with him? Or that other thing, the exciting thing?

She told herself to be careful. It had been a long time since she'd felt so turned on by a man. Not since those early days with Ray back when they were both kids in high school and she was so dumb and didn't know any better. And that didn't last long—just long enough for her to do a stupid dumb thing and marry him, and then there was never anything good with him again. Except for Mandy, of course. She'd always be thankful for Mandy. But she had learned to keep big walls up around her feelings, and she'd decided it wasn't safe, ever again, to feel comfortable with anyone. Especially with men.

She looked again at that light in the window. She really didn't want to go into the house, and she really didn't want this man to drive away from her now.

"My name is Jamie," she said. "It's Jamisson, actually. Jamisson

Sundstrom. I was named for my mother's family. Everyone calls me Jamie."

"I know. Harvey told me."

Like red flags going up, she could feel all those defenses suddenly on alert.

"Then I guess you know all about me."

"I sure don't know all about you, ma'am. It would take a lot more than what Harvey said for me to know all about you." He smiled broadly. "Old Harv never talks much anyway. It's like birthing a calf to try to get something out of him. So why don't you and me just take a ride and you can tell me whatever you feel like. Or not. Either way, suits me. It's such a pretty night, it shouldn't get wasted. Someone ought to be out there appreciating it."

Again, it was a judgment call. She reasoned that he'd already pulled her out of trouble a couple of times tonight. She actually had this good feeling while he was around, and there were few enough good feelings in her life to let this one end. She took one last look at the light in the window and that must have decided her.

"Okay," she said, mentally crossing her fingers. "Okay, let's take a drive."

"All *right*!" He closed her door and went around back to his side of the truck. As he climbed in, he pointed to the Oreos on the seat.

"And we even have some grub with us, so we're fixed for dinner."

Chapter Three

Minutes before she'd been angry and resentful, digging deep inside herself to find the strength once again to fight back against an unfair, harsh fate.

And then this man she'd just met—she couldn't even remember his name—suggested a drive in the moonlight, and she felt sixteen years old again. No, much better than sixteen. At sixteen, she'd already known too much anger and misery. Right now, cruising along in Cal's big old Ford pickup, she was feeling *good*!

She knew it was risky to take this drive, but this man beside her just felt so safe, so comfortable, so—she couldn't put her finger on it—so *right*! There was something about the way he fit the seat of the truck, his long legs easy on the pedals, the way he handled the wheel. He smelled of leathers and hay and horses—a good, manly scent that belonged to honest work and open skies. The radio was picking up KSOP all the way from Salt Lake City—her favorite for country music, when she could get it. The signal was coming in clear even though the truck was already well into the canyon, climbing the steep grade that wound back and forth between the tall red-rock walls that rose up high into the moonlit sky, and Cal was humming lightly with the music.

She felt as though she was making an escape.

She felt like a girl on her first date.

He offered her the package of Oreos and she took one.

"I ought to have remembered your name," she said, "but I'm afraid I didn't catch it."

"It's Calvin Cameron. Everyone calls me Cal. Like I told you, I just hired on at Harv Jackman's place for a while. He's got that spread just south of town."

"Sure, the old Winder ranch. I guess I did hear Vern Winder had sold it a couple of years ago. After his wife died. Heard he'd retired and moved down to Phoenix with his daughter."

"That's the one. Harvey's the one bought it."

"I never met the new owners. The last few years I guess I've sort of avoided the folks around here." Instantly, she was afraid she'd said too much, afraid she'd just spoiled the good mood.

"Why's that, Jamie? What's wrong with the folks around here?"

Cal turned to look at her and she decided right away she *had* said too much.

"That's a long story. I'll tell you about it sometime."

Maybe.

"Okay." He looked back at the road. "Any time you feel like it."

He was tapping his hand lightly at the top of the wheel, in time to the music, and just as lightly he changed the subject.

"You know this canyon," he said. "Any place up ahead where we can see down to the valley? Should be real pretty from up there."

He turned again, smiling at her.

"Yes, the road will open up about a quarter of a mile from here where you can get a good view." She hadn't spoiled anything, after all. She took a bite of Oreo. "It's been kind of a private place of mine ever since I was a kid. It's where I go when I have to think or maybe if I just want to get away from everyone. I've always been completely alone up here." She paused, remembering. "Except once . . . there was just this one time—"

She stopped dead, her eyes suddenly wide, staring straight ahead, up the road.

"Oh my God!"

Instinctively, unconsciously, she put one hand over Cal's on the steering wheel, to stop him, while with the other, she pointed ahead of them to the top of a rocky escarpment that rose about thirty feet into the moonlight.

"That's so spooky!" She could barely speak the words.

At the same moment, Cal saw what Jamie was staring at. Instantly, he brought the truck to a silent stop and switched off the headlights. His eyes narrowed slightly, and he cut the engine and the radio. "Now *that's* something you don't see too often," he whispered into the sudden silence.

A mountain lion! Nine feet easy, from nose to tail tip. The bright moonlight shone silver on his sleek coat marked only by black tufts of fur at the point of his ears. The lion stood attentive to them, waiting, poised for their next move.

Jamie's eyes were wide and her fingers gripped Cal's hand tightly, still unconsciously.

"He's watching us," she whispered.

She was unable to take her eyes from the beautiful animal, his powerful muscles held in check, his graceful, dangerous form gleaming in the moonlight. The big cat lowered his head slightly, his eyes still fixed on them, and his tail never stopped its slow switching back and forth, back and forth. Otherwise, he remained immobile. Around them all, a soft wind stirred the leaves of the quaking aspen, their bright circles quivered against the dark, still background of the spruce trees. Jamie's senses were quickened by the cougar's presence and she was aware of the sharp scent of spruce.

She became aware, too, of her fingers, gripping Cal's hand so tightly. It had been a long time since she'd held a man's hand in hers, and as she eased her grip, she felt the warmth of his skin, the long tendons strong against her palm. She pulled her hand away, stunned by a sudden current that seemed to flow between them, an actual, physical reality, and she was embarrassed and confused by the rush of sensation that reached up through her arm to wrap itself around her heart.

If Cal noticed, he gave no sign. He just pushed his hat way back on his head and rested his chin on his hands, clasped now at the top of the steering wheel.

Cal had given no sign, but yes, of course he had noticed. How could he not? That kind of current flows two ways, and it carries its own message. But Cal had already figured out that this girl needed careful handling, not sudden moves, so instead he just rested his chin on his hands and peered up over them to watch the enormous cougar.

"That sure is one good-looking animal. Just about the biggest cat I've ever seen. But why did you say spooky?"

"I'll tell you later." Jamie was still too stunned to explain. "But shhh. Look. He's leaving."

The lion had taken his eyes from them, as though dismissing them, as though he was satisfied that he had fixed them safely in their

place. He padded downward along the ridge, and then, in an uncon-
cerned slow motion, mysteriously he vanished into the brush, his
moon-silver coat blending into the sage and scrub oak.

The cougar's disappearance released Jamie and she shivered,
coming out of the spell of the big cat's hypnotizing beauty.

And Cal whistled soundlessly. "Well, that's something you can
tell your grandchildren about!"

"Oh, Cal, you don't know the half of it."

She was still shaken by the cat's mysterious appearance, just at that
moment, just as she'd been thinking of that other time so long ago.

Cal made no move to start the engine. The warmth of her hand on
his had been nice. He was eager to feel her touch again, but he knew
too much about nervous animals to take a chance on scaring her
away. Instead, he turned and settled himself back against the door,
one arm resting on the wheel, the other on the back of the seat. He
was glad of an excuse to sit quietly in the unlit interior of the truck so
he could watch the way her fine, white-blond hair captured the silver
flashes of cool moonlight.

She's as beautiful as any wild animal.

"I guess I should explain." She hesitated.

Cal said nothing; he was wishing he could reach over and touch
that beautiful hair, but he remained still and just waited.

"I mean, I should explain why I said it was spooky. I'd just been
saying we could go to this place that I like, sort of my own private
place, where no one had ever been with me before. And then, just
when I said that, I remembered something that had happened there,
when I was really little, about seven or eight years old."

She paused, remembering. She took another cookie and ate the
whole thing while she thought it over. Then she decided to tell him.

"I was really little," she began, "like I said, and my dad used to let
me run wild, pretty much. I don't think he ever cared what was happening to me. I used to play up here in this canyon all the time, so I
got to know it pretty well and I always felt safe here.

"But there was this one time, something had happened at home,
and I ran away up here and wound up getting lost."

She paused again, thinking about that day, and Cal waited, not
asking what had frightened her. When she was ready, she went on.

"The school bus had left me off down by that clump of cedars,
where the dirt road begins, where you turn off from the highway, and

after the bus drove off, I started walking up the road to the house. It was just one of those freaky things; there was this rattlesnake curled up in the dirt, sunning itself I guess, and I didn't see it till I was practically on it. Well, I knew enough to be scared of rattlesnakes and I guess I jumped a mile in the air and the snake jumped too, trying to get away from me. Well, it took off right into the field, but when I landed, I came down on a rock and twisted my ankle pretty bad.

"I was still scared the snake was going to get me, even though I'd seen it trying just as hard to get away from me, and I couldn't run because my ankle was hurting so bad, so by the time I'd limped to the house, I was crying and calling for my daddy. I saw his car outside— we had an old beat-up Chevy convertible then—so I knew he was home, but when I came in, he was just sitting at the kitchen table, and he was drunk, of course. I tried to tell him what happened and he got real mad, and he yelled and yelled and when he tried to get up his chair fell over and that made him madder. He kept yelling about how much trouble I was and couldn't I look where I was going, and why was everyone always picking on him. He was stumbling around and things were falling on the floor, dishes, the newspaper . . .

"I was afraid he'd come after me and I ran out. I guess I was so scared by then, I didn't even feel my ankle hurting anymore. I came up here into the canyon, where I always felt safe. Only this time, everything was so confused and seemed so dangerous, what with the snake and my ankle hurting and beginning to swell up and my dad so mad. I lost my way and I wound up not knowing where I was. I just kept climbing and slipping and sliding around and I was getting scratched by the branches and the stones, and I lost my shoes. I guess they came loose with all the slipping and sliding around and I didn't even stop to find them, but I just kept climbing and climbing until I found an open space, where there was this big flat rock. And I got up on the rock to rest, and I could see down into the valley. I could see the road to my house and the town all laid out in front of me, like a big picture.

"So I started to feel better, like being all alone was okay, sort of safer, even. There was something about having found this place high up over the valley, and being able to see everything spread out, I felt okay, like I'd found my own private place where I was safe and in charge.

"And right then, young as I was, I understood that I really was alone, that I'd just have to handle things by myself, without help from other people. I think I was learning something I had to know; kids who aren't being cared for right have to learn to take care of themselves.

"Anyway, it was just around then, when I was feeling better, I heard this sort of soft breathing behind me. And when I looked up, this huge cat was standing there on the ridge. I just froze and it stayed there, absolutely silent, for a long time, watching me."

She paused, remembering, and then repeated, "For a *long* time."

The next part was harder to describe.

"But it's funny, Cal. As scared as I was, I had the feeling that that big cat was just like me, that we were sort of related, somehow. Like he was there to tell me something. And here's what it was: he was all alone and I was all alone, and just like he could take care of himself, I could take care of myself, too. And like we were, somehow, together. Almost like we were friends or something . . .

It was hard to go on as she struggled to find the words.

"I don't know how to explain it. Like I didn't need to be afraid of him."

She needed to be silent for a few moments as she realized she just couldn't express the mystery of the experience.

"But anyway," she said at last, "the cougar never did anything. He just watched me for a while—it seemed to be a long time, but maybe it was only a minute or two—and then he went away. Didn't even twitch his tail or anything, just quietly walked on."

She was suddenly aware of how long she'd been talking.

This sounds so bizarre. He must think I'm crazy. But talking about this—talking to him—it feels so good.

She took a breath and went on.

"So that was it. I did get myself back home again, eventually. I kept looking for my shoes, all the way back, but I never did find them, and I was scratched up and when I told my dad what I'd seen, he was so angry, said I was nothing but trouble, and he really walloped me. He said I was making it up about the cougar. He said anyone as much trouble as I was *should* have been eaten up by a cougar. So I shut up and I never said anything about it again."

Another deep breath.

"Until this very minute," she said. "With you."

She was swept by a wave of shyness and a sudden sense that she'd made herself very vulnerable.

In the shadows of the truck's cab, it was too dark for her to see the response that lay deep in Cal's black eyes.

"Lucky that cat wasn't hungry," he said. "Though I've never heard of a cougar attacking a child unless he wasn't able to find his regular game. Like if he was injured, or something like that, and wasn't able to hunt. There's plenty of fat game around and as long as he'd had his fill of deer, or had gotten a calf on the range, he wouldn't have bothered you."

"I suppose." She laughed a little. "And I guess I was kind of a scrawny kid at that. Anyway, that was a long time ago, but the funny thing is, every time I come into this canyon, I think of those shoes I lost, and I keep looking for them. Like I still expect to get a licking for losing them. Like maybe they're going to turn up under a bush or behind a rock or something. Little red tennis shoes. Red and white. I guess some gopher or something took them away—some pack rat or a hawk—who knows what, but they just disappeared. You'd think by now I'd have forgotten them. But still, it always crosses my mind every time I come up here, like maybe that cougar decided to take them instead of me. I don't know. It's just that I keep needing to find my shoes. Isn't that silly?"

"And you never saw another lion up here?"

"Never until this one, just now. They're around, I know; the ranchers are always keeping an eye out for them. Just tonight I heard some talk about Al Wideman seeing a big cougar a couple of days ago and he thinks it took one of his calves. Who knows, maybe it's this same one. But what's so strange is how I was just remembering that time, when I was little, and then just at the same minute I thought of that other cougar, there's this big cat staring us right in the face."

Just tonight, when I came here with you. Like magic.

"And until tonight," she said, "I never said anything about it to anyone. Figured they'd only call me a liar, like my dad did. But somehow, in my kid mind, I thought that cougar had some special meaning for me, only I couldn't tell if it was good or bad. Is that weird or what?"

"Not weird for a kid," Cal said. "Kids think that way. But those big cats are dangerous and—well, like I said, you were lucky."

"I guess you're right. I guess I really was in a lot more trouble that day than I realized. Still, no cat up here has ever done me any harm, which is more than I can say for the two-legged animals down in the valley."

Cal remembered what Harvey had told him. He didn't want to pry, but he sure did want to know more about this beautiful young woman. He could still feel the press of her hand on his; that mysterious electric current hadn't flowed in one direction only and he wondered if she'd felt it, too. If she had—

He straightened around on the seat and started up the engine.

"Why don't you and me just ride on up to your special place you were telling me about. You can show me the view of the town from up there and fill me in on the folks who live there."

He started the truck on its climb up the steep grade.

"Okay," she said. "I like looking at the valley and the whole town and everything just spread out below. It all seems a lot more manageable from this distance."

The radio was on again, and the canyon ahead of them looked so friendly in the truck's headlights.

It really is funny, how the littlest thing can turn your whole mood around.

Chapter Four

The narrow canyon road twisted suddenly, widening onto a clear space that was bounded by clumps of scrub oak and tall spruces and, on one side, a steep cliff wall. Far below them, the broad valley stretched into the distance with the highway running straight through it and the sparse lights of Sharperville winking up at them. At the base of the cliff, the layered red rock formed a natural bench, broad enough to sit back comfortably against the stone.

Jamie climbed onto her favorite roost and pulled her legs up under her.

I can't believe I'm doing this. I never brought anyone here before.

Cal had deliberately lagged behind so he could watch her scramble up the layers of rock, where she made such a pretty, moonlit picture, with her legs crossed, fitting so neatly against the grooved stone. A gentle wind, soft through the canyon, lifted her fine hair and moved it from her shoulders as she looked out over the valley. The air had become nighttime-cold, and Cal realized she was bare-armed and her orange vest was only a thin covering.

"I'll be just a minute," he called to her. He reached into the space below the gun rack and pulled out a plaid flannel shirt. "In case you're getting cold." In a moment he had climbed up beside her and put the shirt around her shoulders.

Jamie tensed as he reached around her, for the protective gesture had startled her, in part because of its unexpected kindliness.

But only in part.

For she had felt again that unmistakable flow of energy, a wave of warmth that closed the small space between them. She'd felt it through her skin. She needed to take a really deep breath, as though to make room inside herself for the sudden flow of feeling that curled deeply into her. Confused by the mixed feelings that were tumbling about inside her—pleasure, desire, and a hefty dose of panic—and needing to conceal her confusion, she turned away from him.

"Thanks," she said, fumbling to pull the shirt around her. "It does get chilly up here at night. I was beginning to feel cold." That was certainly a lie—his touch had brought all the warmth she needed—but how could she tell him that? Her mind made a quick twist and she forced herself to remember that they'd come here to look at the view.

"Well, there it is." She gestured at the valley spread below them, quiet and remote in the moonlight. In the distance, a thin cluster of lights marked the center of town, and across the valley, tiny spots of light were scattered sparsely. An occasional beam from a car's headlights moved along the highway. She spoke as lightly as she could, trying to ignore the sensations that had just been so unexpectedly roused inside her.

"There it is, folks," she said. "There's the hustling, bustling little town of Sharperville you see down there below you, Galena County's busy downtown metropolis, the red-rock jewel of the nation, cattle capital of the world, and the intermountain west's answer to New York and Paris." The wind caught at her hair and she brushed it quickly out of her face. "Where everyone is 'just folks' and God help anyone who doesn't toe the line."

Cal caught the pain behind her sarcasm.

"You lived here all your life?"

"Every damn minute."

He scooped up a handful of sandy earth and let it trickle out of his fist.

"I haven't noticed it seems such a bad place. Didn't anything good ever happen to you here?"

"Oh, yes."

But then she was quiet while she stared out over that silent valley, her gaze held by the far-flung lights. The night was vast around her and was stirred only by the rough, pulsing, high-pitched cricket-sound and the gentle whisper of the firs moving in the wind. Far away, the snow-tipped peaks were touched by the moon. A coyote called and she jumped. Then all was silent again except for the crickets and the wind-whisper.

"One good thing happened."

She felt the whole story rising up, about to be told out loud for the first time, a story she'd carried silently and so painfully for two years. She was astonished that it was happening with this man, this stranger. As though a key had been turned in a lock, as though a door had opened, and she was about to expose her unspeakable shame.

Cal was the best kind of listener. He said nothing; he just kept scooping up handfuls of sand, absent-mindedly, and letting them slide through his fingers. He sensed that he was hearing—in this time and in this place—what had never been told before.

She needed a few moments before she could start—and Cal waited silently.

"I have a little girl. Her name is Mandy—Amanda, actually—and she's four years old. Four years old this May. Mandy is the good thing that happened. The best thing in the whole world that ever happened to me. The bad part is, her daddy is Ray Nixon. Maybe you know the Nixons. Everyone in Sharperville knows the Nixons. Pillars of the community."

She made no effort to hide the bitterness in her tone.

"It's an old story, I guess. I was just so damned young and there was so much I didn't know. But there was one thing I *did* know, ever since I was a kid. The 'good' people of Sharperville didn't think much of us Sundstroms. People watch each other pretty close around here and they've got this thing—from the Bible, I guess—about visiting the sins of the fathers on the children, or something."

"Unto the third and fourth generation," Cal nodded thoughtfully, looking down at the faraway town.

"Well, the sad truth is, my daddy's a drunk and hasn't done a days' worth of real work in his life. And all I got from my mom were my blue eyes and my hair and her family name."

"What happened to her?" Cal had a feeling he already knew what happened to Jamie's mom.

"My mom ran off with some trucker from Idaho when I was a baby"—she kept up her brave pose for a moment or two and then she finally let her feeling show—"so I guess my folks really aren't any good." She turned away from him, embarrassed. "I don't know why they turned out the way they did," she went on quietly. "They both came from real good old Scandinavian stock. The Sundstroms and the Jamissons were well known around here, used to be good, solid people. They settled this part of the country way back, more than a hundred years ago and they worked hard and built up their farms, prosperous places, well-cared for. Everyone knows both families were real respectable. Reliable, hard-working people who went to church on Sunday and knew right from wrong.

"But something must have gone wrong in the later generations. All of them just disappeared, God knows where, and there was nothing left around here of that whole line—both sides—except my dad and me. And that left me, like it says in the Bible, with the sins of my father . . ."

"Oh, Jamie, that isn't what it says—"

"Well, whatever. My dad never did work the farm and he just lets the house fall down around him. He lives on whatever odd jobs he can pick up around town. When he's sober, that is. So now the place is an eyesore and, like I've heard plenty of times, a 'disgrace to the community.' I've been hearing that one since I can remember. And some people in this town can be pretty unforgiving. They don't let you forget.

"Anyway, by the time I got to high school, I was real glad when Ray Nixon started hanging out with me. I figured it would make me look respectable, what with his folks being such upstanding pillars of the community, like I said. Can you imagine I could be so dumb? But I was just a kid and I thought they must be good people, I mean they do their church work regularly and Ervil—he's Ray's father—he plays the organ for Sunday morning services. Nobody can touch Edna's needlework at the county fair and they're always the ones to see to it that there's no liquor at the high school dances."

Jamie's smirk gave Cal a pretty clear picture of the "good" Nixons.

"You can imagine Edna wasn't exactly happy when Ray told her we were getting married. She kept prissing up her mouth and whining about how she never would understand that boy. Of all her kids—there were eight of them—he was the wildest of the bunch, she said, always into some sort of trouble, keeping her life a misery. And now here he was marrying Lee Sundstrom's daughter."

Jamie's voice became a whining, sarcastic mimicry of her former mother-in-law. "'Ever since that no-good wife of his ran off, Lee Sundstrom has just got worse and worse, and that Jamie, that daughter of his, is going to turn out to be no better than her mother, you just mark my words, you see if I ain't right.' And then she'd poke Ervil to make him agree with her. 'Ain't I right, Ervil? Ain't I?' And Ervil always agrees with Edna so he'd nod his head, up and down, obediently. And then she'd point to Ray and say, 'But there's never been any stopping that boy from doing whatever he wanted,' like she thought he was just the cutest damn thing that ever happened."

"So you and Ray went ahead and got married?"

Jamie shrugged.

"It didn't seem so stupid at the time. I'd known him ever since kindergarten, and I thought the Nixons were really respectable people. I was too dumb to know that being prissy and small-minded isn't the same as being decent. It took me a while to figure out that Edna's front parlor was plenty clean but the spirit inside her was mean.

"So, that very summer, right after we finished high school, we drove over to some little town in Nevada and quick got married and Edna got to tell everyone how her boy had 'run off with that no-good Sundstrom girl.'"

"So you had no fancy ceremony?"

"No way. There was no one on my side to make a regular wedding, and we knew Edna and Ervil would never approve. It just seemed like a good idea at the time. Like I said, we were so young, we even thought it was kind of a kick in the ass, you know? Be the talk of the whole senior class. I mean, imagine"—she smirked—"I wasn't even pregnant.

"But it turned out Ray wasn't just some wild kid. I mean, it wasn't just high spiritedness, you know. The marriage was in trouble right away—like that's a big surprise."

"What kind of trouble?"

"Well, right away Ray got a job at the hydro plant and it seemed like he always had to work crazy hours, and somehow he always needed to be out of town for days at a time. We had this little trailer home—Ray's still living there now—and it got so I never knew when he'd be coming home. He didn't care when I told him I was worried or that I didn't appreciate the way he was treating me. There were all these phone calls at all hours, and meetings with people I didn't like the looks of. And when I tried to find out what was happening, that's when things started to get real nasty."

"He hit you?"

"Sure, he hit me."

"And you stayed with him?"

"I know it sounds real stupid, but I actually *was* pregnant by then. I'd already figured out things weren't likely to work out, but I guess

I was so miserable and so confused, I thought having a baby would make us a real family." She needed to stop. The memories—and the shame—hurt too much, and she felt the tears starting. And she was *not* going to cry in front of this cowboy, and she needed a moment to get her brave face back on.

Cal understood. He stayed quiet so she could continue when she was ready.

"But honestly, Cal. No matter how bad all the rest turned out, having Mandy was wonderful. She's the greatest little girl. I just don't see how someone so wonderful can come from Ray Nixon. Must have been something good left over from my side.

"Anyway, I thought I was somehow going to make it all work out—for her sake, you know? That's another dumb old story . . ." with both hands she gestured the futility, the frustration.

"And it didn't work out that way, did it?"

"Does it ever?"

"Not as I've ever seen. So what finally happened?"

For a long time, she stared into the darkness while the moon climbed higher above their heads. The crickets filled the night with their sandpaper music, and far below them, in the valley, the lights of a car moved along the highway. She didn't speak again until it disappeared into the dark.

"Things just kept getting worse between us. I knew something was going on—though to this day, I still don't know what he was up to. There were a lot of people coming and going in that little trailer, and he was making all these trips and not telling me where he'd been, just telling me to shut up and quit asking questions. He was getting nastier and meaner and, after a while, I couldn't stand to be around him. I decided to get a job, get out of the house more.

"That's when I started to work down at the feed store. I got Ray's mom to take care of Mandy during the day while I worked. I really needed to get away from Ray and I liked earning my own money. And for her part, Edna liked having Mandy under her wing, so she could be a 'good influence' on her and see to her spiritual life, but I figured Mandy was still too young for Edna to do her any harm or to turn her against me.

"The trouble was, the more independent I became, the madder Ray got. And the madder Ray got, the rougher he got, and the rougher he got, the more I started staying away from home whenever

I could. At night, after work, I'd pick Mandy up from her Grandma's and we'd go get a hamburger or something instead of going home for dinner.

"Then, one Friday night, we got back to the trailer later than usual, maybe around eight o'clock. We came in and Ray was there and so was this girl. Tina."

It felt so strange, the whole story pouring out of her, and now she couldn't help the burning tears that came with it.

"The trailer was dark and I thought Ray was working the night shift. Mandy had run on ahead of me—I can still see her, waving that little lunch box she always took to Grandma's—and I got in just behind her and turned on the light, and there they were on the sofa, Ray and Tina, and there wasn't a stitch of clothes on either of them. Ray grabbed his pants and Tina was laughing like she was having high old time, looking right at me and *laughing*!

"That did it. I started to yell that I'd had it, that I wasn't going to take anymore. I said, 'I'm taking Mandy and I'm walking out of here right now!" But Ray was too fast, and as soon as I said I was taking Mandy, he grabbed her by the arm and practically threw her behind him and yelled at me like he was going to kill me. 'You think you're just going to up and walk out on me? No way, baby. No one walks out on me. You do any walking, it'll be when I tell you to!' Mandy was crying by then, and he yelled at her to get to her bed or he'd really whack her and she was so terrified, she ran away into the bedroom where her crib was, at the other end of the trailer.

Jamie turned her head away from Cal, shaking her head as though to rub the scene out of her memory. "She was still carrying that little lunch box."

She couldn't speak for a few moments, just holding her hand over her mouth, and Cal waited silently. Finally, she wiped her tears from her cheeks.

"I tried to run past Ray, to get to Mandy, but he threw me back against the door and I could hear the glass breaking. I punched at him and I was screaming at him to cut it out and my foot slipped and I was just grabbing at anything I could and he was yelling, 'Just get the hell outta here, bitch! Just get the hell outta here!' And he was dragging me to the door and I was pounding on him and I could hear Mandy crying. I managed to hit him once really hard in the mouth, so he was bleeding down onto his shirt"—by now the words were rushing from her—"and I kept yelling 'Just let me get Mandy!' He kept saying, 'No one walks out on me!' and he kicked at the screen door so it came loose off the hinges and he threw me so hard I couldn't catch my balance, and I landed in the dirt outside the trailer.

"I was so scared, and I was bleeding, and I ran for my car and all I could hear was Mandy crying from the bedroom and Ray still yelling, 'You hear me, you bitch!' Only his language was a lot uglier than that. 'You ain't walking out on me 'cause I just threw *you* out! And I don't want to see you around here! You understand that, bitch?' And he was slamming the door again and again, so the rest of the glass fell out, and he was yelling, 'Go on! Go back to that no-good father of yours! See how much good *he* does you!'"

The pain was too much and she needed to stop. She ducked her head against her shoulder to hide her face from Cal so he couldn't see as she brushed at the tears. He waited silently, letting her have the time she needed. A full minute passed before she could go on.

"So I came up here, like I always do. All the way, all I could think was how Mandy was crying for me—that and the disgusting sight of Tina, laughing at us.

"I knew there was no use anymore trying to keep the marriage together. I was just sitting here—right here where we are right now—just looking out over everything—and it was a Friday night, just like tonight"—she waved a hand vaguely toward the town—"and I tried to figure out what I had to do.

"But Ray was already a couple of steps ahead of me. I stayed at my dad's house over the weekend and on Monday morning I drove over to the county seat, in Flintlock, to try to find a lawyer. That's when I found out that Ray had already filed a divorce complaint against me. Can you imagine? I never knew it, but Ray already *had* a lawyer, and they just got together over the weekend, and first thing Monday morning, that lawyer of his was in court, claiming I was an unfit mother."

She was staring blankly into the valley as though the whole awful memory was playing itself out there, below her.

"At first I thought he was just trying to hassle me, you know? Make me miserable. I knew he wasn't really interested in having custody of Mandy. But there was more to it than that. It was his mom, Edna, sticking her nose into the whole mess. What she really wanted was for Mandy to be with her. She never approved of me and she saw a chance to do some more of her famous 'good works.' His lawyer got a court order, keeping me from seeing Mandy until the divorce hearing, and that suited Ray just fine. He handed Mandy over to Edna so he wouldn't have to be bothered taking care of her and he got to drive me crazy at the same time."

"But how could he get away with that?"

"Cal, you know how things work in these small towns. Everyone knows everyone and the Nixons are the kind they call 'fine, upstanding people.' And the judge was Edna's sister's father-in-law. Judge Joyner. Judge Whitaker S. Joyner. Like I'll ever forget him. He's dead now. About six months ago. Too bad it didn't happen a whole lot sooner."

She sucked in her breath, ashamed of her bitterness, ashamed to realize how poisonous she sounded. But there was no taking it back. The pain was too great, and she was letting Cal see it all.

"You should have seen the order he wrote. It's right there"—she couldn't control the sarcasm—"about how a mother who's out of the home every day, working in an office, when she should be with her little child, wasn't providing a 'properly stable environment' or a 'suitable role model and moral standard'. He said I was negligent, leaving my little girl in the care of others, failing to perform my maternal duties. The whole thing is so full of that kind of stuff. Hell, I've read it over so many times, I know it by heart!"

"But what about your lawyer? Didn't he fight for you?"

"My lawyer? Now *that's* a laugh!" Jamie wasn't laughing. "That poor bastard didn't know the first thing. Almon Reed"—she made an impatient sound—"hell, he was just a young kid himself, about two minutes out of law school. I didn't have a ton of money and I didn't know how to find someone better, someone who knew how to really be a lawyer. Someone who wouldn't be afraid to take on the Nixons and all their 'standing in the community.'"

She scraped her hand along the rock, trailing her fingertips in the dirt, dragging along fragile little bits of twigs and dried pinyon, unconsciously building up a little pile.

"Then, when it came time for the divorce hearing, Ray and Tina had me all set up." She paused for a long time, unable to bring herself to tell Cal about it, feeling the revulsion that always swept over her whenever she let herself remember.

"It was so sleazy, Cal. It's hard for me to talk about it."

Cal stayed quiet.

So she took a deep breath and braced herself to continue.

"Ray needed to set up something about me that would make me really unfit to have custody. That's where Orrin Fletcher comes in. That's the man you tangled with tonight, back at the Canyon Rim."

Orrin's showing up like that, right out of the blue, had wrenched her memories painfully. Maybe that's why she couldn't stop herself from talking about that other night, two years ago.

"In a million years, I wouldn't have seen what was coming. My mind just doesn't work that way, I guess. Anyway, it was only three weeks before the divorce hearing, and I was pretty wound up. I could see my lawyer didn't know what he was doing. You could tell, just walking into his office. It was in a row of cinderblock offices, down by that strip mall out the other side of Flintlock—that's the county seat—where it runs into the interstate. The windows had these metal blinds that were always a little cockeyed and a poor old dusty tree in a pot, standing up in a corner, trying to decorate the place. And he had this desk all covered with manila folders and papers and yellow pads and about a million pieces of pink slips with telephone messages. And these books from law school sitting on shelves nailed to the wall, looking so hopeful. Poor kid, you could see it was all too much for him. I knew I'd made a mistake, getting a kid like Almon to represent me, but I had no money and by then I thought it was too late to change.

"I don't know why I feel so sorry for the poor guy. If he'd known his business, my life might have turned out a lot happier. And if I'd known what was coming, I sure *would* have found a way to get a different lawyer. But Almon was all I could afford and anyway, I just couldn't believe that the judge wouldn't finally give Mandy back to me. Almon kept telling me there was always 'a presumption in favor of the mother of a child of tender years'—doesn't that sound fancy?—and I believed him.

"So I figured I just had to get through those last weeks before the trial without losing my mind, and that's when I made my really big mistake. Though honest, there was no way I could have known—"

Now Jamie was talking out into the night, as though Cal wasn't there at all. The sound of her own voice seemed remote, as though it was someone else talking about the disaster of her divorce.

"By that time, I was working for Gordon. We were doing a job up near Salina, cutting a frontage road through the ranch country just north of the Koosharem Reservoir. Most of the crew, me included, were staying in trailers that were parked in a camp near the town, but there was this one fellow, Orrin Fletcher—didn't mean a thing to me at the time—who had signed on just a couple of days earlier, said he was staying in a motel. No one knew anything about him, and no one cared much. Gordon needed a flagman for a couple of weeks, and Orrin was passing through town and said he wanted to pick up a few bucks before he moved on.

"It wasn't till later I found out the whole thing had been set up between Ray and Orrin—and Tina, of course. She'd known Orrin from long ago when she'd been working in California.

"The way they'd done it, Orrin had gotten to my car while I was working and seen to it that the distributor cap got cracked. Well, you've seen that old wreck—it had been giving me problems for months, so I never suspected it had been deliberately messed with. It had happened so many times, and I'd needed a lift back from the job site so often, I didn't give it a thought when this new guy said he'd take me down to the service station. But when we got there, it was too late for the mechanic to get to it that night, but he said first thing in the morning he'd send someone out to pick it up.

"Orrin seemed okay and anyway my mind was on other things. The hearing was coming up soon, and I was supposed to drive down here to Sharperville the next day to see Mandy—that damned judge's preliminary order allowed me to see Mandy only every other Saturday—and now it looked like that stupid old car wouldn't be ready in time to make the trip. So, with everything else, I just wasn't paying much attention to this guy."

Another pause. She lifted her head and squared her shoulders as though trying to settle a great burden more comfortably on her back.

"I know. I should have been paying attention. I should have noticed, down at the service station, how he acted real friendly, like we were heading out for a big evening on the town, but I thought he was just kidding around and I didn't realize how it looked to the guys who were working there.

"And I should have been paying attention when Orrin wanted to stop—just for a minute, he said—at the Silver Saddle. 'There's this fellow I need to see,' he said to me, just as cool as could be. 'It'll only take a minute. Why don't you come on in, have a Coke or something.'

"And I didn't give it a thought. I mean, it wasn't a big deal. Most nights all of us in the crew would go out together for a drink after work. So I went into the Silver Saddle with Orrin and we sat at the bar together, for just a few minutes, and I had that damned Coke and he went off for another couple of minutes with a man who'd come in a little bit after we did. And then Orrin and I left together. That was all. I wasn't there more than maybe twenty minutes. Just long enough to be seen with Orrin, having a drink, apparently friendly. Seen by about two dozen people."

Jamie wasn't looking at Cal, so she didn't see him nod his head slightly. She didn't see his anger. Cal understood already what was being done to Jamie that night.

"And I still didn't get it when he asked me, about a mile or two down the road, if I'd mind waiting for him while he stopped in at his motel to pick up something. It wasn't out of the way. He'd have me back at the trailer in no time, he said.

"'Sure,' I said. 'No problem.' Can you believe I could be so dumb? I figured it was the least I could do—the guy was doing me a favor. So we pulled off the interstate into this sad little row of seedy motel rooms. It's such big, windswept country up there, so empty, and the way traffic moves along, usually doing eighty-five at least, you could drive past it a hundred times and never notice the place.

"The rooms were set way back from the road, in two rows facing each other, and up at the front there was this office, a separate building from the motel rooms, and it had a plate glass window facing out to the dirt parking area. I remember it had this sad little neon sign saying VACANCY, like that might stop any of the folks who were zipping by on that road. That time of the year, couldn't have been a hundred cars a day passed through there.

"So Orrin went into the office—'just for a minute,' he told me. He said, 'The rooms don't have any phones and my cell phone is dead. I just need to make a quick call. Will that be okay? Won't be more than a minute.' Can you believe? Just as slick as a lizard. And I said, 'Sure, Orrin, go right ahead.' I could see him there, behind that VACANCY sign, talking to the desk clerk, smiling, sort of waving friendly-like at me, nodding his head. I even nodded and waved back at him. I didn't realize what they were saying, until later, at the trial. The clerk was called as a witness, and then I understood what was really going on."

Jamie paused. It was a bitter memory and not easy to repeat. "He testified that Orrin came into the office and said he needed to use the phone. And he said Orrin also wanted to get some ice. He said Orrin pointed to me, waiting in the car. He said he saw 'this cute blonde' in the car and he identified me, of course. Said he saw me wave, like Orrin and me were real pals. He testified that Orrin said we had a bottle, and we were going to have a little party in the room. And the way he said it, you could tell what kind of party he figured Orrin was talking about. He said Orrin told him not to wait up, that it was going to be a long night—oh God, that damn clerk was all leers and smirks and kind of locker room smutty. And then he told the judge he looked at the clock and saw it was eight o'clock and he was about to close up for the night, turn off the VACANCY light, and go home." Jamie was quiet then, remembering. She was staring at nothing at all, and was picking at her fingernail. "And he said he told Orrin the two of us should go ahead and have a good time. There'd be no one around to bother us.

"Oh, I was just so clueless. They were setting me up. It was all so carefully worked out and I had no idea at all. I saw Orrin make his call and then he came back to the car and drove it up to his room, which was all the way at the far end of the row. He parked the car, turned out the lights and took the keys with him, and he said to me, 'Won't be but a minute.'

"I saw him open the door of his room, I saw him go inside, and I saw the light go on. He left the door to the room open a little, like he'd be right out. He didn't ask me to come in. Nothing at all happened to warn me, I swear. He was really so slick. And I was really so innocent.

"So, while I waited, I had plenty of time to look around at the empty parking lot and at that little collection of sad, lonely rooms. I saw that there were no other cars parked in the lot. I saw the clerk, down at the other end, turn out all the lights and come out of the office, lock the door behind him, get into his little VW and drive away. And I figured, with so little business, it made sense for him to leave early.

"And then I began to wonder what was taking Orrin so long, must have been fifteen minutes, at least, and finally—I didn't even *think*—I just got out of the car to go looking for him. The door was open, like I said, and the light was on, but when I looked inside, I couldn't see him so I called to him.

"I said, 'Orrin. Are you okay?' I was beginning to feel concerned. He couldn't have vanished into thin air and I was thinking maybe he was having some kind of problem. An accident, maybe. So I went ahead into the room. Then I heard his voice. 'Well, well, well. I thought you'd never get here.' And right away, I knew I was in trouble. Real trouble.

"There he was, sitting in a chair over on the other side of the open door, where I couldn't see him at first. He stuck his boot up against the door and pushed it closed behind me. And before I could do anything, he was up and locked the door behind me. I tried to get at it, but he was blocking it and he was too strong for me. He was just laughing and I was yelling at him to let me out. I can still hear that nasty voice of his, every single word: 'Hey, darlin'. You might as well lighten up a little. We're gonna be here for a while, so you can just take it easy. No reason we can't have a little fun.' And I can still see that face of his, like a photograph stuck in my head. His crooked teeth, and no shave, and those eyes of his, so pale, like there was no life in them. I kept trying to get to the door but he had his hands digging into my arm. I remember his dirty fingernails, and I could smell the beer on his breath.

"I knew that yelling for help wasn't going to do any good. I'd already seen there wasn't anyone around. I tried to stay calm, tried to think. I made myself take a couple of deep breaths so I could stop struggling and just quietly look into those cold eyes of his. And I said as calmly as I could, 'Listen Orrin. I really want to get out of here. I'm a married woman and I'm not interested in fooling around. If you thought—'

"And that's as far as I got. He started laughing right out loud. He said, 'Hey, honey. I know all about how you're a married woman and you got a kid and everything.' He was looking down into the top of my shirt, and—oh! he was so disgusting—he put his arms around me and he pulled me really close against him so I could feel his hip bones. And he said 'Don't see how that should get in our way. Don't see why we couldn't have a little fun for ourselves here, and then you could leave whenever you want.' And I told him, 'Orrin, I don't want to do this.' I was trying to keep the panic out of my voice. I knew if that creep saw how scared I was, he'd make it even worse."

Jamie stopped, took a deep breath and looked long and hard at Cal.

"I know what you're thinking. You're thinking I got raped that night."

Cal didn't say yes or no. He was just waiting. And looking hard at her.

"Well, I might just as well have been raped. It sure felt like it. But raping me wasn't part of the plan. Of course, I didn't figure it all out till long after."

"What did happen?"

"Well, there I am, trying my best to be cool, and trying to ease myself out of his grip"—she shuddered, still revolted by the memory—"and all of a sudden he lifts his hands off me." She made the gesture, raising her hands, palms out, fingers spread. "And he looks at his watch, and he says, 'Well, I was hoping there'd be a good time in this for both of us. But hey, darlin,' if you don't want to party a little, why hell, that's *your* loss.'

"And I just stepped back from him, just as easy as that, and he turned and unlocked the door. 'If you want to leave'—he said it just as cool as could be—'if you want to leave, I'm not stopping you.' Well, you better believe, I got out of there right away. There weren't any lights in that parking lot and I could hear him laughing behind me, calling after me, 'Just thought we might liven it up a little.'

"I walked all the way to the trailer site, I don't know how many miles, in the dark, and it was really late by then, so no one saw me get there. And anyway, I didn't want anyone to see me, I felt so slimy and so stupid. I felt I'd come real close to getting raped, and I felt so humiliated, like somehow it was all my fault, I wouldn't have talked to anyone about it. Not then, anyway. Today, maybe I'd be smarter.

"But still I didn't understand what was going on. I didn't even think to connect it with the divorce hearing. At the time, I figured Orrin was just a guy who'd guessed wrong and made a move on an unattached female and was willing to let her go when she made it clear she didn't want to play. I even congratulated myself on how cool I'd been. Like I thought any girl ought to be able to talk her way out of any ugly situation."

She paused again and sighed deeply.

"Like I said, I had other things on my mind. Next day, O.D. disappeared from the job site—no surprise there—and I made myself forget all about him.

"Then, it was three weeks later, at the divorce hearing, I finally caught on to why he had let me go so easily. He'd enjoyed scaring the hell out of me, but his only real purpose had been to be sure the desk clerk saw me with him and then to keep me locked in that motel room until he was sure the desk clerk had closed down for the night. That way, when the clerk was called as a witness, he could testify that he'd seen me in Orrin's car when we arrived. He told the judge he'd got a good look at me and he described me, and he said we looked real friendly. And he also testified that he saw me the next morning, waiting in the car while Orrin checked out. He said, under oath, that I was in that car. That he saw the cute blonde who came in with Orrin the night before, only now she was wearing dark glasses, and he told himself, 'She must have had a busy night. Guess she didn't get much sleep.' And he sort of smirked at the judge and I saw the judge was totally taken in. He looked over at me like I was so beneath him I didn't even belong in his courtroom. And I nudged Almon because I thought he'd say, "Objection," or something, like they do on TV, but Almon was so nervous, I saw he didn't know what to do. I tried to get him to say *something* but he didn't open his mouth—poor incompetent kid—and when I tried to speak, the judge shut me up. I knew that motel clerk was lying and I thought he must have been paid off to say he'd seen me in Orrin's car that morning. And I was sure Ray was behind this, but I had no way to prove it."

Jamie paused. It was painful for her to remember that trial, and she needed to take a couple of deep breaths before she could go on.

"After that, it was all downhill. The guys from the service station were called as witnesses and they testified how Orrin and I looked so friendly and they got from him that we were going out partying that night. He'd even made a point of going into the little convenience store they had there, buying some condoms and saying something to the clerk about how he'd be needing them later that night. And the bartender at the Silver Saddle told how we'd been drinking together, and that he saw Orrin go over and talk to someone who slipped him something that the bartender thought looked like what could have been a little packet of cocaine. And again my dopey lawyer still said nothing, and by then I was just trying to keep from crying and I knew it was all over for me.

"As for the desk clerk at the motel, it wasn't until months later that I realized he hadn't been lying. He *had* seen someone in the car." Jamie paused. Again, she needed to take a deep breath. She still had trouble believing what had been done. "I went to pick up Mandy for our Saturday visit, and she was playing dress-up. And she had on a blonde wig. It looked just like my hair, light blonde and straight, same length. Mandy said she'd found it on the floor in the back seat of Ray's car and I guess he didn't see her take it. And that's when a light bulb went off in my head and I put it all together. The clerk *had* seen someone in that car, someone who looked like me, someone who was with Orrin that morning. Obviously, some woman joined Orrin that night, after I left, and I'd bet anything it was Tina. Ray probably left her off and she just slipped in without anyone seeing her. The place was dark, practically no traffic on the road, the rooms were empty. And then, the next morning, with the wig and dark glasses, and maybe her face turned away so the clerk couldn't get a good look, he really might have thought the woman he saw was me.

"As for the rest of the trial, on top of everything else, because I hadn't been able to get my car fixed in time to pick up Mandy the next day, that was used against me at the hearing too. I'd telephoned, of course, to explain the delay, but Edna testified that I just never showed up. 'But what could you expect from a tramp like that one, coming from the kind of family she does!' That's what she said, with that righteous smirk of hers. And Judge Joyner just nodded his head like he of course agreed with every single word she said."

"So Edna and Ervil were at the hearing?"

Jamie stared blankly across the valley—and across the two years, back to an orange-carpeted courtroom with wooden chairs, and the blue and gold state flag at one side of the judge and the American flag at the other.

"You bet Edna and Ervil were there. They were called as witnesses, too, and of course they had plenty to say about my family and my background, and how they never did approve of Ray's marrying me and how they were prepared—right in a minute!—to look after Mandy every day while Ray went to work and that way they could save her from my wicked influence and see to it that she was set on the path of righteousness."

The sarcasm of Jamie's little laugh was only paint-thin over her profound humiliation and loss.

"The judge really liked what Edna said. Around here, church-going carries a lot of weight, and when Ray's lawyer questioned me, I had to admit that I hadn't had much religious upbringing." She picked up some pebbles and tossed them at her little pile of twigs. "The judge didn't like my kind of work, either. Hell, he didn't like the idea of a mother doing any kind of work. He had plenty to say about how I was 'contributing to the instability of the home environment and creating an unsuitable role model.' He said he didn't hold with all these 'working mothers'—the way he said it you'd think it was an obscene expression—and as far as he was concerned, a woman's place was at home with her children and for sure not doing work that only men should be doing, like road construction."

She peered at Cal, trying to guess at his reaction, but his face was in the deep shadow of his Stetson and the pale illumination revealed only a few small highlights of cheekbone set above the more deeply shadowed planes of his face.

What am I doing? Why am I telling him all this?

But she plunged on.

"The truth was, if I *had* won custody of Mandy—well, I couldn't have provided much for her. There was surely no way I could have let her live in the same house with my dad. You saw that house. You can probably guess how he is. I can handle my dad all right, but you don't want to be around him when he's had a few drinks. I couldn't have admitted it in court, but back then, I really didn't know how I was going to manage, what with having to work and all."

She picked up a long stick that lay close to her feet and as she talked she slowly stripped the dry bark down its sides, leaving only a reedy wand of green to be torn apart by her nervous fingernails. Suddenly she snapped the remnants of the stick into several pieces and tossed them away from her onto the dusty soil.

"Looking back, I realize I was just so scared. Now, I know, I'd have found a way. It wouldn't have been easy, but I'd have found a way."

"What about your husband knocking you around? Didn't the judge react to that?"

"My lawyer tried to get in some testimony about that. He called Tina to the stand, of course, and she just lied. Said she'd gone to the trailer just to help Ray take care of Mandy because I stayed out so late, and she said she'd seen how I threw things at him and attacked him. And would you believe, that stupid judge believed her? He said that he didn't see where Ray had done anything wrong. That Ray had been justified in hitting me because he'd been 'highly provoked.' That's what he said. 'Highly provoked!'

"So the judge decided I had demonstrated an improper moral standard and I was unfit to be Mandy's mother. Ray got to have custody of her, which meant, of course, that in reality, Edna and Ervil got to have custody of her, which was what they wanted from the beginning."

Cal was pinching his lower lip.

"There's one thing I don't get," he said. "Why didn't Fletcher just let you go earlier, as soon as the desk clerk left? If he wasn't going to force anything on you, and only needed for you to be seen coming in with him. Why did he come on to you at all?"

"I've thought about that lots ever since. If he just needed to delay me, there were plenty of ways he could have done it. So at first I figured he just wanted to have a little fun being mean to me, scaring me. But then I realized, the plan was slicker than that. They wanted to be sure I didn't mention anything about being with him, like to the guys on the crew, for example. They knew that if he really scared me, roughed me up even a little, then I'd shut up about him—it can be hard for women to talk about things like that. And especially me, what with the hearing coming up soon. So when it came out in court, they'd made it look like I'd been sleeping around secretly." She put a hand over her eyes and turned her head away, fighting to shut it all out, fighting not to cry again. "And every bit of it worked!"

Then suddenly, Jamie was sorry.

Sorry and angry.

Furious with herself—for having opened it all up to be seen by a man who had just appeared out of nowhere and was completely unknown to her. Like a kid, as if she'd learned nothing at all, she'd been pouring out all her secrets. She had trusted a stranger with the whole ugly mess of her life. And now, she had no way to take it all back.

He's not talking. Of course he's not talking. What can he say? 'Gee, you must be a jerk, getting into a mess like that.' Or maybe 'What a slut—like mother, like daughter.'

Look how I just rode with him right up here into the canyon—a guy I just met tonight, a complete stranger. Jamie, don't you ever learn anything?

A sudden wind sliced through the canyon, a cold draft that blew through the trees and bent the top branches so they waved like silhouetted warning signals, black against the moonlit sky. She stiffened up, making her back as straight as a fence post, crossing her arms over her chest, clutching herself tightly.

"I'm getting cold," she said. "I want to go home now."

Chapter Five

Jamie was wrong about Cal's thoughts. He understood easily enough the hell she'd been living with. He understood she'd been handled too roughly and that her feelings were on a hair trigger. He understood why she had learned to protect herself by drawing high fortress walls around herself.

But Lord, she looks so picture-pretty in the moonlight. It's hard to be close and not touch that wonderful hair. Just a touch—not more. Just an arm around her to pull her close, hold her safe.

But he had seen how she stiffened when he'd put the shirt around her shoulders. And from the beginning he had seen the angry, inward expression of her eyes. He remembered a lesson he'd learned, back when he was a kid. His dad had made a mistake that time by hiring Jack Lyman to break the new string of young horses. There had been this one pretty palomino filly, and Lyman, who had a harsh way with animals, had done everything wrong with that palomino. Used the wrong bit, the wrong spurs, and finally the fool had taken a club to her. She'd been a strong, high-spirited animal to start with, full of spunk, but not a thing mean about her. When Jack Lyman finished with her, she was tough and unwilling, always looking for a fight. They never were able to gentle her down after that.

And this girl's the same. She's already been handled too rough. Isn't going to take much more to ruin her for good. One thing is certain, she sure as hell doesn't need another sonofabitch in her life.

He'd seen how tense she was, her tight little form almost quivering there next to him, her breathing coming shallow and quick as she told her story. He lifted his hand and, meaning to reassure her, let it rest as lightly as possible on her hair. He felt the silkiness against his fingertips and, unable to resist the pleasure of that touch, he stroked gently down her sleek, flaxen hair, starting a shiver in the palm of his hand that spread through his body.

Instantly, Jamie stood up from the rock, getting away from him. "Don't do that! Please! Don't do that!"

He stood up, too, with his hand lifted away from her, where she could see it, not touching her. "I just thought-I mean"—he fumbled for the right words—"I mean it's been so rough for you, and I just wanted—"

"I don't want to hear about it. I just want to go home. Take me home. Right now."

He heard the panic in her voice. He heard how scared she was.

"Sure thing, Jamie." Cal kept his voice as soothing as he could. "I'll drive you back right now. No problem."

She was already heading for the truck.

Jesus, Cal. Take it easy. Don't move so fast. Let her calm down.

He waited a moment where he was, giving her a chance to put some distance between them, and then followed her to the truck.

You knew she'd spook. Couldn't keep your hand to yourself, could you?

Even as he whipped himself, Cal knew the answer. No, he hadn't kept his hand to himself. Like it had a mind of its own. But if ever a woman needed comfort and support, some plain old tender loving care, he could see that Jamie Sundstrom was that woman.

She had already climbed onto the front seat of the truck and was waiting tensely, her legs drawn tightly together, her hands clutched fiercely in her lap, the white hard hat set on the seat next to her, a barrier between them. He was silent as he drove down the canyon, letting her be alone with her own thoughts and her own feelings. It wasn't until he'd driven into the ragged driveway in front of her house, overgrown with scruffy weeds, and she had opened the door, apparently eager to leave him quickly, that he turned to her.

"Wait a minute, Jamie."

She paused, her right hand on the door handle, her left holding her hard hat. Cal got out on his side and quickly came around the front of the truck. He held the door open and put out his hand to help her as she stepped down.

She hesitated, the confusion of her feelings showing clearly in her eyes, and when she accepted the gesture, it plainly made her nervous. But she let him help her out of the truck and when her feet were on firm ground, her hand remained in his, and she let it stay there. The moon was high above them now, making Jamie's face glow pale and silver in the dark, and her glistening eyes, full of the moon's reflection, at first tried to avoid his, looking once to her right, back up the canyon road, and then left, over his shoulder, to the cedar trees down by the highway. But then she let herself look into Cal's face—and she knew he wanted to kiss her. In her head, warning sirens were screaming at her and she was too tense to let herself ignore its message. She made no move, her eyes remained wide open, fixed on him, and Cal felt the tension of her hand in his. He held it for only a moment more as he spoke to her, as gently as he could. "Jamie. I'm not going to hurt you." He took his hand from hers and stepped back. Instantly, like a freed animal, she went past him. Without a word, she went directly into the house, letting the frayed screen door slam shut behind her.

Cal watched her until she disappeared into the house.

He resettled his hat forward on his head,

If ever there was a woman needed some tender, loving care . . .

He got back into the truck, and headed south across the valley, back to Harvey's ranch.

The door slammed behind her and, out of an old habit, she made her usual quick check of the front room, first thing always as she entered the old house. To her left, in the front room, the television was on, the sound turned low. Her father was on the sofa, his shoes off, his bare feet up on one arm of the couch. His head was turned toward the TV but he was sound asleep and snoring loosely.

At least he hasn't burned the place down . . .

But this time she only half paid attention; her thoughts were elsewhere.

She went into the front room but didn't even consider waking him. He preferred sleeping downstairs; he needed the companionship of the background sound and the flickering light. A half dozen or so empty beer cans were scattered on the wooden floor and she gathered them up, not bothering to wipe the spilled drops. Long ago, there'd been a flowered rug there, but it had become so stained and frayed she'd finally got rid of it and he had never noticed. Another can lay wedged between his hip and the back of the couch and there were wet splotches on his pants and on the dirty cushion. She reached over him, pulled out the can, and tucked it into the crook of her arm, along with the others. She carried them outside, at the back of the kitchen, put them down on the dirt, stamped hard on each one to flatten it, and then tossed them all onto the pile that was already there. At the end of the month, she would throw them all onto the bed of the old pickup and cart them away.

Back in the kitchen, she poured a glass of milk and slowly drank it all, standing in front of the open refrigerator, illuminated only by its interior light. Then she washed out the glass, dried it and put it back into the glass-fronted cabinet, and went upstairs to take that shower.

The hot water was a blessing. It stripped away the accumulated grime of the day and worked its magic, letting her tensions ease, her anxieties settle down. As she relaxed, her mind went back over this strange evening, so full of surprises. Beginning with O.D. Fletcher appearing out of nowhere, like a recurring nightmare. And the cowboy who had come to her rescue, also out of nowhere.

Cal Cameron.

With her eyes closed, she remembered the look of him there in the canyon, while she'd waited for him to join her in the truck. He'd stood quietly in the cool light, silhouetted against the great boulders and the jagged firs. Like some mountain animal himself, like the sleek elk that foraged in the hills. Or like the lion that preyed on the gentle deer. His lean body had that same primitive, natural strength and patience, a kind of supple, easy, elemental grace. She opened her eyes, embarrassed, frightened by the confused direction of her feelings.

Cal's touch, as gentle as it was when he held her hand, had frightened her. But now, away from him, she dared to know that her response was more complicated than fear alone, and she was stunned to realize she'd also, at the same time, felt safe with him.

A lifetime of shielding herself against the aching need to be loved had made her unwilling—perhaps unable—to accept this new sensation. His hand on her hair, she could still feel it, warm, comforting. No, more than comforting.

She scrubbed impatiently at her neck and around the back of her shoulders.

Nothing but trouble. It always turns out to be nothing but trouble.

She lathered up the cloth again and rubbed it over her breasts and down her stomach, the smooth skin of her torso a pale contrast against the deep tan of her shoulders. As the rough cloth passed over her exposed body, the image of Cal, standing on the rock, his sleek form lit by the moonlight, was there again in her imagination.

No!

She closed her eyes.

Why would this one be any different?

She tried so hard to force her thoughts away from him, but she remembered how he'd looked, earlier tonight, when he'd walked away from her across the dance floor, those long legs in the tight jeans and the plain boots . . .

Plain old shitkicker boots, nothing special about that, just what everyone else wears.

She turned off the water and stood motionless for a long time, aware of the hunger that cried through all her body. She tried to tell herself it was only the hot water, the strong soap, the rough cloth. Or maybe fatigue.

And I'd been afraid of the cougar! As though that big cat would have hurt me. It's not mountain lions you have to worry about.

She stepped out onto the mat and wrapped a towel around herself. In the dry desert air, cool in the evenings, it was hardly necessary to rub herself dry, the moisture on her skin would evaporate quickly. She walked down the hall to her bedroom, leaving a faint trail of wet footprints behind her on the rough wood floor.

A glimpse into her bedroom would have uncovered Jamie's best-kept secret. Though her manner had been made hard and tough—rough around the edges and increasingly sharp-tongued, a protective shell to keep her safe—in this room could be seen the truer side of her personality. A peek over her bare, damp shoulder would reveal much more of the real girl.

There was little furniture in the room, but Jamie had done what she could with it. It was as clean as frequent dusting and sweeping could make it. There were two windows, one looking south, toward the town, the other facing the mountains to the east, where each morning the coming day announced itself. Ruffled curtains hung at the windows and spread on the twin bed, a matching bedspread. Jamie had bought the curtains and the bedspread when she was fifteen years old, after saving up what she could out of paychecks from her first job down at the Gas 'n' Goodies, down by the Chevron station. It had seemed to her then to be a big deal and very grown-up, picking out the first linens to decorate her room. She had driven up to the Kmart in Spicer's Wells and had spent a couple of hours in maddening, sweet indecision, going through all the stacks of linens in the housewares section. Carefully, she matched this one with that, mixing colors, holding up one colorful package after another, walking away down the aisle and coming back again. Finally she had decided on the set with the soft blue flowers on a peach background, all trimmed with a peach-colored eyelet ruffle.

There was also a small dressing table in the room, set in front of the southern window, and on it she had put a mirror she'd found in the attic, in an old trunk. The mirror had a wooden frame, carved into a wreath of flowers and ribbons, a treasure brought from Sweden long ago by one of her great-great-grandmothers. There were other items on the table, pretty things she'd acquired from time to time. A glass candlestick held a peach-colored candle and next to it was a round bottle of perfume she'd bought in Janssen's drug store in Butcher's Fork. She liked to touch the perfume behind her ears before she went to bed, and sometimes, after dark, her only light would be from the candle, and she'd sit at that table and try to see beyond the mountains that rimmed the valley all around.

Tonight, too, she preferred the softer light. Still wrapped in the towel, she sat at her little dressing table and lit the candle. She ran a comb a few strokes through her hair—it never needed more—and she touched a drop of perfume into the hollow of each shoulder. Then she leaned forward on her elbows and looked thoughtfully into the mirror.

Why was this night different? Usually, what she saw was her anger, her increasing sharpness. Usually, when she sat before her mirror, she saw the lines beginning, the marks of fatigue and chronic resentment. She would frown at her hair, cut roughly and only when she remembered, always in her eyes, always needing a trim. She would hold her hands out before her and scowl at her ragged fingernails—she couldn't stop biting them! And how much longer would her skin stay good, always working out in the sun and the sand of the desert?

So why was this night different? Why, tonight, did her reflected self please her? Why, tonight, did she lift her head, holding it a little sideways, showing herself that she had inherited the good bones of her Scandinavian ancestors, the fine jaw and high forehead and the graceful hairline? Why, tonight, did she think she was beautiful?

She blew out the candle, leaving only the silvery shadow of herself reflected in the mirror. She saw her shoulders, narrow and delicately formed despite her strength, exposed above the towel, remembered Cal's eyes, holding her immobile, and she wondered why she'd been so afraid, so tense.

—I'm not going to hurt you—

She closed her eyes.

Stop this, Jamie!

She stood up and turned away from her reflection. She dropped the towel onto the chair and slipped a fresh nightgown on over her naked body, letting its lacy straps settle into place on her shoulders. She lifted the pale blue blanket and the flowered sheet and as though she were fleeing to a hiding place, she slipped quickly under them, eager to sleep and avoid her thoughts.

But they came anyway.

First, a memory of his body, as though her hands were moving over him, running down his arms, his back, up under his shirt and around to his chest. He was probably not tanned—cowboys never took off their shirts when they worked. Then she thought of *his* hands; they were the kind of hands she liked, strong fingers, with a good reach to them and fine black hairs along the back, hard-working hands, but clean—she'd noticed that. And his face—a good face, thoughtful—she could still see the black eyes, the steady gaze . . .

But then the other thoughts, the demon thoughts, the spoilers, hurried in quickly to fill her mind.

Why am I in such a hurry to trust him? He didn't tell me a thing about himself, practically. Drifted into town from Nevada. Hired on to the old Winder place. Drifted in, he'll drift out again. They all do.

He could have a wife up in Idaho or in Wyoming. Or both, for all I know. With a bunch of kids somewhere. He could be a divorced man, paying alimony to a couple of wives. And child support for a mob of kids. For all I know.

He could be a hatchet murderer. Or a bank robber. Honestly, Jamie, you told him practically your whole life story and you didn't find out a thing about him.

He hurt himself, somehow. He favored the one leg, remember? And he rubbed his knee like it was really aching. But you never asked him, did you? No, you were too busy pouring out your guts. And he never told you much of anything, did he?

Cal Cameron. Nice name.

Wonder how he hurt himself.

Cal. Calvin. Nice old western name. The Callisters, Gordon and LaRaine, named their third boy Calvin. Always call him C.C.

Cal Cameron. Seems like I heard that name before. Was it something good? Something bad?

But Jamie was asleep before she could remember.

Chapter Six

Saturday morning started with a fast cup of coffee and a telephone call to the service station.

"It's the fuel line, Charlie. Just totally rotted out on me, just like you said it would. It's down at the Canyon Rim, in the parking lot there."

"Jeez, Jamie, my guys are real busy this morning." Charlie Bitts's voice, high-pitched and harassed as always, crackled through the telephone. Behind him she could hear the flat, mechanical voice of his radio, putting out the morning weather report and the end-of-the-week futures quotes on grains and precious metals. In the background were the usual body shop sounds of banging tools and the spitting noise of the air compressor. She could almost smell the sharp tar of grease and oil and diesel fuels rising up from the blackened concrete floor.

"Charlie, you've got to help me out. I've got to have the car by eleven-thirty this morning, quarter to twelve at the latest."

"But jeez, honey, it's Saturday."

"I know, Charlie, and I wouldn't ask, but it's my day to be with my kid."

There was a silence on the other end, and Jamie knew old Charlie was doing his best.

"Well, tell you what I can do," he said at last. Then another longish pause. She could picture him pulling the kerchief out of his back pocket and rubbing it over his balding head and down his long, lean, stubbly face. "I'll pull Jimmy off the job he's doing now and send him down with the tow truck. Meantime, I'll take a look, see if I got me a kit for that old Honda of yours somewheres here on the shelf. We get a little cleared-away space here this morning, I might could get that line replaced for you in an hour, hour and a half."

Before she could even say thank you, he added, "If we get it to-gether in time, I'll send someone over to pick you up. Are you to home now?"

"I am. And Charlie?"

"Yep?"

"I surely do appreciate this."

"Well, don't thank me yet. Let's see first can we get her working in time. I better get hustling right now."

"You bet, Charlie. And Charlie, say hello to Darlene for me, okay?"

"You betcha. I'll just be sure and do that." And he hung up.

She poured a second cup of coffee and sat down at the kitchen table to contemplate the day that lay ahead of her.

If all else failed, she told herself, she could take the old pickup out back, but it wasn't an idea she liked. First of all, her father would probably insist that he was going to need it today. And second, everyone in town knew that old wreck was Lee Sundstrom's vehicle, and she didn't want Mandy to be seen riding around in it. The more distance she could keep between her father and her daughter, the bet-ter for Mandy.

She wondered sometimes if Lee himself understood that. Maybe that was why he never talked about his granddaughter, never asked about her, never seemed even to want to see her.

But you'd think a man would want to know his granddaughter, and would want to see her. Would want to love her.

But there's only one thing that man wants.

Someday, Jamie figured, Lee's drinking was going to be a prob-lem for Mandy—maybe it already was. In fact, the chances were good Edna Nixon was making sure that Mandy knew all about her rotten granddaddy. That sort of "doing-good" damage came as nat-ural to Edna Nixon as spit to a hound dog. All the more reason to get Mandy away from her.

As though in an accompaniment to her thoughts, Lee was waking up noisily. She heard him in the front room, the couch was creaking as he dragged himself upright, head hanging, and coughing, cough-ing. She heard him rummaging for a cigarette, heard the striking of a match, and then he was stumbling, shuffling, toward the stairs. He stopped when he saw her sitting in the kitchen and took a step or two to lean against the door frame, looking at her dizzily, his sandy hair hanging thin over his eyes, the cigarette dangling from his mouth, smoke drifting upward over his face.

"What time did you get in?"

"Not late."

He made a sound, a bad-tempered grunt, turned, and went heavily up the stairs.

She called up the stairs to his retreating footsteps. "I may need the truck today."

"No way. Got to see a man later—" The door slammed hard behind him.

That sonofabitch! Didn't even ask why. Wouldn't know or care, of course, today's my day to see Mandy.

She sat there silently for a couple of minutes. Feeling sad.

But jeez, it's like a poison in the system, hating your own father.

Too much hating, Jamie. Hating your father, hating your kid's father, hating the town fathers. Ah, shit!

There must be decent men, men who feel good about their kids, men who are careful of their wives, their marriages, careful of their families.

Well, sure there are. Gordie Callister is one of the good ones. And Charlie Bitts, he was another. But jeez, they're so rare and you have to be so careful.

Like last night.

What about last night?

How would Cal Cameron be with a wife, with a kid? How much could you tell from the way a man holds your hand?

Not a good way to be thinking, Jamie. So he held your hand. And he let you talk your heart out, which you did, like a jerk. And what does all that mean? Could be you'll never hear from him again.

Her phone rang.

And Jamie jumped, really startled, and then laughed at her own response, as though she'd think for a minute there was some magical force out there in the world that would put Cal Cameron on the phone just as she was thinking about him.

She pulled out her phone, but it was only Charlie Bitts to let her know he had in fact come through for her and Jimmy would be by with the old Honda no later than eleven-thirty.

* * *

She could see the little blonde head in the window, bobbing up and down, even as she drove toward the house on Fourth East.

Inside, Mandy had been squirming impatiently for the last twenty minutes, kneeling on the sofa that stood in front of the parlor window, peering over its back. The moment she saw Jamie's car pull up to the house, she slid off the sofa and ran to the front door, her red tennis shoes slapping on the polished wood floor.

"Mommy's here! Mommy's here!"

Jamie was just getting out of the car when the screen door banged open and Mandy came running down the front steps and across the yard.

"Hey there, sweetie!"

Jamie held out her arms and knelt in the edged grass as Mandy's greeting almost knocked her over. The child locked her arms around her mother's neck, her white-blond head snuggled up against Jamie's, the corn silk of their hair mingling and shining in the noontime sun. "Let's go let Grandma know we're leaving now," Jamie said, standing up and taking Mandy's hand.

They went up the front steps and Jamie waited on the porch while Mandy ran to tell Edna that Jamie had arrived. Even Mandy knew Edna wouldn't willingly have Jamie in her home.

Edna came to the door, wiping her hands on a dish towel. Her distaste for Jamie marched before her, a gray rigidity that pinched her face and stiffened her back.

"Do you think maybe this time when you bring her back you could see to it she's not filthy dirty." Sniping at Jamie was the only way she knew to talk to her. "Last time I had to work for hours trying to get the stains out of her shirt. Finally had to just throw it out and buy her a new one."

Jamie rarely responded to Edna's jabs. Certainly not in front of Mandy. She let her eye meet Edna's hostile gaze only for a moment and then she looked past her former mother-in-law into the dark parlor where Ervil could be seen sitting in his usual straight-backed arm chair, pretending to read the newspaper. A steep shaft of mote-filled sunlight, the only light in the shadowed room, cast its musty beams into the corner behind Ervil and lit up a large and ancient rubber plant that had stood there for as long as anyone could remember. Edna's needlepoint pillows were all over the place and on the wall there was a cross-stitched sampler.

The Lord's Blessing Dwells
Where the Righteous Reside

It was a tidy, hateful house, full of its own dry rectitude and there wasn't a day that Jamie didn't suffer with the pain of having Mandy call this dark place home.

She took Mandy's hand in hers and together they turned to leave the porch. "Let's go, sweetie."

Mandy was already tugging her down the steps with Edna's voice crackling after them.

"And don't bring her back late! I'll have dinner on the table at six! You hear?"

Jamie let that slip past her and, as they crossed the yard, Mandy whispered to her, "I *wasn't* filthy dirty!"

"I know that, honey." Jamie leaned down to kiss Mandy's cheek. "I know you weren't filthy dirty." It was bad enough how much she and that wicked old witch hated each other. At least she could try to keep Mandy out of their war. "Grandma just really works very hard keeping everything super clean, so I guess even a tiny little bit of ketchup looks like a whole bottle to her."

She opened the rear door and got Mandy buckled into the car seat. Then she went around to the front and got behind the wheel. From the back seat, Mandy said, "I didn't mean to get dirty. Maybe if we got me a new shirt, Grandma would be glad."

Jamie started the car. "Tell you what," she said. "What we really need to do first of all is get us a big hamburger and a chocolate shake. How about that? And then we can go for a ride all the way to the Big Buy over in Butcher's Fork and we can get you a new shirt."

Then the old biddy can't complain about having to buy a shirt for her granddaughter!

"And if I promise I'll be real, real careful," Mandy said, "and I don't spill a single drop of ketchup, cross my heart, can I get some fries, too?"

"Oh, honey" Jamie slapped her hand impatiently on the steering wheel, her anger at Edna Nixon almost too great to restrain, "You can have all the fries you can eat, and you don't have to worry about the *ketchup!*"

At the plastic-topped table inside the IceeFreez, Mandy dragged the last fry through the puddle of ketchup on her paper plate, swirled it around a couple of times, and then held the soggy thing over her head, turning her face up to let it drop into her mouth. Jamie was glad Mandy had already forgotten about trying to stay spotless.

Such stupid nonsense. You can't expect a little kid to be clean all the time. Isn't that why God made washing machines?

And especially on her one day out of every fourteen that she got to spend with her mother, not even the whole day, she ought to be able to be just a kid!

Is it any different when she gets to see Ray? He can get to see her any time he wants and he wouldn't even notice if the child rolled around all day in a corral. What does Edna say then?

Jamie sipped at the chocolate shake once and then slid it across the table to Mandy, who took a long pull on the straw, almost draining the big paper cup.

And just how much time was she spending with Ray? And what did they do together?

"Sweetie, have you been over to Daddy's place lately. Do you get to see Daddy very much? Does he—do he and Tina—take you out?"

The cup was empty but Mandy kept sucking, sweeping the straw around and around the narrow base. She kept her eyes lowered, as though the inside of her cup had suddenly become very interesting. When she didn't answer the question, Jamie, concerned now, spoke as gently as she could.

"What's the matter, honey. Is there something you don't want to tell me?"

Mandy's fine little brow puckered up before she spoke, and she kept staring into the cup. "Mommy," she said finally. "I feel funny at Daddy's house."

"Funny?" Jamie asked. "At the trailer?"

"They act funny when I'm there."

What's going on? If that bastard is doing anything to hurt her . . .

"Who acts funny? Daddy? Or Tina? It's all right to tell me sweetie. I know you didn't do anything wrong."

Mandy's little face looked so serious and she was keeping her eyes away from Jamie. "Well, once when Grandma was real sick and Grandpa had to drive her all the way to Salt Lake City to go the doctor—"

Jamie hadn't known about that. But even if Edna was seriously ill, no one would have bothered to tell Jamie about it.

"I didn't know Grandma was sick. When was it? Was it after I saw you last time?"

"Yes. Grandpa had to take the day off from work to go with her. So I had to stay with Daddy and Tina and I had to sleep overnight."

Suddenly she got down from her chair and came around the table to climb into Jamie's lap. She started to play nervously with the buttons on Jamie's shirt.

"They have a lot of parties, Mommy, and the people act funny. They sort of laugh a lot, and they cry too, and they run out of the trailer like they don't know where they are. And there was this one man, he wanted me to do something. I didn't know what he wanted. He said to me, 'Here, kid, sniff some of this stuff. It's real good stuff.' And Daddy was laughing and he said, 'Hey lay off her, she's only a kid.' And Mommy, I was scared. And then Daddy and Tina went away and I didn't see them anymore."

Jamie had to hold her tongue against the rage that blazed through her. Her arms went around Mandy who snuggled closer and put her thumb in her mouth, something Jamie hadn't seen her do for a long time.

"And Mommy," Jamie almost couldn't hear her now, "I got under the bed and slept there all night and I wanted so bad for you to come and get me. And the next day, there was only Daddy and Tina, and they were sleeping on the sofa, and they didn't even know I'd been under the bed all night." A couple of tears rolled down Mandy's round cheeks and her tiny chin was all dimpled and quivering. Jamie took a paper napkin from the tray and wiped the child's face.

"Mandy, honey, you were really good to tell me. Don't be afraid at all, sweetie. You didn't do anything wrong. Not a single thing. You were a good girl. You *are* a good girl." She pressed the napkin around the tiny nose. "Now, blow." The child did, and Jamie hugged her. "There. That's my good girl."

"That's not what Grandma says."

"What do you mean honey? What does Grandma say?"

"I don't think Grandma likes me very much. She's always saying I'm *not* good. Only she says I'm a no-good."

Jamie felt as though a hammer had slammed her chest. "Well, Grandma *can't* say that. You're a very good girl. Maybe Grandma just wasn't feeling well. Didn't you say she had to go to the doctor?"

"Why can't I live with you, Mommy?"

The pain in Jamie's throat was making it hard for her to talk. "Sweetie, Grandma and Grandpa love you and they'd be so unhappy if you didn't live with them."

"That's what you always tell me, Mommy, but I told Grandma I want to live with you and she said she was going to wash my mouth out with soap if I said that again. She said the devil was going to take me away and I'd never see *anyone* again. Why can't I stay with you, Mommy? I'd be so good. You'd see, I'd tie my own shoelaces and I wouldn't be any trouble. I know how to wash dishes. I'd wash all the dishes and you wouldn't have to. Please Mommy. I'd try so hard. I'd be such a good girl. You'd see, Mommy. Please!"

She had locked her hands around the back of Jamie's neck and her eyes were fastened on Jamie's.

I could just take her out of this place, just get into the car, and drive with her, far, far away, away from this damned nightmare. It isn't fair. Things like this shouldn't happen to innocent little kids. I should just put her in the car and go!

And we'd wind up fugitives. I can just see it, Mandy's picture in an Amber Alert. And then, after they drag us back, I'd never see her again!

She put her hands around the little face—God, was there anything sweeter than the velvet feel of your own little girl's face in your hands? She hoped the child could see the seriousness of what she was about to say to her. "Someday, you *are* going to live with me, honey. You'll see. I promise you, sweetie. I promise!"

Somehow, somehow I will make it happen!

"And I want you to make a promise to me. I want you to promise me you'll remember that you *are* a good girl, darling. You are a *wonderful* girl. Don't ever let anyone tell you any different!"

She held her tightly, almost terrified by the fragileness of the little body in her arms, and she pressed her cheek against the feathery fine hair.

"Now, you promise me," she said, "if anyone says you're not good, you'll say to them, 'Yes, I *am*. I *am* a good girl.' Promise me, sweetie?"

Mandy whispered firmly right into Jamie's ear.

"I promise, Mommy."

What am I going to do? I don't want to scare her, but she's not safe. I've got to see to it that Ray stays away from her!

And if I don't do it right, I'll make it worse for both of us!

She forced herself to put on a light-hearted face and hugged her little girl. "Now, sweetie, you and I are supposed to be having a good time today. So don't you worry about Grandma. It's going to be all right. And don't worry about Daddy's parties or going over there. That's not going to happen again."

Jamie hadn't a clue how she could stop them, but it was all she could think of to tell Mandy. "And right now, you and I are going shopping and we're going to find you the snazziest new shirt. Okay?"

Mandy sniffled a little bit, but her face brightened. She felt safe with Mommy and Mommy said everything was going to be okay. She put her plump little hand into Jamie's, and together they went back to Jamie's car.

Saturday was family shopping day, the day when everyone from fifty miles around drove into Butcher's Fork to stock up. All the moms and dads and trailing-along kids, babies being toted or riding in shopping carts. The air at the Big Buy was filled with the sounds of piped-in music, the soft whirr of the air-conditioning, and the muted buzz of the shoppers.

Jamie and Mandy made their first stop, as they always did, to buy a bag of popcorn. Jamie carried the bag and Mandy had her fist crammed with popcorn.

"I want a shirt with Hello Kitty on it, Mommy. Okay, Mommy? Can I have a shirt with Hello Kitty on it?"

"For sure you can, if they have them." Jamie steered her toward the racks of children's T-shirts. "Let's see what's here."

Jamie was glad to have something silly to think about. One little corner of her mind could deal with Hello Kitty on a T-shirt. The rest of her mind was being wracked with tough, tough problems. And she didn't have forever to solve them. Every day that Mandy was exposed to the Nixons, all of them, was another day for them to harm her daughter.

As she searched through the hanging shirts on the circular racks, with Mandy bouncing excitedly around her, she was trying to think of a plan. First of all, she would have to just sit down and think this through carefully. And the best way to do that would be to go to her favorite retreat. After she took Mandy back to Edna's tonight she could grab a sandwich and a coffee and head up to the canyon. A few hours up there would clear her head and help her figure things out. And don't even talk to her anymore about finding the strength to just bear her troubles. Those days had just come to an end.

But now the canyon wasn't hers only. She had allowed Cal Cameron to share it with her. A mistake? With everything else on her mind, there in the midst of the T-shirts, there was now also the sudden memory of him from last night, a good-looking cowboy, with the canyon wind blowing the trees and the grasses around him.

And the memory of how she'd run away from the touch of his fingers on her hair and the warmth of his hand holding hers.

"Here's one, Mommy! I found one!"

Mandy was reaching into the display of shirts above her head, excitedly trying to pull out her prize from amidst the mass of hanging T-shirts. "Is this my size? Is it, Mommy? Is it?"

"Hey, good for you honey. You found one all by yourself." Jamie came around the rack to where Mandy was bouncing up and down. "Let's just check the label and see if—"

She was brought up short, forgetting what she was saying. Far down the aisle, near the other end of the store, there he was!

Cal Cameron was walking slowly, apparently trying to find something on the shelf in front of him. He was running his right hand along the labels on the shelf edge.

And his left hand was holding a tiny baby against his chest.

A *baby*? Jamie's mouth opened in astonishment. The infant was sound asleep, her little round head nestled on Cal's shoulder, her little round bottom in its puffy diaper not even filling Cal's big hand. Even at this distance, Jamie could tell the baby wasn't more than a few weeks old. It was dressed only in the diaper, a lightweight knit top and tiny pink booties. A frilly satin headband decorated her fuzzy scalp.

Jamie saw him pull a big pack of diapers from the shelf, and then he turned away, apparently calling to someone to join him. In a moment she saw a shopping cart propelled by a little boy arrive at his side, and Cal dropped the pack into the cart.

"Is it my size, Mommy? Does it fit me?"

Mandy was pulling at the shirt that Jamie had abstractedly removed from its hanger.

"What?" She looked down at Mandy, bringing her thoughts back to the T-shirt. "Oh. Oh, yes. Just a minute."

She looked at the label, and then held the shirt against Mandy's chest, spreading it across the child's shoulders. Involuntarily her eyes rose again to watch Cal, following his jeans-and-boots-and-Stetson-topped figure as he and the boy left the aisle, the infant unmoving on his big shoulder. She watched him walk to the checkout counter where, at the end of the line, a young woman was waiting, along with a little girl of about two or three. Cal came up to the woman and leaned his head close to her as she turned toward him. His arm went around her shoulder, drawing her close in a quick embrace and Jamie felt as though she'd been smacked across the face. His Stetson obscured her view for a moment, but not before she'd had a chance to see that the dark-haired woman was very pretty, a little taller than average height, and that her shape was attractive in her jeans and western shirt. A bright bandana had been rolled into a headband and was knotted around her short, curly hair. As Jamie watched, with a bad feeling of seeing something she wasn't supposed to have seen, Cal reached into his pocket with his free hand and pulled out a wallet that he handed to the woman. She took some bills from it and handed the wallet back to him.

For a moment, Jamie came to a wrong conclusion.

My God, the man has a wife and three kids. Wow! Was I ever close to a big mistake there!

Then she remembered.

Of course. I completely forgot. That must be his sister and her kids.

"Mommy, are we going to buy it? Can I have it, Mommy? Mommy?" Mandy was yanking on Jamie's hand, trying to get her attention. "Mommy! Mommy! You *said!"*

"You bet, honey." She bent low and scooped Mandy up into her arms. "We're going to go pay for it right now. You can tote the shirt, and I'm going to tote you."

She came up behind Cal on the line.

"Well, hello there."

Cal turned and his face lit up.

"Hey, how about that," he said, surprised to see her. His smile was big and broad. "And this," he said, looking down at Mandy, "must be the little Mandy-girl I been hearing about?"

"Yes, this is Mandy. And who is this?" She smiled at the baby, who was still snoozing innocently on Cal's shoulder.

Cal didn't answer right away. He turned to the curly-haired woman who by now was looking Jamie over.

"Ellie, look who's here. This is Jamie Sundstrom I was telling you about." Both women's eyes opened wide, surprised. "This is my sister, Ellie. Ellie Jackman. And that little tyke over there," he said, pointing to the little girl, "stuffing Oreos into her mouth, that's Samantha Susie. We call her Sissy. This big fellow"—he put his hand on the boy's head—"this is A.J. That's short for Andrew John. And this here"—he ducked his chin down toward the baby—"this here's Christina Estrelita. Don't know why they hung such a big name on such a little thing, but they wanted to name her for both her grandmothers. I call her Pissy."

Ellie punched his shoulder.

"Don't listen to him. We call her Chrissy."

"Chrissy looks very comfortable," Jamie said.

"She'll be yelling soon enough," Ellie said, moving ahead in the line. "Twenty minutes from now, like clockwork, I'll be feeding her again. So I really got to drag this crowd on home right away." She was loading things onto the checkout conveyor belt. "But I told Cal here to bring you down to visit. And Mandy, too. She's just about right between A.J. and Sissy, isn't she?"

"Just about."

"How about it, Jamie?" Cal said.

"Well, sure. Maybe some Saturday."

"Oh, I forgot. You and Mandy don't get much time together. So we shouldn't keep you now."

"Well, yes, we were just going for a drive together"—she paused—"into the canyon, maybe . . ."

Ellie had taken the baby from Cal and was herding her kids to the door. She called back, "We've got to run now," and she was out into the parking lot.

Cal started after his sister, pushing the bag-filled cart.

"I'll call you," he said.

Sure. We'll see.

"Where are we driving, Mommy?"

Mandy was holding one hand out the window, letting the wind press against her fingers. A sad, sad song was coming to them on the Kanab station and she and Jamie had been singing solemnly along.

"I'm going to show you the best place in the whole world,"

Jamie turned the car onto the ranch road that would take them to her canyon.

Mandy pointed to the field just south of where they were driving. A young calf was standing near the road, its skinny legs splayed out and its neck stretched way up as it lifted its head to the sky. It was bellowing loudly, calling over and over again.

"What the matter with him, Mommy? He sounds like he's crying."

Jamie stopped the car and searched the field as far as she could see. There was no cow in sight.

"It looks like the little fellow got separated from his Mommy."

Mandy's little brow puckered. "Does that mean he's lost, Mommy? Won't she be able to find him?"

"She'll be able to find him." Jamie looked into the rear view mirror so she could look into Mandy's eyes. "When the Mommy cow and the baby calf get lost, they have a way to find each other again."

"What do they do?"

"They go back to the last place where they were together. It may take them a day or two, and they don't always get to the exactly right spot, but they get pretty close, and then the Mommy moos as loud as she can, and the baby bellows, like that little one is doing, and pretty soon, there they are, together again."

Jamie started up the car and continued toward the canyon. In the rear view mirror, she saw that Mandy had her thumb in her mouth.

When did that *start? She hasn't sucked her thumb since she was an infant.*

"I'll bet, sweetie, by the time we come back this way that calf's Mommy will be there already, giving him his dinner."

Mentally, Jamie crossed her fingers, hoping she wasn't setting Mandy up for a disappointment. In the mirror, she saw a beaming smile break out as Mandy let go of her thumb.

"Yes!" Mandy was all good cheer again. "His Mommy knows how to find him, and she'll come along soon with a big hamburger and a bunch of fries."

"You silly!" Jamie laughed. "You know they only drink chocolate shakes!"

Mandy squealed happily as Jamie gave her a big smile in the mirror, and by the time Jamie had driven to her spot in the canyon, they were both singing again, at the top of their voices, this time to a lively bit of foolishness. Soon she was at her favorite place and Jamie was feeling quite giddy with the pleasure of being in the canyon with her favorite person.

"This is where I come whenever I want to be in a really pretty place. Or when I need to think real hard about something. We can just sit here for a while and listen to the birds. We still have a couple of hours before we have to get you back to Grandma's."

She lifted Mandy onto the flat rock and sat down next to her, cuddling the child up to her side.

Together, they enjoyed the peace and the beauty that surrounded them, the lovely isolation of this mountain roost, far above the valley, far from all people. The cool air rustled the fragile, round leaves of the quaking aspens.

"They look like a whole tree of shaking pennies," Mandy said, pointing to the aspen leaves.

Jamie's arm around Mandy tightened.

I'm going to figure out a way. Somehow, there has to be a way to get her back.

They talked of this and that for a while, and Mandy even put her head in Jamie's lap and snoozed for a bit until it was time to return to Sharperville. On the way out of the canyon, Mandy pointed to the field, where the little calf had his head tucked up under his mother's belly, nursing contentedly.

"His Mommy found him," Mandy said, "just like you said she would."

"Of course she did. Didn't I tell you she'd find him? All he had to do was to go back to the last place where they were together."

Jamie was mighty happy that cow had showed up in time. Things didn't always work out all that smoothly, but at least this was one time she got it right.

Chapter Seven

Her phone was ringing just as she was pulling up in front of her dad's house.

Cal was calling and he wanted to see her.

She sat there, behind the wheel. Thinking.

"I don't know, Cal." She chewed on a fingernail nervously. "My Saturdays after I see Mandy are always kind of hard. I'd be real bad company."

"That's just what I figured. Figured you could use a little cheering up."

"I don't know. I'm feeling more poisonous than usual tonight. After seeing my ex-mother-in-law. Anyway, I've got a lot on my mind. There's some stuff has come up and I've got to spend some quiet time by myself so I can think it through real careful."

"Well now, Jamie, you know two heads are better than one."

Why did she hesitate? Why didn't she just tell him to make it some other time?

"Listen," he said, filling in the space of her hesitation, "Ellie here'll make us some sandwiches and we can take them up to your place in the canyon and see if we can't work out some answers for you."

Still she hesitated.

"I'll swing by in about a half hour," he said. "We'll still have a couple of hours of daylight."

"I'll put some coffee in a thermos," she heard herself saying.

"All *right*!"

He hung up and she sat there, staring out over the steering wheel.

"Well, I'll be damned," she said to the empty air. "How did he manage to do that?"

*   *   *

The day had been a hot one and the valley behind them was sending up shimmering images, water-like, reflective. Overhead, just skimming the thin treetops, a turkey buzzard moved slowly, its wings steady, easy, tipped up slightly at the edges, its sharp eyes watching.

It would be good to get up into the canyon; it would be cooler there, easier to think things out. This time Jamie had a jacket with her.

Cal's hands rested lightly at the bottom of the wheel, steering with only the tips of his fingers as the truck climbed the canyon road. He took his eyes from the road for a moment, glancing over at Jamie, whose face was turned away from him, looking out her open window. She was resting one elbow on the frame and was absent-mindedly chewing on her thumbnail.

"You're biting your nails," he said.

He smiled at her, like he got a kick out of her having such a childish habit, and she pulled her hand abruptly away from her mouth, embarrassed to have been caught in the act.

"I was preoccupied,"

"I know. I could see that."

There were little crinkles at the corners of his eyes and they deepened, along with his smile, as he turned back to look at the road.

"I do that sometimes," she said. It had been a long time since anyone had cared. "I bite my nails when I'm thinking—"

"Doesn't bother me. I don't care if you chew 'em up to your elbow."

"It's a bad habit. I only do it when I'm really worried."

"Then I guess you better tell me what's up before you don't have any hands left."

She kept right on biting on that thumbnail, absent-mindedly, occasionally looking out the window in order to avoid looking at him while she told him about her visit with Mandy.

"I don't know which one scares me more," she said finally, "that ex-husband of mine or his rotten mother." She kept looking out the window, trying not to cry. "I mean, can you imagine Ray and Tina doing that stuff in front of Mandy? It's so awful. Not only is she just a kid, but Jesus, she's *his* kid. Doesn't he care at all? I mean, I wouldn't care if they killed themselves with their drugs and whatever other disgusting stuff they do, that's their funeral. But they're endangering my daughter's life with that crap.

"And as for that mother of his, not only is she trying to poison

Mandy's mind against me—that's wicked enough—but she's trying to poison my daughter's mind against *herself*! How can she do that? How can people be like that? What pleasure do they get out of hurting a little girl?"

"That ex-husband and his girlfriend, sounds like they're downright dangerous. What you need is a good lawyer."

"Sure! You know what a good lawyer costs? And anyway, I don't know how to find a real good lawyer, even if I had the money, which I don't. I'd have to take off a few days, go to Salt Lake or maybe St. George. I don't even know how to begin."

"You got *any* money?"

"I've saved some."

Cal shook his head. "Not many so-called 'good' lawyers will even turn on their meters for less than about twenty thousand. Case like this, probably much more."

"That's what I figured."

"So what are you planning to do?"

"I don't know yet. I have to figure out something."

"Well, we better do just that," he said, the big smile spreading across his face again as he watched her chewing hard on that nail. "Or you'll wind up looking like that statue. You know the one, in some museum over in Europe. The naked lady with no arms."

She didn't laugh. Impatiently, irritated with herself, she yanked her finger from her mouth and made herself keep her hands in her lap.

"What do you know about naked ladies?"

He didn't answer her right away, just kept looking at her, and his smile settled into something different.

"I know about naked ladies," he said at last.

There it was again, that confusion of feelings tumbling through her. She wanted to respond, she didn't want to respond. She tried to look into his eyes, she tried to look away from his face. He was so attractive, she was so afraid. She wound up staring at his boots, stretched forward to the floor pedals. His long legs were lean and hard and a little bit bowed, like all true cowboys' legs, which made him walk with a slightly rolling gait, graceful, like a sailor.

That made her remember.

"How'd you hurt your leg?"

"Nothing special. I got in a wreck. Tell you about it sometime.

Anyway," he said, pulling the truck off the road into the clearing that overlooked the valley, "here we are."

They had arrived at Jamie's private spot.

In the daylight, the place seemed even more solitary that it had under the nighttime blanket of moon and stars and cricket sounds. Solitary, that is, if you didn't count the lizards and birds and other critters.

Again, Cal let her go ahead of him so he could watch her as she climbed up through the dry brush to her red-rock bench. The shafts of sunlight, beginning to lengthen as the sun moved westward, caught at her hair, making it go through all its golden changes from bronze to the purest white. His eyes traveled over her, enjoying the rhythmic movement of her body.

Maybe, if he'd kept his eyes where he was going, maybe then he'd have seen the pointy little rock that was sticking straight up from the yellow-red ground, right in his path. The tip of his boot caught at the base of the thing, and he went suddenly flying forward, out of control, landing hard on his left knee.

"*Aaaahhhh.*"

Jamie turned sharply at the sound of Cal's half-strangled cry, his gasp of pain, and she saw him down on the ground. The color had drained from his face, his eyes suddenly staring and hollow.

"Jesus," he whispered.

He was lifting himself on his right knee, bracing himself with one hand dug into the ground, the other clutching at his left leg, just above the knee, trying to keep his weight off it. His hat had gone flying when he fell, and as he bent his head in agony, trying to catch the breath that had been stunned out of him by the piercing pain, the thick black curls fell forward over his forehead.

She ran back and dropped to her knees next to him.

"Cal! What is it? Are you all right?"

He lifted his head toward her as he tried to catch his breath and she was alarmed by his color, suddenly gray beneath the dark tan. A cold sweat was standing out on his forehead, brushed by his hair, and a film of pain glazed his eyes.

He focused slowly on her eyes, and he took several very slow, very deep breaths as the color slowly came back into his face. At last, like a boxer clearing his head after a knockdown, he shook his head sharply a couple of times, exhaled heavily once or twice, and slowly, gingerly, pushed himself up to stand on his right leg, keeping his weight off the left one. Then he limped stiffly over to where his hat had fallen, bent awkwardly to pick it up, and set it firmly back on his head.

"Come on, little lady." He was climbing painfully. "Let's get up to that rock. I think I need to sit down a mite," he muttered under his breath, "before I faint."

Jamie scrambled up behind him, wanting to help and not knowing what she could do. She reached him just as he sat down heavily onto the red sandstone and stretched his legs in front of him, pressing his hand hard on his thigh, trying to ease the pain that was knifing up and down his leg.

"Whoo-ee." He wiped his hand across his forehead. "Doc said it would hurt if I banged it. He didn't tell me about seeing stars." He tried to smile at her. "That'll teach me to watch where I'm going."

"You scared me. I thought I was going to have to carry you down the mountain."

She didn't know she'd put her hand over his, as though trying, unconsciously, by her touch, to heal the injury. He looked down at the small hand, with its nails ragged like a child's, resting on his big rough one. He took another deep breath.

"Why don't you tell me what happened, Cal? Tell me how you got hurt."

"I got in a wreck."

"A wreck?"

"Yeah. That's what they call it. A wreck. I got wrecked by about twelve hundred pounds of the meanest piece of devilment on God's green earth. Goes by the name of Whipcord."

"I don't understand."

"Well, I guess now it's my turn to tell the story of *my* life."

He looked up to where a hawk was leaning into a canyon updraft, cruising high, letting it carry him west beyond the mountain. Cal watched the hawk and imagined it could see, from up there, all the way to Nevada, all the way to Bennion, up in the northeast corner of the state, all the way to the C-Bar Ranch.

"It's a big spread," he said, "a couple hundred thousand acres, all cattle, and it's been in the Cameron family for four generations. Dad always had a couple of rough-string riders on the ranch to break the young horses, and from the time I was just a tad I just couldn't get enough of hanging around those fellows. Some of those guys could watch a horse real close and understand it as plain as if it was talking English. They could read every move, like an ear just flicked a little forward would catch a man's tone of voice, or how they'd lift up a lip or tighten it down against their teeth when they're nervous, or crimp their tail down between their legs, or you'd see the tension of a shoulder muscle or a change in their breathing. I got so I could read a horse as well as any full-grown man.

"I wasn't no more than eight or nine years old when my dad let me start helping with the young foals, breaking them to the hackamore, coaching them real gentle to a proper lead. Riding just came natural and I was breaking the yearlings to the saddle by the time I was ten. And the rougher the horse, the more I wanted to take him on. I just couldn't say no to a challenge. Just let one of the hands point to some ornery animal and say, 'Hey, Cal, bet you ten bucks you can't ride old—whoever—over there. Sonofabitch is the meanest damn thing on four legs," and right away I'd just have to climb right up on him, and if the mean damn sonofabitch had already cracked a few cowboy ribs or heads, why, I'd be that much more eager to take the buck out of him.

"Of course I'd already had some practice. I'd started in the Little Britches events when I was just eight, and then later rode with the Elko High School rodeo team."

"I'll bet you were good."

"Well," he was obviously embarrassed, "I took the state titles in the bareback and saddle bronc events in my first year on the team, when I was thirteen. My dad said it was important to find out what it feels like to be a winner and he thought I ought to have the chance to pick up a little money along the way. So we built a little arena and a practice chute and I worked my way up to finally getting my PRCA card. That made me a professional rodeo cowboy, and I started competing in the big events. My mom fretted some—you know how moms worry—but she knew there's no way to tie a cowboy down unless he's willing to be tied, and I was starting to win the big championships, so she just congratulated me and I guess she held her tongue that time I smashed my wrist up in Ogden. And then again when I broke my leg at the Nationals in Las Vegas." His smile was maybe a little triumphant, understandably. "That wreck in Vegas cost me the world championship, but I made it up the next year, and pretty soon I was getting to be a really big-money winner.

"Then, last July, down in Mesquite, there was this small event they called the 'Mesquite Stampede,' and I figured it was a quick opportunity to pick up some easy points before heading up to Salt Lake for the Mormons' big Days of Forty-Seven celebration on the twenty-fourth. That was one rodeo I never missed and I was looking to make some real money on it."

"I'm guessing something changed your plans."

Cal was silent for a long time, his eyes staring into the past, his mouth tight with the anger that was still hard to control.

"Yeah," he said finally. "Yeah, my plans got changed, all right. I hadn't counted on Whipcord.

"There was this big storm coming on—you could see the lightning getting closer—and the air felt funny, even had a funny smell to it. Like it was getting heavy, full of electricity. There was something unhealthy about it. Unnatural."

Cal nodded his head slightly, remembering.

"The guy producing the Stampede, Scotty Matthews, he kept riding around the rails, banging on them, telling us to hurry up, wanting to finish all the events before the rain got to us.

"I'd drawn this new horse, Whipcord, and I was already up on the rails, getting ready to lower down onto him. He'd just been added to Scotty's rough-stock string, and none of us had any book on him yet, but right off I didn't like the feel of him. Not that he acted wild or anything—would have been better if he did, maybe—but he just didn't feel right. That horse was too damn quiet. I could feel it as soon as I was on him, and all the time I was fixing my rigging and the guys were getting the flank strap placed, all the time I was trying to get a feel for him, he just seemed too quiet. Not peaceful or anything like that, just quiet—like a bomb with a fuse burning closer. And mean, like he had a plan. "Not that I mind a rough horse. Hell, that's what you need if you're going to get points, and points is what it's all about."

Jamie knew enough about rodeo to know what it took to get those points. It took finely-tuned reflexes, a delicate touch that lets the rider pick up the animal's natural rhythm, and plenty of suppleness. It took the strength and the readiness for one hell of a bone pounding while riding that half a ton of throw weight. It took breathing and patience and superb coordination to be slammed backward repeatedly, back and back flat against the horse's bucking hindquarters to keep that free arm always in the air, keep his boots raking up forward of the horse's heaving chest.

Jamie could see from Cal's face that something must have gone awfully wrong that day, back in Mesquite. He'd gone completely quiet, just sort of staring into space, and his body rocked a bit, back and forth, while his hand gripped the aching leg

"If you'd rather not talk about it." She paused, expecting an answer. But Cal seemed not to have heard her. His face had gone pale and there was a light sweat above his lip. For a long, long time, he was silent and he seemed to have forgotten she was there. She realized Cal had disappeared into the memory of that awful day.

Even as he held the top of the gate with his free hand, steadying himself in the saddle with his rigging-wrapped fist in position between his legs, he wished this horse would do something to start his motion, start reacting to the man on his back, start reacting to the flank strap, start something! But this damned animal was too quiet. Not like he was going to sleep or anything. Nothing like that. This horse seemed to be all attention, all mean intelligence, too smart to telegraph his plan. Cal could feel the tension in the animal's big muscles. The horse made only the tiniest shift of his weight, a kind of hitch of his shoulder. Nothing more than that, but it felt ominous. Like the damned animal planned some kind of a surprise for his rider.

But you can't wait around all day to converse with a horse. He had to get this show on the road. Cal knew he was as ready as he was going to be. He leaned back on the horse, digging his crotch up tight against his hand, positioning his spurs well forward, where they would have to be when came out of the gate, up against the horse's neck. He concentrated on the animal—getting ready to read the moves that were coming—and on settling himself just right, alert, not tense but with the adrenaline moving. He knew he was ready. What he didn't like was how he still couldn't pick up any signal from the animal.

Just too damn quiet.

Cal nodded. "Okay! Let 'er go"

And the gate opening to his left was released.

Cal knew to expect the explosion out of the gate, the whip-ping turns around the ring, the blur of spectators and pick-up men and colors and noise, the nothing-else-like-it crashing union of man and horse, waiting for the eight-seconds signal when the ride was over and—on those special days when every-thing was going just right—almost wishing the buzzer would never come, that the magnificent ride could go on forever.

But Whipcord hadn't read that script. Or, if he had, he'd just torn it up. Whipcord had a script of his own.

A good horse will come out of that gate into the arena and right away he'll proceed to do his stuff. But not Whipcord. You could almost hear him snickering. He didn't even try to come forward into the ring. God knows how he got the power to do it from a standing start, but Whipcord went straight up, with all four feet propelling himself powerfully into the air. And he didn't just go up. As he went up, he twisted to his right, and he didn't just twist. He had something special waiting for Cal. With all his leaping, corkscrewing, half-ton weight, that sonofabitch leaned to the left! He ground his withers right into the metal hinge of the gate, and right there, between horse and hinge, Cal's kneecap caught the full crushing, twisting, split-ting impact.

The pain that screamed through him knocked him out in-stantly and he was already unconscious as Whipcord's motion spilled him like a handful of matchsticks into the dirt.

The blessed blackout didn't last long, and he opened his eyes to see rodeo clowns and pick-up men bending over him, their faces intent, talking to him, but he couldn't figure out what they were saying. Then their faces receded as they moved back to let the ambulance attendants get the stretcher to him.

As the medics lifted him, in the moment before he passed out again, he imagined he could hear that damn horse laugh-ing maliciously.

Jamie waited through all his silence until finally Cal straightened up and took a deep, deep breath. His color came back and he returned to the present.

"Happened a year ago," he said. "I just drew a bad horse and he messed me up. Permanently. It took a lot of surgery to repair the damage, and they had to put in some artificial parts. I just came out of the cast a few months ago and the knee is still pretty tender." The hand that was still gripping his injured leg was white at the knuckles and his free hand, resting on his other knee, was clenched into a tight fist. She watched the muscle in his jaw working as he stared out over the valley, and she saw that he was struggling with an intense anger. "I'll be just about good as new in a few months, but the doc says I'm not going to rodeo anymore. That's the part I haven't got used to yet."

"That's rotten luck."

By now of course, she had recognized his name. The rodeo tour didn't reach into her remote part of the state, but the fame of its stars got some circulation, even in Sharperville. But she'd never heard the report of his accident, and she probably wouldn't have paid it much attention if she had. A rodeo wreck was a common enough story, and Jamie had other things to think about.

"Really rotten luck," she repeated. "To have it all end like that—" She didn't know what else to say.

Cal nodded. "What the hell," he said, trying to conceal his bitterness. "I guess I got enough trophy saddles and silver buckles and other doodads to show off to a hundred grandchildren. And there's plenty of people would say the rodeo circuit is too tough a life anyway, that I'm lucky to be out of it. That's what my mom says. I was traveling all the time. Only time I'd get to see my folks in Nevada was if there was a rodeo nearby. You've got to put a lot of points together if you want to make money in the rodeo business, and that means you got to hit as many events as you can. I bet I entered maybe fifty rodeos a year, all over the country, from Madison Square Garden in New York City to little county fairgrounds in Oregon."

"I read about you," Jamie said. "I remember now. You won the Nationals, in Las Vegas. Three years running."

"That's right." He didn't smile or even seem happy about her recognizing his name. "The thing is, I just wasn't ready to give it up. I really like riding the rough stock. I like the competition. I like the look of the arena on a hot afternoon, with the girls all in shorts and sunglasses and the kids eating their cotton candy. And the smell of the animals and the guys getting ready, stretching, checking their riggings, getting to see each other, shootin' the shit. I even kind of like the fuss people made over me."

"And the women?"

Cal sort of squinted thoughtfully and looked upwards, away from her, his hat shading his eyes, as though he might find the right answer somewhere up in the sky. He considered for a few moments before he went on.

"Yeah, and the women," he said, finally. "When you're traveling all the time, and passing through some little town, maybe only a few days at the most, yeah, there are always women. The kind of women who hook up with a guy for no more than a day or two. I didn't mind that part, and that's the truth.

"And I'll tell you something else I like. I like when I walk up onto the stand, with the sound of the announcer on the mike, coming like from somewhere up in the sky, and they give me that big check for my winnings and I wave it at the crowd and give them a big smile and I wave my hat and everyone cheers like crazy. Yeah, I like that part, too."

Then he paused again, like something was hurting him really bad and it wasn't his knee.

"Some folks hate all the fuss and all the stuff that starts once you make it big. You know, the TV interviews and the endorsements and your face in the newspapers. And there's the business stuff, the meetings with the accountants and financial manager and the investment advisors. Some guys really hate all that. But not me, Jamie. I *liked* being a champion, and I liked everything that went with it. And I sure as hell wasn't ready for it to be all over."

He couldn't continue. It went deeper than that; it wasn't just seeing his championship days at an end. With his rodeo career down the tubes, it seemed to Cal his youth had been taken away. He felt like the one wicked move from that horse had turned him into an old man. His head knew better, but in his heart, in his gut, it seemed his young days were suddenly done . . . and the loss was unbearable. And he didn't know how to say it, couldn't even find the words for it. Cal Cameron had never been an angry man; he had, by nature, an ease and patience that had served him well through all the challenges he'd taken on. But ever since the accident, ever since the strength and suppleness of his body had been compromised, he'd been filled with rage. He didn't know how to get it out of him, and he knew he couldn't go on living with it, but he'd been raised by a code that gave him no language for the tangle of feelings that struggled inside him and he would have sooner cut off his hands than expose the misery of his loss to this lovely girl who was sitting next to him.

For her part, Jamie was also silent. She wanted to say something that would help, like maybe saying that no one could ever take his championships away from him, that he would always be a champion, whether he ever rode again or not. She wanted to say that he must have known, always, that someday he'd have to stop, and if he had money in the bank and a home to return to, he already had more than most people ever get. But she held her tongue. He must have heard all that from lots of people. There was more to it, and she could only guess at what he was feeling.

Cal took a deep breath and sat up straighter. He abruptly relaxed his clenched hands, lifted his hat from his head, and resettled it low over his eyes, as though that would change the direction of this conversation.

"Jeez, Jamie. You should have stopped me. Don't know what got into me, running on like that. You sure you're not sound asleep by now with me talking your ear off?" He really was embarrassed.

"What are you talking about? After all that whole sob story I've been pouring out in your ear. It's the least I can do, is let you complain all you want."

"But that's just it, Jamie. I've got no right to complain. I know how good I've got it. I've done and seen a hell of a lot more than most men ever do, I've put away plenty of money, got it all invested real smart, and it's not as though I don't like the ranch life. Right now, Harvey needs a hand on his place and Ellie was all hot to get the chance to fuss over her kid brother—nothing she likes as much as bossing me around—and I need a place where I can recuperate and do a little light work, keep myself busy.

"And as for the C-Bar, back at Bennion, that's going to be mine someday, and I always expected I'd go back there when my traveling days were over. I like working with my dad and I'd want to take good care of the place like he does. There's a nice little house down by the creek that's waiting for me whenever I want it, and it's a perfect place to start raising a family."

He smiled and his smile, somehow, was sad.

"And how else am I going to get all those grandkids to show off my trophies to," he said, making a stab at a lighter touch. It lasted only a moment. "So, when my knee is better, and Harv gets a regular hired hand, I'm going to move on back to the C-Bar."

Then he said nothing for a long time. Just looked out toward the ranges of mountain peaks, far off, across the valley and beyond. That delicate time had come, that brief time just as the sun sets, between the day's heat and the evening cool, when the air itself seems to pause and no breeze stirs. The canyon was quiet and even the shivery leaves of the aspen trees were still. Finally, he spoke again, quietly, but she could read the anger on his face clearly now, a painful contrast to the peace around them.

"It's just, I guess I figured all that was something I'd do later on, you know, when I got old. Well, older, anyway. I just didn't think I'd have to get so old so early."

What could she say? Jamie wished her own life and Mandy's held the measure of safety that were already in place for Cal. His future looked pretty sweet to her. But no matter. Cal was in pain and she was sympathetic to that.

She looked quickly away from him, instantly unsettled, instantly grasping for a way to deflect him. She forced herself to remember that there had been a reason to come up to this place. She forced herself to set aside all that Cal had just told her and all the emotion that flowed between them. She turned from him, straightened up—all business now—and raised both her hands to lift her hair from her shoulders, flipping it back, stirring a tiny, cooling breeze at the back of her neck. Her gesture made Cal's heart twist around in his chest, but she didn't know about that.

Now he, too, remembered why they were there, and knew it was just as well if he got deflected. There'd been enough talk about him.

"Hey, I thought we came up here to figure a way to get your daughter away from those creeps." He settled back on the rock, stretched his legs out into the dirt, easing the strain on the injured knee.

"Right." She, too, was glad for this change of subject.

"Well," he said, "let's get to it. I think maybe I can help. Here's the thing; like I said, seems to me you need to talk to a good lawyer."

"Sure. But like I said, I don't have the money for a good lawyer. And what's more, I don't know any good lawyers. The only lawyer I ever ran into who knew what he was doing was working for the other side!"

"Well, right there is where I can help you. I know a crackerjack lawyer, absolutely first rate. A lady lawyer, and sharp as a tack. Up in Salt Lake. Her name is French. Elaine French."

"How do you happen to know a crackerjack lady lawyer up in Salt Lake?"

"That's another long story, and I've already chewed your ear off enough. The thing is, you don't meet many lawyers you can like, but Elaine French will be completely straight with you, and if something can be done, she'll tell you what it is. I think you could meet her and see what she can do."

"Will she even talk to me if I can't pay her fee?"

"Elaine's been handling all my legal work for a couple of years now. She'll talk to you if I ask her to. We can worry about the fee later."

We?

Such a small word—and it felt like an alarm bell going off in her head.

All her nerve ends went on alert.

She was scared, but knew she shouldn't back away from this tiny turn in her luck. She took a mental deep breath and kept her voice as steady as she could.

"Maybe I could take off some time from work. I think Gordie wouldn't mind, and I could drive up to Salt Lake on Monday. If you give me Elaine French's number, I'll give her a call when I get there."

"Sure thing. Only, you don't need to do that. I'll call her. And you're not going to drive up alone. I'm going to take you up in the truck."

"I can't let you do that. It's at least five hours each way, and it could be a couple of days." A bundle of mixed emotions tossed around inside her—she was grateful, wary, embarrassed, comforted—both excited and frightened by the thought of a few days alone with this man she barely knew.

What am I doing?

"Why, shoot, Jamie, that's nothing. Harvey can spare me off the ranch for a while and as for the drive, why hell, I've been driving all over the country, from coast to coast, for the last seven, eight years. You think a little bitty ride up to Salt Lake is a long haul for me? Anyway, that old car of yours would never make it. Could be something else will conk out again, and I can't let some other cowboy come along to give you a hand." His face creased into a big grin. "Why shoot, ma'am, that's *my* job. So I'll just pick you up Monday morning early. We'll give Elaine a call on the way, let her know we're coming."

"I don't know what to say. I don't know why you're helping me like this."

She was turned toward him, letting herself explore his face, his eyes, openly. There was a long silence between them. Then he spoke. "Sure you do, Jamie."

Suddenly, everything was still. It seemed the very leaves on the trees were holding their breath, and the grasses paused in their gentle motion. Cal made not even the slightest move toward her, and yet all Jamie's defenses were on a hair trigger.

Of course she knew. All her attention was locked on this quiet-talking, easy-moving man, while her emotions flew every which way.

He leaned, just the tiniest bit, closer to her. Her eyes were locked on his.

A sharp, sweet heat tightened her throat and spread through her whole body. Everything, the stilled trees, the ancient stones, the valley below them, seemed to spin away and she was lost, somewhere in the endless, cloudless sky. His hunger for her was palpable and it terrified her.

In that moment, Jamie panicked. All her familiar fears and inhibitions flooded through her and her defenses sprang into their accustomed place with a terrible force. She was instantly rigid, her heart froze.

What am I going to do! Oh, God! What am I going to do!

For a long, long, minute neither of them moved. Cal had seen the terror in her eyes, seen the anger and denial that chilled their brilliance. He saw her lips shut tight and she looked ready to fight. He waited as long as he could, the struggle inside him keeping him immobile until he accepted that she would not let him come closer. He held himself in check. It was like braking a runaway locomotive, but he willed himself not to ruin everything.

When he felt he could speak safely, without making a fool of himself, he managed to whisper hoarsely. "Let's go, Jamie. I'll take you back to your house now."

They were magic words, and they broke the spell. Jamie's panic gradually eased up. Relief replaced the tension that had stiffened her muscles.

Cal stood up and held out a hand to help her.

"Elaine will want to see all your papers," he said, returning to a neutral subject, giving her time—and space—to recover her sense of safety. "Your divorce decree and all that stuff. Any notes you have. And I'll fill her in when I call her. She'll have plenty of questions. You need to prepare, think through everything she might want to know."

They walked to the truck, he held the door for her, she climbed in, and they drove down the canyon silently. She'd seen how painfully he'd walked, and when they got to her house, she said, "Don't get out. You need to rest that knee." She got out and came around to his side. She put a hand on the edge of the window.

"I'll need to talk to Gordon," she said. "If I don't get him tonight, I'll have to catch him before church in the morning."

"Okay. And I'll let Harv and Ellie know I'll be away for a few days."

"Okay."

Then she did something that astonished them both. To her own amazement, she stepped up onto the running board, leaned in, and kissed him lightly on the cheek. He reached for her, knocking his hat off against the window frame, but she was already running toward the darkened house.

"All *right*!" He was grinning broadly as he retrieved his hat and set it firmly back on his head, where it belonged. He watched her go into the house, saw a light go on inside, knew she was home safe.

"All right." This time it was a whisper.

Chapter Eight

LaRaine Callister had the kids loaded into the big van and was strapping the next littlest into a car seat just as Jamie pulled up in front of the house. Young Gordie was holding the baby, waiting for her to come around to the other side to get the baby settled into his seat. And Gordon Callister, wearing his best white Stetson and his Sunday morning tie and jacket, could be seen just inside the front door, talking on his cell phone. Jamie got out of her car and waved at Gordon, glad to have caught him before he left for church.

He pointed to the phone in his hand, signaling her to wait, so she stopped at the van in the driveway and ducked her head inside, waving a brief greeting to the passengers.

"Morning, LaRaine." Then to all the kids, "Hey, you guys." A whole field of sandy-haired, gray-eyed Callisters waved back at her. "Sorry to hold you up, LaRaine. I see Gordie's busy on the phone. I just need to talk to him for a minute."

"No problem, Jamie. Gordie had to make some calls before we left but he must be about finished now. Something's up at the Henson ranch and we'll have to wait a minute while he takes care of it, so you just take your time. They're not going to start services without him."

Even as she spoke, Gordon came out onto the porch and Jamie ran up to join him just as he was closing the front door behind him.

"Morning, Gordon. LaRaine says there's been some trouble."

"Yep." He looked serious. "Cougar's taken another calf, down at Lou Henson's this time. Took him right out of that little pasture Lou has just back of his house. His 'sick bay' where he keeps any livestock needs doctoring. He's real upset. His kids play out there and the cat's tracks are all over the place, even in the yard up by the children's swing set. Must be a real big one, judging by the prints he left, and he doesn't seem to be afraid of anything, coming right up to the house like that."

"Do they think it's the same one got Al Wideman's calf the other night?"

"No question about it. Same big tracks, same nerve, coming so close to folks' homes."

Jamie thought of the cougar she and Cal had seen, beautiful and bold in the moonlight, and for a moment she thought of keeping silent, as though that big cat was part of a secret that ought to be kept.

"I'll bet it's the same one I saw the other night, in the canyon up by my place," she said at last. "Huge animal, looked like he could take down a grown horse, easy."

"Up by your place?" Gordon shook his head incredulously. "Might just be. If so, he sure is getting around. I don't like it, a big cougar like that, doing his hunting where folks live."

"Are you going after him?"

Gordon seemed preoccupied. He took his hat off and rotated it a few times, staring at it as though it were a crystal ball.

"Well, I hate to do it on a Sunday, but we've got to start tracking him soon. I've been calling around to get some of the men together this afternoon."

He remained thoughtful for a minute. Then, as though he'd finished one piece of business and was ready to start on the next, he put the hat firmly in place on his head and smiled at Jamie, focusing all his attention on her.

"So, Jamie. What's up? What can I do for you?"

Jamie did a quick shift, forgetting the cougar and remembering what brought her here. "I know it's short notice, Gordie, and I'm real sorry, but I'm going to need to take a couple of days off. Tomorrow and Tuesday at least."

Gordon seemed to forget right there that eight people were still waiting for him and that services were supposed to be starting soon He frowned as he pushed his hat toward the back of his head, and peered closely at her.

"What's the matter, Jamie? You're not sick are you?"

"No, Gordie. It's nothing like that." If only it could be something so easy. "It's personal stuff. I've got to go up to Salt Lake for a couple of days. Something just came up, and I wanted to let you know right away. That's why I came by so early. I wanted to catch you before you left for church."

"Well, Jamie, I surely do appreciate that." He pursed his lips, calculating his possible moves. "Sunday morning, might be a little tough finding a replacement." He thought for a moment. "I'll call Craig Larsen over in Flintlock. He's just finished a job up by Delta and if he hasn't signed up for something else right away, he might could send someone over to fill in for you. Two days?"

"Two days. I expect to make it back by Tuesday night, late."

Gordon waved to LaRaine to wait some more. He pulled out his phone and started dialing.

"I'm real sorry to keep you, Gordie. I know you need to get to church."

"LaRaine's used to it," he said as he waited for Craig to pick up. "In this family, it's always something. Not one thing, it's another."

Craig must have answered just then because Gordon turned away, toward the house, and worked it out for Craig to send a man over to Sharperville for a couple of days. Before he was finished, he turned back again to Jamie.

"It's okay, Jamie, honey. We'll manage it, somehow. You go on up to Salt Lake and take care of whatever have to and I'll expect you back on the job Wednesday morning."

"You're a peach, Gordie. I surely do appreciate this."

"No problem, Jamie. You just take care, you hear?"

Jamie turned to head back to her car. Then paused.

"About that cougar," she called back to him, "the one I saw had black ears. Black tufts up at the points of his ears."

"Thanks," he said. "I'll remember that. And Jamie, do me a favor, honey, and tell LaRaine I'll be there in a minute, soon as I take care of this."

"You betcha."

She stopped one more time at the van and delivered Gordon's message.

"That man! You'd think just once in his life he could get somewhere without any interruptions!"

Jamie didn't wait to hear all about it. She wished them all a good day, and hurried to her car. Things were moving smoothly now. The first piece of the plan was taken care of, and now they could get on with the rest.

Chapter Nine

The offices of Larrabee, Slaughter, and French took up the whole ninth floor—the top floor—of the Stilton Building in Salt Lake City. A lot of money had been spent by the firm to make their offices the most impressive in the city, and the Stilton Building had been selected because it was a turn-of-the-century masterpiece, built when the territory was just beginning to flex its muscles as a newly admitted state. The original blueprints had been located in the architect's archives back east and were used to make accurate restorations of the plaster moldings, the fine old woodwork and the elegant brasses. The original marble, quarried from the nearby mountains for the lobby's floor and staircase, had been scrupulously matched upstairs for the firm's entryway, its fireplaces, and even in its bathrooms. The brass fixtures matched their lobby counterparts that after more than a hundred years wore a fine glow of age and dignity. Every detail had been designed to impress the firm's clients—and their adversaries—with the old-fashioned western elegance and solid conservatism of the Stilton Building and its premier tenant, the law firm.

And impressed, indeed, was Jamie, who had never before traveled beyond the red-rock country around Sharperville, except for that quickie elopement in Nevada. She'd never been to Salt Lake, she'd never seen a big city except on TV, and she'd never seen the traffic, the urban pace, the masses of people.

And she'd never been in an elevator. She felt very sophisticated as she entered the stately old machine that carried them with unhurried dignity up to the ninth floor. Both the start and the stop, though not abrupt, did surprising things to her stomach, making her eyes open wide in nervous surprise.

They stepped out into a reception area, where cream-hued marble, deep carpets, and wood paneling were meant to intimidate and impress—and that's just the effect they had on Jamie.

"Jeez," she whispered to Cal. "Some difference from Almon Reed's dumpy little place down in Flintlock!"

A coolly pleasant receptionist, in business suit and high-heeled pumps, was sitting at a leather-topped writing table. She took their names and pointed to the leather couch.

"Ms. French is in a meeting just now, but she's expecting you. She'll be with you in about ten minutes. Would you like some coffee while you're waiting? Or a cup of tea?"

"Coffee's fine for me," Cal said. "Jamie?"

"Sure. Coffee. Thanks."

The receptionist left the room and returned with a small tray bearing cups and saucers and a silver coffee service. Jamie's taste for lady-like things was touched by this deliberate display and she tried to look comfortable though she was suddenly aware of her Sketchers and her jeans and her plain blue cotton shirt.

She and Cal drank their coffee silently, leafing through the magazines on the table in front of them, until the intercom on the receptionist's desk buzzed. The girl pushed a button, listened briefly to the crackling message, and then looked up at them.

"Ms. French is out of her meeting now," she said. "She'll be right with you."

And only a minute later they heard a woman's voice, sharp, high-pitched, and fast-talking.

"Cal Cameron! It's good to see you here in town."

Jamie looked up from her magazine and saw a tall woman, dark hair peppered with gray, coming toward them through the reception area. The woman moved quickly, as though time was money, but she was smiling genially, and she approached Cal with her hand reached out in greeting.

"And this must be the friend you called about."

"Yes, ma'am. I'd like you to meet Jamie Sundstrom."

Cowboys so seldom take off their hats. But now Cal removed his and Jamie realized she'd hardly ever seen him without it. His hair, black and wavy, caught the eyes of both women.

"And Jamie, this is my lawyer, Elaine French. Elaine is the fastest legal gun in the West."

The two women shook hands and each did a quick, wordless appraisal of the other.

Jamie noted the perfectly tailored suit, a dusky rose linen, and the filmy, pale rose blouse cut in a deep vee, just lining the opening of Elaine's suit jacket. Women didn't dress that way in ranch country, and Jamie was seeing, for the first time in real life, a style she'd known only on television. Elaine was wearing jewelry—big chunks of gold at her ears and around her wrist—that looked expensive and, Jamie figured, probably *was* expensive. Her manner was all quick, informal ease and extraordinary confidence. Jamie liked her right away.

"Come on into my office." Elaine started quickly out of the reception area. "Cynthia," she added over her shoulder as she strode past the writing table, "if Mack Brundage from Jenner and Brand calls, you can tell him those transcripts will be delivered whenever I get around to them and not a minute sooner."

"Yes, Ms. French. I'll tell him we'll messenger them to his office first thing tomorrow morning."

Elaine laughed. To Cal and Jamie she said, "That girl is always one step ahead of me."

She led them down a wide, thickly carpeted hall lined with floor-to-ceiling shelves that were filled with fat law books in beige and black bindings. Through a succession of open doors associates were visible, young, good-looking, and intense, each one hard at work at their computers or on their phones, their desks covered with bulging files. None of them looked up as Jamie and Cal passed. A set of double doors revealed the firm's law library, the walls lined with stacks of books and computer stations, several more banks of books housed on movable tracks, and in the center, two rows of long tables at which more associates were working at their laptops. At the end of the hall, a wood-paneled door opened into an enormous office. There were windows on two sides, one pair looking west to the Great Salt Lake—a flat, reflective sliver in the distance—and the others facing the southern end of the valley where, twenty-five miles away at Bluffdale, the ridged promontory called Point of the Mountain reached a brown, treeless paw into the valley. The state prison at Bluffdale was clearly visible through Elaine French's windows.

Elaine pointed to couple of chairs facing her big mahogany desk, inviting Jamie and Cal to get comfortable, and sat down in her big chair behind the desk. She leaned back against the soft leather and gave them one careful, appraising look.

"Okay, Jamie. I know you and Cal drove a long way to see me today, and I'm glad I was able to free up an hour this afternoon. Tell me what brings you here."

So Jamie began her story and Elaine French turned her full attention to the young couple seated a little nervously across from her desk.

Elaine French had no difficulty concentrating on more than one thing at a time, so even as she listened closely to Jamie, interrupting her every now and then to ask a question and to make a note on the long yellow pad in front of her, she was also paying attention to Cal. She saw that his eyes never left Jamie's face. He was sitting way back in the chair, his left foot, in the black, tooled-leather boot stretched forward, his white Stetson perched atop his right knee. She noted that although his posture was relaxed, his attention to Jamie was intense.

Cal is obviously mad about this girl.

At the same time, she evaluated her potential client, this girl that Cal Cameron had totally fallen for, even as she made note of Jamie's account of the divorce, the events of the last two years, and Mandy's disturbing report of activities at Ray's trailer.

She's definitely a bright girl. Nervous, of course; it could be she's never even been outside of that town—Elaine looked down at her notes and found it—*that's it, Sharperville. But still, she knows how to think on her feet. Well-prepared, has all the necessary papers with her. Anticipates my questions. Gives me intelligent, thoughtful answers. I like her.*

And I can see why Cal likes her, too. He's no fool. And what man wouldn't react to her looks. Good shape. Wonderful hair. What I would have given for hair like that when I was her age. And those blue, blue eyes. Vivid, pure blue, like they describe in books, like cornflowers.

Her sharp eye noted Jamie's ragged fingernails.

A little rough around the edges, probably never had a minute's pampering in her whole life. But dress her up right, add a touch of makeup, and with those cheekbones, she'd be a knockout.

But what a load of trouble she's in! Who was her lawyer in this mess?

Elaine glanced down at the papers Jamie had brought her, riffling through them with her fingertips.

Here it is. Almon Reed. Must have been a real jerk. How could he let it get this bad?

I need more information, local stuff. See what's going on with that husband. Sounds like a real bad actor.

She let her dark gray eyes flick over to Cal, sizing up how much he'd be willing to help.

As much as Jamie needs, I'd bet. That boy is solid as a rock, and if I'm any judge, I'd also bet he'd like to give Jamie some of that pampering she's been missing.

But first we have to get her out of this mess. So let's see what we can do for her.

Everyone sat quietly for a moment, while Elaine looked quickly over the notes on the legal pad in front of her. Then, abruptly, she placed her pen onto the yellow pad, making a sharp sound.

"Cal, I'd like to talk to Jamie alone. Would you mind waiting outside?"

He was up on his feet instantly, lifting his hat from where it had been resting on his knee.

"You betcha, ma'am. I'll just go right on down to the front room there, and let you two get to know each other a little better." He crossed the room quickly, the thumping heels of his boots silenced by the thick carpeting. He closed the door as he left, and Elaine brought her full attention back to Jamie.

"He's a doll, isn't he?"

Jamie said nothing, but Elaine noticed the flush that rose to her cheek. Elaine turned to the file on her desk, abruptly all business.

"Okay, Jamie. I'm going to need to review this record carefully before I advise you. But whatever we decide to do, it looks to me like Cal's help is going to be important." She paused thoughtfully, giving careful consideration to what she was about to say. "So there's something I need to know first. Just how does Cal Cameron figure in your life? What is this guy to you?"

With one finger Jamie traced the fine leathery creases in the arm of her chair, suddenly having difficulty looking directly into Elaine's eyes.

"I hardly know him," she said uncertainly. She knew she was being evasive, but it was herself she was evading as much as the probing questions. "I just met him Friday night. Two, three days, it's hardly time enough to know someone well."

"That's bull."

Jamie flinched at Elaine's abrupt response, and felt her hackles rise. Fancy lawyer or not, Elaine French was not going to bully her.

"It's not bull," she said firmly, looking directly into Elaine's eyes. She was not evasive now. "I've known the man only a couple of days. So far, he's been decent and that's real nice. So pin a medal on him! But I don't know why he's putting himself out like this for me, and no one does something for nothing. I've got too much to deal with to take a chance on bringing any more trouble into my life."

She found she was gripping the leather of the chair's arms, and she forced herself to ease up. A small smile softened her mouth. "Cal seems to be a pretty good guy. But I can't tell if he's just another horny cowboy or if he really means to help me out. Like I said, I've known him only two, three days."

Elaine was not at all put off my Jamie's sharp response. Confrontation was her bread and butter and it pleased her to see a display of backbone. The girl was going to need it to get through this mess.

"'Two, three days.'" Elaine repeated Jamie's words. "That's plenty of time." She smiled at Jamie as though they were co-conspirators. "Let me tell you something about Cal."

She put down her pen, folded her arms on the desk top and leaned forward toward Jamie.

"Now, you grew up in ranch country, so you know how these cowboys are. They're a rough bunch. They can be as foul-mouthed as anyone anywhere. On the rodeo circuit, they'll sleep around with anyone who opens her legs. They'll drink and fight and brawl just for the fun of it, and if it comes to shooting—well, a lot of them won't stop at that, either. But they live by a code and it's a serious one. When it comes to a woman in trouble, or a woman they love, there's no messing around. They turn into knights in shining armor, ready to slay dragons." She peered at Jamie, hoping her point was getting across. "These guys are like a modern version of those old stories. They'll ride into any kind of danger for a woman in trouble and they'll defend her all the way if she needs them to.

"As for Cal Cameron, if you ask me, you've got yourself a genuine knight in shining armor. Cal is one hell of a good guy. Honest as they come. And I'll tell you something else. He's got a first-rate business head screwed onto those gorgeous shoulders. That's where he's different from a lot of those other rodeo cowboys. The trouble with most rodeo cowboys is they're so damned independent. Every one of them just has to be his own boss. Some of these men could be making big money, like football players and basketball players, if they played their cards right. If they let the right kind of pros help them. But they refuse to let anyone represent them. You can't get these guys to use a lawyer or an agent. They insist on handling all their contract negotiations—endorsements, promotional appearances, that kind of thing—they handle it all themselves. They always think they know what they're doing. So of course they get screwed.

"But that's where Cal is really different." She leaned across the desk closer to Jamie, making her point with a tap of her fingernail on the desk. "Cal knew enough to do it the right way. He came up here to Salt Lake, all on his own, sat right there, in that chair"—she pointed to the empty chair—"and told me he figured he could use a little professional know-how. Seems there was this cereal company wanted to put his picture on their box of oat flakes, and he came to see me about it. We got him a sweet deal, much better than anything he could have done on his own."

With another tap of her finger for emphasis, Elaine continued.

"I've been handling all that boy's work for a couple of years now. I know how his mind works in the clutch. He's tough and smart and honest. A good combination." She smiled wickedly. "*And* he's got good legs, too."

Jamie couldn't help returning Elaine's smile, woman-to-woman, agreeing.

"And," Elaine said, "he comes from a good family."

Elaine heard herself and she stopped abruptly.

I sound like a matchmaker. What the hell, it's no business of mine! This girl needs legal help, not a maiden aunt! Back off, Frenchy!

"I guess he's been pretty straight with me," Jamie said, cautiously, a little contritely. She wasn't accustomed to women who talked so tough, but still, she was reassured by Elaine's style; it made her feel this was one woman who could handle anything. "So I have no complaints. So far."

Elaine laughed briefly at the grudging admission.

"Well, that's a beginning." She picked up her pen and got back to work. "And I'm glad to hear it. Because I think we're both going to have to rely on him to help us out with this matter of yours." The red fingernail tapped the manila folder Jamie had brought. "Now, about your custody problem." She made a note on the yellow pad. "I want you to come back tomorrow morning, let's say at ten, and I'll be able to advise you then. I'll have reviewed all these papers you brought and checked out your lawyer. And your ex's lawyer, too." With one lifted eyebrow cocked at Jamie, she seemed to ask if that arrangement was satisfactory.

"That'll be fine. Ten o'clock," Jamie agreed, glad she'd cleared a couple of days' absence with Gordon.

Elaine punched a button on her phone system. "Cynthia, Ms. Sundstrom has an appointment tomorrow at ten. Mark it down."

She stood up and came around the desk. "I'll walk you to the door." As they headed toward the hall, she added, "That'll give me a chance to say goodbye to that cowboy of yours."

"What do you think, Cal? Is she going to be able to help me?"

The sun was blinding as they came through the big glass-and-brass doors onto Main Street.

"I've seen that woman work, Jamie. If it can be done, she can do it. We'll find out tomorrow morning. In the meantime, we have an afternoon to kill." He waved an arm, taking in Salt Lake's downtown—a few modern office buildings among the much older ones, all fronting the broad streets and centered around the Mormon temple that raised its white spires into the clear blue sky. The whole scene seemed to have been hung, like a huge picture postcard, right up against a backdrop of spectacular granite mountains. "Let's take a look at what we've been missing, living out in the desert," Cal said.

"But first," Jamie said, "I have to find a place to stay for the night, something not too expensive."

"Hey, we can talk about that later," Cal said. "Right now, let's you and me go look at the fancy stores. They got places here in the big city that'll knock your socks off."

There was music in the air and the chatter and buzz of hundreds of shoppers; escalators climbed up through light-filled spaces lined with shops, and all was a confusion of color and action more dizzying than anything Jamie had ever seen before. Babies were being pushed in strollers, older children ran in and out of the crowds, chasing each other, laughing, spilling their popcorn and their ice cream cones, and teenagers cruised the shops and the food stores, trying to look savvy and succeeding in looking bored.

"Isn't that *something*?"

Cal looked around at the bright spectacle and tipped his hat back, his face beaming as though he had, himself, produced this fantastic show just for Jamie's benefit.

"There's just about everything in the whole world you could want here. Let's just start at one end and work our way all the way through."

Jamie was speechless, dismayed, delighted, all at the same time. There surely was a lot going on in the world beyond the Sharperville valley.

"Wait a minute," she said. She held him back with a hand against Cal's arm as they approached the escalator. "I've never been on one of those things before."

"Nothing to it, Jamie. Just take it slow and easy."

He waited with her while she figured out how the damn contraption worked. They both laughed when a little boy, not more than two or three years old, holding his mommy's hand, stepped casually on ahead of her.

"All right, all right," she said. "If that little tyke can do it—"

It took a couple of false starts before she finally got herself safely onto the moving step, clutching awkwardly at the handrail, and when they reached the top and the escalator deposited her relentlessly onto the second floor, she was thrust back against Cal's chest and into his arms as he arrived behind her. Momentarily, they created a human bottleneck as the people behind them almost ran them down. They were both giggling as Cal pulled her to one side to clear some room for the folks behind them and helped her get straight on her feet. Then he waved his arm to take in the whole clamorous display that surrounded them.

"Now, Jamie, let's pretend we're just in from the ranch, making our annual shopping trip into town to stock up, and it's been a great year, beef prices are way up and we've made a fortune. And on top of that, we struck oil on the south forty. So we've got tons of money to spend."

"I could get into that."

Like kids at a carnival, they strolled along the store fronts, enjoying the music that played in the air above them, pretending they were buying this and that—"I'll take one of those and one of those and one of those"—expensive watches and perfumes, elegant fashions and children's toys. Jamie got dizzy imagining that she was gathering up clothes and jewelry and electronic gadgets, loading up the bed of Cal's truck and arriving back in Sharperville with goods enough to fill up an equally imaginary new house for her and Mandy. As if imagining could make it so, she was soon spending that make-believe fortune with as much relish as if it was really hers, a bulky wad of dollars bulging in her pocket.

"This place makes the Kmart up in Spicer's Wells look pretty puny," she said. "I've seen these malls on TV, but it sure feels different when it's all around you. A lot noisier. A whole lot of racket and—"

And then—and then—she was suddenly silent, transfixed in front of one particular window. It was filled with a profusion of the frilliest, prettiest lingerie she had ever seen. There were tiny panties, trimmed in black lace, and pink lace, and white lace. Fragile bras and silky gowns and negligees displayed in luscious extravagance, accented with exquisite perfume bottles and fancy soaps and ribbons and bows and tiny flowers, all suggesting Victorian images of femininity and delicacy.

Cal would have kept going, but he saw Jamie's face and he changed his mind.

"Let's go in," he said, "and see if all that dainty fluff feels as good as it looks."

"Oh, no, I couldn't."

"What do you mean you 'couldn't'? I don't see any signs saying down-staters aren't allowed."

"It's not that. Really. It's just—" She couldn't think what it was. Too rich, maybe. Too indulgent. Maybe—too intimate. Whatever it was, she was sure it wasn't for her. But Cal had a hand on her arm and, there she was, in the midst of all the satin and silk and ruffles and frivolous frou-frou and charming little wisps of fabric that filled the racks and counters. She was embarrassed to let him know how timid she felt, so she made herself touch the delicate bits of finery, and in only one minute she was running her fingertips over this item and that, delighted by the silver flasks, the flowered picture frames, the fragrant bath oils and gels, the soft fabrics, the filmy gossamer wisps in pale hues.

She wanted it all! The paisley-printed panties, the pale-blue silk pajamas, the long robes of creamy white satin with broad ribbon ties, the matching nightgown with the thinnest straps, cut to the waist at the front. The bras, so pretty, you could almost be seen in public in them.

She was totally seduced. And she was totally unaware of how Cal was watching her, for he recognized her hunger for beautiful things, for all the things she'd never had, and he was indulging a fantasy of his own, a fantasy of giving her everything she'd ever been deprived of, everything she could ever want.

A huge basket on the floor was filled with a pile of peach-colored sachets filled with fragrant potpourri and tied with thin satin ribbons, each decorated with the tiniest of satin roses.

Such a pretty, silly thing, and not expensive. Mandy would love to have one of those.

She picked one from the basket and turned toward Cal. He was standing at a nearby glass-topped counter. He was holding in his big hand the flimsiest pair of panties she had ever seen.

"How about this?" Cal dangled them from a finger as she came over to him. "Isn't this the prettiest thing?" It was just the barest whisper of dark green and red silk and black lace, and it hung from his hand, saucy, intimate, and seductive.

"Oh, Cal. I couldn't." But she wished she could, and she could see he was eager to give her something pretty. "You mustn't—really—" But Cal had already turned to the salesgirl, across the counter, handed her the panties, and pulled a hundred-dollar bill from his wallet.

"We'll take this, ma'am."

The girl had sized up the cute cowboy. She flashed him a coy smile and disappeared.

"Cal!" Jamie's hand was on his arm, involuntarily. "I can't let you do that."

"It's already done." He smiled warmly at her. "That's the kind of thing you should have lots of. It suits you."

Jamie was blushing and that made him laugh.

"I don't know," she said, feeling wary and confused. "It seems so personal."

"Sure it's personal," he said, making light of her objection. "Don't worry about it," he added casually as he took the small sack from the salesgirl who was back with his purchase and the change from his hundred. He took the sachet out of Jamie's hand and handed it to the salesgirl.

"We'll take that, too."

She gave him another coy smile as she rang it up. Cal counted out the difference from the bills he was holding, handed it over, and dropped the sachet into the bag. He put the sack into Jamie's hand and turned to leave the store with her. But as they stepped outside the store, Jamie stopped him.

"Wait, Cal—" Jamie held back. "Wait! It's just—I shouldn't—" She was stymied. She was trying to figure out what she was trying to say. She loved the little panties. She knew she shouldn't allow Cal to give her such an intimate gift—it was too much—and it was also a kind of challenge. And then, to her own surprise, she decided to plunge ahead.

"Wait outside for me, Cal. I'll be just a minute."

She turned and ran back into the store. She had a moment's conference with the salesgirl who obligingly clipped off the sales tag. Then Jamie ducked quickly into a fitting room. She unzipped her jeans and stepped quickly out of them. She peeled off her plain-white Kmart panties and stuffed them into the little sack. Half-naked in front of the mirror, she removed the little fragment of green and red silk from the bag and, for a long minute, held it up to the mirror, savored its rich color and smooth texture. Then, with a delicious sense of permissible naughtiness, a new sensation and not at all childlike, she stepped into the panties and pulled them slowly up her legs, enjoying the sensuous feel of the silk as it slipped over her bottom, the soft lace lying flat, low across her belly. She stared at herself, turning this way and that, surprised by her pleasure at being the pretty image in the mirror.

Then she stepped back into her jeans and pulled them up to cover the lace and silk, zipped up quickly, and hurried to join Cal.

The escalator took them to a lower level where a courtyard of tables and chairs was served by a variety of restaurants. Over pizza and Cokes, Jamie reminded Cal that she needed to find a place to stay overnight.

"I have to keep my costs down. I saw some hotels nearby, but they look pretty fancy. What do you think, Cal? You've been here before. What do you recommend?"

Cal had wolfed down one slice of pizza and was taking a big bite off the point of the second. He paused, wiped his mouth and swallowed.

"Here's what I was thinking. The C-Bar is only about a hundred and fifty miles from here. I haven't been home in ages and I'd like a chance to see my folks. I know they'd be real pleased to meet you. Wouldn't take but a couple of hours to drive there, and you'd have a free room for the night."

"A couple of hours! Jamie was astonished. "Are you planning to *fly?*"

"Don't need to fly. It's a straight shot on I-80 from here. It's an easy drive and I promise I'll hold it to the speed limit. And I'd really like for you to meet my folks. Anyway," he took another bite of the pizza, "these big cities are too noisy for me. I'd kind of like to sleep at the ranch tonight."

Jamie agreed about the noise. The traffic racket outside and the indoor clatter of shoppers and the music had begun to feel like a smothering blanket of sound. She made a quick calculation, balancing her own shyness at the prospect of meeting Cal's parents against the oppressive clamor of the city around her.

"Okay, Cal." Her decision was impulsive. "Let's just do it. Let's drive to Nevada!"

Chapter Ten

He didn't quite keep his promise. He held the big pickup down to about eighty-five, zipping straight-arrow past the Great Salt Lake and the Bonneville Salt Flats, stopping only at the state line at Wendover to get gas and call his mother to tell her he was on his way and to let her know to expect company. It was near sundown when they turned off the interstate highway onto the secondary road that took them to the Cameron spread. The sun was huge against the distant mountains, almost blinding them, when Cal turned the truck west again onto a dirt road, passing through the gate and under a wooden sign that marked the entrance to the ranch.

"This is it," he said. "This is the C-Bar."

In the glowing last warm rays, the change that came over Cal was visible; he was glad to be home. He settled comfortably back against the seat and pushed his hat back letting the wind blow against his face. Behind them, a cloud of dust rose high as the truck moved along the dry road, through the gray and silver-green of the sage, made rosy now by the approaching sunset. Ahead of them, high in the blue sky, a hawk was scanning the sparse foliage, lazily finishing off his day's hunting, and to the north, along a slope of hill, a herd of elk grazed quietly, one or two of them lifting a casual head to examine the passing truck. On the flat, a rough air-strip had been laid out and a small Cessna was parked there. In that big country, the plane looked as small as a child's toy, as though it were waiting to be picked up and put away in the toy box, now that the day was over.

"Helps cut the place down to size," Cal said, waving airily at it.

Moments later they reached a compound of several buildings surrounded by a white-painted rail fence. They turned into the driveway and in front of them was the Cameron home, painted white like a Midwestern farmhouse and two stories tall under a gabled roof. It had a broad porch and a large, well-watered lawn all around, a tidy patch of green in the surrounding desert. Behind the main house were bunkhouses, a cook house, a slaughter house, and a tack room. Two enormous cottonwood trees shaded the southern side of the lawn and between the two trees, in a gazebo, a white lawn swing rocked back and forth, gently, lazily.

A small woman, slightly plump and light-haired, perhaps fifty years old, in jeans and plaid shirt, was in the swing, reading a book. She looked up as the truck arrived inside the fence in a cloud of dust, dropped her book on the seat beside her, and came quickly toward them, beaming. At the same time, the front door of the house opened and a man came out onto the porch, calling, "Hey, Christina, they're here!"

"Let me get that door for you," Cal said to Jamie, and he was quickly out of the truck and around to her side to let her out. Then he ran to his mother, lifted her off the ground and swung her around a couple of times.

"You fool boy! Put me down! Watch that knee, Cal! You hear me? I don't want you banging that knee again!"

Cal gave his mother a big hug as he stopped swinging her and set her back on her feet.

"Stop babying the boy, Chrissy. He's just fine. The knee's just fine, isn't it, Cal?"

"You bet, Dad. It's coming along just fine. Doc says I'll be busting horses again in no time." The men's hands met in a warm grip, followed by a big hug, muscular and affectionate. Over Cal's shoulder, Big Cal saw Jamie, who had remained near the truck. Christina Cameron was already sizing her up.

"Let's meet your friend, Cal." Mr. Cameron's weathered face, lined by deep creases at the corners of his eyes and around his mouth, turned to examine Jamie, a genial smile masking whatever his thoughts might be.

"Mom. Dad. This is Jamie Sundstrom. Jamie lives down in Sharperville, and she needed some legal advice, so I drove her up to talk to Elaine French. She has to see Elaine again tomorrow morning, so I convinced her to come and stay here tonight."

Jamie shook the proffered hands. "I sure do appreciate your having me here tonight. I don't know my way around the city and I didn't know where I was going to spend the night."

"Why, Jamie, we're happy to have any friend of Cal's." Mrs. Cameron led Jamie to the house and up the porch steps. "And any excuse that gets that boy here is a special treat for us. We don't get to see him often enough."

Jamie stayed quiet during dinner. The Camerons were cordial, but mostly they chattered away at each other, sharing their news, their concerns, the events of the community and the ranch. The parents wanted to hear all about Ellie and the kids, and they wanted to be assured that Cal's knee was healing well. They all had so much to catch up on, they left Jamie free to listen quietly and to get over her shyness. And that gave her a chance to look around her at Cal's home.

In Jamie's experience, ranch families worked hard the year round and usually had far too little to show for all their work. Luxuries, even small ones, were hard to come by, and many a ranch owner thought he'd had a good year if enough was left over after the calves were sold to buy a new Stetson and maybe a pair of boots.

But obviously it was different here on the Cameron spread; this was one family that was making cattle ranching pay. Comfort and financial stability were evident even in the simplicity of the big kitchen where they ate their meal. By Jamie's standards, the room was sumptuous, with its thoughtful design, sleek stainless-steel appliances, and airy space. This was not the hardscrabble lifestyle she was accustomed to.

And she had time now to reflect, and to realize that, in fact, this whole remarkable day had been one introduction after another to a more attractive way of living than she had ever known, beginning with the drive up from Sharperville. Cal's reliable, solid vehicle made the long drive and not once did it heat up or break down. Then there'd been the imposing offices of Larrabee, Slaughter, and French, where the aura of power and money was laid on in a layer as thick as the firm was able to create. And that had been followed by the abundance of goods in the stores at the shopping mall, where there had been almost a surfeit of things, things, and more things. To say nothing of the lingerie store and all it lacy frippery—a tiny bit of which had come away with her, even now snug around her bottom like a secret memento. And finally, this casual, oh-so-ordinary Monday night dinner with the Cameron family, luxurious in its ease, almost opulent in it warmth and honest generosity.

The comfort, the sense of natural, unforced affluence that had gathered around her this day was seductive in its casualness. Even the dinner, which was ranch style—big portions of pot roast, gravy, and potatoes, with cherry pie for dessert—was solidly substantial without being overwhelming. When she declined seconds, Mrs. Cameron didn't press her, though Big Cal did tell her, with obvious pride, "Those cherries are from our own trees, right out in back. Best in the county."

When dinner was over, she offered to help with the dishes, but Cal interrupted her, taking out of her hand the dish towel she had already picked up and putting it back on the wood-topped counter.

"Mom, do me a favor and excuse us from doing the dishes. Or leave them, and we'll do them when we get back." He was already leading Jamie out the door, not even waiting for his mother's response, not even stopping, on his way out, to pick up his hat from the hook next to the door. "I want to take Jamie for a ride. I'd like her to see the place."

Jamie's protest was evident but ineffective as Cal propelled her out through the kitchen door. Mrs. Cameron was smiling, shaking her head indulgently as she started to clear the table.

"You could at least let the girl catch her breath," she called after him, knowing Cal wasn't listening.

The screen door banged behind them and Cal and Jamie disappeared in the direction of the truck. In the kitchen, Big Cal picked up the dessert dishes and carried them to the sink. He ran some water over the plates to rinse them and placed them into the dishwasher. Then he straightened up and looked out the window over the sink, watching the taillights of the truck already far down the road.

"What do you think of her, Chrissy?"

His wife came over to where he was standing and joined him, watching the taillights disappear.

"I'm not sure, Cal. She's young, of course, but it seems like she's right on the edge—like she's just about to go one way or the other. I think she's had some hard times, and it's put a rough edge to her, but underneath, there's something really ladylike about her. Sort of smooth and gentle, if you know what I mean."

"Just what I was thinking, too. She sure is a pretty little thing."

"She is, indeed. I think I like her."

"Me, too."

"And I think Cal is in love with her." She went back to the table, collected more dirty dishes, and brought them to the sink. "Be the best thing in the world for him," she said, "to start thinking about the future. This last year's been so hard on him, and I'm worried about how hard he's taking it—he hasn't accepted what's happened to him at all. I was never happy about his rodeoing, but I hate for him to have it end this way."

"Not easy," said her husband. "Having it all be over so sudden, and so young. Takes a man a long time to get used to that kind of thing." He remained quiet for a long time, preoccupied with another idea that was taking shape in his mind. At last, almost to himself, he said, "I never believed in spoiling my children. You know that, Chrissy. But this friend of Cal's, now that's something else. I do believe a little comfort would do that girl some real good. Looks to be like she could use a little spoiling."

He kept staring out the window for a long time while his wife went back and forth, picking up the dirty dishes and loading up the dishwasher.

At last he turned around and leaned back against the sink.

"You know, Chrissy, one of these days, Cal is going to be needing that house down by the creek. I've been thinking about it and I believe I'm going to do that kitchen over again. Put in a dishwasher and maybe a washer and dryer. It's a nice little place, but it could use a little fixing up. What do you think, honey?"

His wife came over to him and clasped her hands behind his neck. She kissed him lightly on the mouth and said, "I think you ought to talk to Cal about it. I think he may be having some ideas of his own about that house. Wouldn't surprise me the least bit."

Cal switched off the engine and waited for Jamie's reaction.

"I wanted you to see this. It's my favorite spot on the whole ranch."

He had brought her to a sweet oasis that lay, recumbent and sensuous, hidden in an almost invisible pocket in the harsh desert, dotted with shadowed foliage that bristled in the moonlight. Not more than a hundred yards away, a long, low cliff rose into the night, its harsh face cleft and jagged, with spiny bushes and stunted trees clinging tenaciously to the sides of the rugged rock. Along the base of the cliff flowed a broad stream that flashed in the moonlight, its waters fed by distant mountain run-off from the melting winter snows. The stream's music could be heard, running its endless scales, singing its timeless songs, bringing life to its patch of the desert. A broad band of vegetation grew along the waters' banks, and at its far side, tall cottonwood trees formed a kind of grove, cool, touched equally by moonlight and shadow, a lush and private hideaway in the stark openness.

With the engine silent, Cal turned toward Jamie and rested his arm along the back of the seat, waiting to see if this lovely place affected her as it did him.

She was unaware of his eyes on her for her senses had been captured by the enchantment of the stream's song, the grove's sheltered beauty. Her lips parted in response to the shimmering, magical setting, and her breathing slowed, her gaze caught, as though she had been hypnotized. She turned to look at Cal and noticed that without his hat, he looked naked, somehow, like a man just coming out of the shower. He was watching her—so intently—his eyes exploring her face, eager for her response. And she knew why he'd brought her here. Before she could stop him, his hand moved toward her and stroked up through her hair, lifting it away from her neck, smoothing it back as though it had a beautiful life of its own, as though it were a delightfully, magnetically attractive adornment that he, like a curious child, couldn't help touching.

But the pressure of his hand at the back of her neck frightened her. All her inhibitions were once again solidifying inside her.

"Cal, wait. I have to talk to you."

She put a hand against his chest.

To Cal, her touch felt like the closing of a circle, the forming of an irresistible connection between them, and he heard nothing she said. Instead, his arms went around her, enfolding her, and in the same movement, his mouth came to hers, hungry and demanding.

"Please, Cal," she was whispering now, stopping him, turning her face away from him, "please, I really do need to talk to you." She felt as though there was a hand clutching her heart, a barrier against any feeling, a guard against any response. She looked intently into his eyes and she was more forceful. "Please, Cal. Please let me talk to you." Her hand remained pressed against his chest, a silent, clear rejection.

And now he paused. He closed his eyes momentarily, as though he were in some deep, private communion with himself, and then he took a long breath, opened his eyes. He wasn't smiling now and she was sure he was angry.

"I can hold you while you talk, can't I?" His tone was cool.

"No. This is hard enough for me as it is."

Reluctantly, he let her go. He sat back into the seat, resting his hands on the wheel.

"All right. Go ahead. Talk."

"This isn't easy."

"I got that already."

"I don't want you to be angry."

"I'm not angry." Not yet, he seemed to be saying, but the wary set of his face told her he was getting there. "But you know what I want, Jamie." He looked beyond her, toward the stream. "I want to go with you over there, where those cottonwoods are. Tonight. In this place. I want to make love with you."

That stopped her. He spoke those words so easily; would he be able to understand that for her the language of love—and of love-making—lay trapped behind great, inhibiting barriers of sad memories and lost innocence?

"That what I mean, Cal. That's what I have to talk about." She could barely make the words audible. "I have to talk to you about"—she could barely say the words—"about making love."

She didn't know how to interpret the way he was looking at her. He was silent, eyeing her cautiously. She could do nothing but continue, now that she'd finally started.

"Making love—even the casual way you say it, like it's something so easy. I know, it *should* be easy."

Tears burned against her eyelids and she looked away from him, out the window at the gentle grove of trees.

Her voice was faint now, but Cal heard her perfectly.

"Well, dammit," she was whispering, her face still turned away from him, "it's just *not* all that easy. Not for me, anyway. I'm not saying this right but I don't know how to say it. It scares me to tell you this. I know how I feel when you hold me. I know how I feel . . . inside . . ." Now the tears slipped down her cheek.

"But I get scared. It's like something bad is going to happen. And I get afraid I'll be all numb and nothing will work right, and then I feel so ashamed. I know it's not supposed to be that way. And I think something really *is* wrong with me."

She kept looking out the window, unwilling to let him see her face.

"Has it always been like that? I mean, with other guys?" His voice was very quiet.

"Well, it's not like there have been a hundred men in my life." She laughed briefly, bitterly. "In a town like Sharperville, a girl like me learns early to be careful. You sleep with one guy, soon the town'll have you sleeping around with everyone. Not that there weren't boys who tried . . ."

"I'll *bet*."

"But Ray was the first." She closed her eyes. "And the first couple of times it *was* good. I thought I was in love, and I was so damned young and so damned dumb. But then, after we got married, Ray didn't care anymore one way or the other . . . and sometimes . . ." She really couldn't continue.

"Did he hurt you?" Cal spoke through clenched teeth.

She pressed her forehead against the window, ashamed of the memory. She could only whisper an answer. "Sometimes."

She didn't see that Cal's eyes closed and he lifted his chin as though he'd absorbed a blow. "And since Ray? Has there been anyone?"

"Are you kidding? After Orrin Fletcher and all that mess? That's all I'd need. The judge gets wind of that, I'd *never* get Mandy back!"

"Hey, Jamie. You're not expected to stop being a normal sexy woman just because you want custody of your little girl."

"Well, that's how it feels. Like I have to be super careful."

"It's not like that, Jamie. Trust me."

She looked around at him and laughed. "That's what they all say."

He laughed, too, briefly. Then he reached his hand toward her and wiped the tears from her cheeks. He rested his hand on her shoulder.

"Come here," he whispered. His arm circled her and he drew her close to him. And he kissed her. At first, just once, very softly. And then, as though he would not allow any barrier, he kissed her again, with a growing intensity.

Poor Jamie tried, she really did try . . . but his hand moved to the buttons of her shirt . . . and his hand slipped inside . . .

And that's when she froze.

The image of those damned panties flashed through her head and she knew that this was what she'd wanted when she put them on, and she was ashamed and afraid.

She went instantly numb. "I can't do it!"

She pushed hard against his shoulders, forcing him away from her with sudden strength. She grasped his hand in both hers, his hand that was already inside her shirt, and she felt its strength, felt his resistance, felt how impossible it could be to stop him. His face was blackening with sudden frustration and as she pushed him back, forcing his hand away from her, she was certain that now she really had made him angry. Confusion and fear raged through her.

"I can't. Please, Cal. Don't be angry. I can't do it. I'm scared." She pulled her shirt closed around her. "I told you how it is with me. I just can't do it." She turned from him, crying now, looking out the window. "I want to go back. Please drive me back." The grove of trees looked dark now, and threatening.

She was rigid with her determination to keep him away, and he understood that she really meant him to stop. His jaw set hard, the muscles working. And then, abruptly, without another word to her, without looking at her again, he turned on the engine. With a grinding of rubber against the dirt, he turned the truck back toward the ranch and got them home in a hurry. And when he got there, he held no doors for her, offered no kisses goodnight. He slammed into the house, letting Jamie trail miserably behind him, and he stormed into his room.

For a long time, Cal stood at his bedroom window, his fists tight against the frame. He felt like a thousand cymbals were crashing inside his head.

What Jamie had done—what she'd said—

That sonofabitch ex-husband of hers—

It had never happened to him before. Never had a woman pushed him away. He knew Jamie was fearful, but he'd meant to be so gentle, so careful—

Guys like her ex should be horsewhipped!

The cottonwood trees looked back at him, and the swing and the fences were all white and silent in the moonlight.

He peeled off all his clothes and threw them at the wall.

No! Horsewhipping's too good for him. He should be strung up from a tree, like in the old days.

A woman like that. So warm. I can see it. Deep down so full of love.

Naked, he continued to stand at his window, glaring for hours out into the silent night, until the moon settled behind the mountains, until the morning's first light began to thin out the darkness.

I'm going to get that goddamned sonofabitch. Whatever it takes, I'm going to get that sonofabitch.

And in the guest room, Jamie was burrowed under the blankets, trying hard to ignore the tears she couldn't hold back.

"I don't care!" she kept telling herself fiercely. "I just don't care!"

Chapter Eleven

They were right on time the next morning, ten o'clock in Elaine's office. Jamie and Cal sat silently next to each other while Elaine reviewed the case.

"What it amounts to, Jamie, is this. We can turn around that custody order from two years ago by showing that there has been what's called a *material change of circumstances.*"

Even while she explained the procedure, Elaine was puzzling out the overnight change.

What's up between those two? Jamie's been crying. And Cal looks like he could eat nails. And they're both awfully quiet.

She decided not to open that can of worms. Whatever it was, it was just between them, and she was pretty sure Cal wasn't going to bail on this girl, even if they had had a lover's quarrel. Instead, she quickly settled the matter of fees, explaining that she was taking the case pro bono and she headed off Jamie's protests by making some brief explanation, saying the firm always set aside a certain number of its hours in order to represent folks whose pockets were not as deep as the firm's usual corporate clients. Every firm does it, she said. Then she pushed up the sleeves of her dark green silk jacket, turning up the cuffs to expose the pale lining, and didn't give Jamie a chance to discuss it further. She went right into the details of the matter at hand.

Despite her puffy eyes, Jamie's expression told Elaine the girl was paying close attention, trying to find, inside all the legal talk, where the possibility lay of bringing Mandy back to her. Jamie had the impression that the situation was not altogether hopeful, and her fears were confirmed by Elaine's next words.

"We don't have a whole lot to work with. Judge Joyner's decision may have been a model of stupidity"—Elaine was not hiding her contempt for the judge's incompetence—"but the time permitted for appeal has passed. That is, it's too late now to change the original order. So now, instead of an appeal, we have to request a modification of the order, based on totally new grounds. A new judge might be sympathetic to your petition to modify, but it's going to take a whole lot more than sympathy. So let's look at what we do have going for us."

She leaned forward, holding up one finger to begin the count of the issues for them. "The first and most important change in your circumstances, Jamie, is that you're in much better financial shape today than you were two years ago, at the time of the divorce. You have regular income now and steady work. Of course, your work is a little bit unusual, but not so much anymore. That may have been a problem for Joyner, but many women are working construction now, and I'm sure we can get around that." Elaine laughed briefly; she had good reason to trust her powers of oral advocacy. "So that's one. Second"—she raised a second finger—"you've managed your money well and you have a substantial amount saved. That's definitely on your side. We'll have no trouble showing that you are a responsible woman and that you're entirely capable, financially, of making a suitable home for Mandy.

"The next thing the judge is going to look at is your present home environment. From what you've told me, the home you share with your father is out of the question. So third, you're going to have to get out of your father's house immediately and get a suitable place of your own.

"Next, if we can, we want to show that the Nixons' circumstances have also changed, and in their case, for the worse. Now, didn't you mention that Mandy said her grandmother had been sick and had to come up to Salt Lake to see a doctor? People don't travel those distances to come up here unless it's something serious, something the local doctors can't handle. Maybe we can get some information along those lines. We might have a shot at convincing the court that the Nixons are no longer suitable custodial substitutes—"

"Ms. French, I know I'd make a whole lot better home for Mandy than Ray's mother is doing. I know I would!" Jamie surprised herself by her outburst, but it was so hard to be patient, listening to all that legal talk. Still, she heard the rising emotional pitch in her voice and she knew she mustn't be out of control, so she slowed down, took a breath before she continued.

"I'm sorry, but Edna Nixon makes Mandy feel bad about herself. And bad about me. That's got to be unhealthy for any child, to feel that way about herself and about her momma." She leaned forward in the chair, her fists clenched on the black desktop.

"You're absolutely right, Jamie, and that will be the next thing we do, but we don't even get to talk about that problem until we first show that circumstances have changed, and I mean changed significantly. Only then, after we convince the court that there's been a real change, do we get an order for a custody evaluation to find out what's in Mandy's best interests. At that point we get the best experts to examine her, and to examine your home and the Nixons'. The other side will try to show that Mandy should stay where she is. Our experts will disagree. The court may appoint its own experts as well. Then all the experts will report their findings to the judge to say which home they think is best suited to Mandy's emotional development and well-being."

Cal had said nothing yet, but he was leaning forward in his chair, resting his arms on his knees, slowly rotating his hat around and around, his dark eyes examining her intently.

"But what about that other stuff?" he said. "About Jamie's ex? And his girlfriend? The things Mandy told Jamie about Ray and Tina? About what was going on at that party the night she had to stay with them?"

Elaine didn't answer immediately. She weighed her response carefully. Finally, she spoke. "I think it's likely Ray is involved in criminal activities, but by itself the child's story is not going to be good enough. We need evidence, Cal. *Hard* evidence."

She was looking at him thoughtfully, as though she were putting him through some kind of unspoken examination. Cal nodded, also thoughtfully, and she decided they understood each other. She laid her pen down across the yellow pad and sat way back into the big executive chair.

"Of course, if we had that kind of evidence, some real proof of what he's doing, we'd have a much stronger case." She didn't dare to be too explicit, but she was pretty sure both Cal and Jamie were getting the meaning behind her noncommittal words. "A private investigator would be able to do it, but it's hard in a small town for him to work unobtrusively. Someone who lives and works in the area could manage it a little more easily. Of course, he'd have to be careful not to do anything illegal himself."

She was now talking only to Cal.

"I suspect we're dealing with some genuinely dangerous people," she said as Cal nodded his agreement. Clearly he had already reached the same conclusion. "Still, with care—and with plenty of nerve—it might be possible for someone who has his wits about him to turn up something useful."

Cal still looked at her thoughtfully, only nodding his head once or twice, following her exactly. "I understand what you're saying, ma'am, and I hope it's real clear that this part of it is something Jamie should stay out of."

Jamie was ready to jump in, but Elaine turned to her, cutting her protest short.

"Absolutely. Aside from the danger—and I know you're not afraid of the danger, Jamie—but I want you to be totally without any involvement in whatever may happen in the course of this—"

She stopped. After all, she couldn't counsel anyone to do anything illegal. Like trespass. Or breaking and entering. Or burglary. To say nothing of risking one's neck. But if Cal chose to snoop around on his own, well, it certainly couldn't be said that Elaine French had said anything to encourage him. She was, after all, a responsible, highly respected attorney—an officer of the court. She let her voice trail off, waving her hand vaguely in their direction.

"In the meantime," she said, "I'll start putting together a petition to modify the original divorce decree. Let's give it a week to see if anything"—she glanced at Cal—"turns up." She pushed her chair back from the desk and stood up, indicating their conference was concluded.

"Well," Cal said to her as she walked them to the door, "I wouldn't be surprised if something does in fact just happen to turn up. If it does, I guess you just might hear about it, ma'am."

Elaine held the door for them. "That's what I'm hoping for. Without some really good information, it's going to be an uphill battle."

Chapter Twelve

They were silent until they reached the front doors of the Stilton Building, but as soon as they were outside, Jamie stopped abruptly and turned toward Cal.

"You can go on ahead, Cal," she said. "I won't be riding with you back to Sharperville. I'm going to take the bus instead."

"You don't have to do that, Jamie." He was obviously surprised—and not pleased.

"Yes, I do," she said. "I've decided."

She was unwilling to try to explain, but after last night, she couldn't face the long drive alone with him. It had been hard enough, driving back to Salt Lake from the C-Bar. Five more hours cooped up with an angry man would be unbearable.

He looked at her hard for a long minute, but all he saw was her fierce stubbornness, the little jaw set unyieldingly, the blonde head held defiantly. His face was grim, but he didn't even try to argue with her.

Shit! But if that's the way she wants it—

He was too hurt, too angry, too ashamed to argue.

"Suit yourself," was all he said.

He pulled his hat down over his black brows, turned away and left her, standing alone on the sidewalk, alone in the press of people hurrying around her. She turned quickly, too, so she wouldn't have to watch him walking away from her.

She was eager to get away from there. She strode along Main Street, a lonely little figure, moving through the uncaring crowd. At the intersection she asked a passerby for directions to the bus terminal, glad to learn it was nearby. She found it easily, waited for the next bus heading south, to Sharperville, and then chewed her nails miserably all the way back, not even seeing the breathtaking, corkscrewing mountain passes through which the bus traveled, or the mesa-skimming blacktop from which the sheer drop on both sides made the road seem a skyway, unsupported by the earth. It was dangerous terrain and one had to be so careful, but she was too miserable to notice.

When he got back to the ranch, Ellie and Harvey saw right away that something was wrong. Cal looked like he was ready to kick the cat—or anything else handy—and since he was usually so even-tempered, everyone just stayed out of his way; they knew he'd talk when he was ready. Ellie asked if he'd had dinner, but she couldn't get more than a preoccupied mumble. He poured himself a mug of coffee, drank about half of it standing at the kitchen counter, looking fierce. Then he said something about there being a couple of hours' daylight left and he was going to go work on those fence posts and then he disappeared into his room, changed his clothes and stormed out to the road that went through the alfalfa field. The sound of the sledge driving fence posts into the ground could be heard for hours, long after everyone had gone to bed.

"Where you been?" Lee Sundstrom barely looked away from the television to acknowledge his daughter's arrival. A beer can, already empty, dangled from his slack fingers, and in his eyes, brooding and dull, squinting through the cigarette smoke that veiled his face, there was no interest at all in her response.

"I told you. I was going to Salt Lake to see a lawyer."

He made no answer, only puffed listlessly on his cigarette, his sharp face made garish by the television light.

It's pointless to explain anything to him. He doesn't care if I come or go, he doesn't care why I went or what I did while I was away or what I'm going to do now.

Her glance slid past him and past the awful reality of this crumbling place and its useless occupant. With a terrible sense of a shattering collapse, of brittle, over-stressed defenses crashing within her, she hated it all. She wanted to erase it, replace it with its opposite, with a lively, happy family like the one she'd seen in the Cameron home.

But it couldn't be done. This was the reality of her home, these were the facts of her life. Against this scene, the memory of the C-Bar was now like a knife, slicing at the slender threads of her self-esteem. She didn't want this shabby place to be her home, but it was. And she didn't want this empty man to be her father, but there was no other, only this one.

She imagined it all through Cal's eyes and she hated it and was ashamed, and she hated herself for her shame. The confusions that were raging through her were cutting her to pieces. She climbed the stairs to the refuge of her bedroom, undressed, and then sat, naked in the dark and cold, for more than an hour, without even the candle's light to warm her hopes or show her the future.

Cal said he'd help. But not, I think, after last night. And so what! I don't need him. I can handle it myself.

She got into bed, still naked, and finally she slept.

Cal's heart was badly bruised, and his brain felt like mush. What's more, his leg had been aching horribly for hours. Despite all the physical therapy, there were going to be days like this, from now on, when the knee would be giving him trouble, and hard work was the only way Cal knew to fight pain . . . *from now on* . . .

The words repeated themselves relentlessly in his head, for his time of grieving for the heedless, happy-go-lucky boy he had been was not yet over. With each blow of the sledge-hammer against a post, he fought an agonizing battle against his demons, struggling to accept the reality of a loss that could never be recovered. He would never be the same—*could* never be the same. And he was beginning to understand: these are the blows that turn a boy into a man. A hard lesson, but Cal was learning it.

And gradually, although his heart still hurt, and he continued to pound those posts with all the fury of a man raging against his fate, the pain in his leg was forgotten, and one idea emerged clearly from the tangle of emotions, a single ray of clarity in the black, senseless hurricane that was twisting through his mind.

Jamie needs help. And whatever else happens, I'm not going to let that ex-husband of hers do her any more damage. I understood Elaine French's message even if she didn't spell it out for me—and I know what needs to be done.

That realization was the first shred of peace he'd experienced all day and it allowed him finally to put away his tools, go back to the house, and get some sleep.

He was up early the next morning and Harvey was glad to see his brother-in-law looking calmer. As soon as the chores were done, Cal said he had something to tend to. Later that morning, Harvey saw Cal had taken one of the saddle horses and was riding west, toward the desert range.

The crew started early on summer mornings, taking advantage of the cooler hours, so by sunup on Wednesday, Jamie was back at work. She tried to concentrate on cutting the drainage trenches alongside the road bed, but her hands pushed and pulled mechanically on the joysticks. Her mind was engaged elsewhere.

A new place to live. That's number one. How long do I have? Elaine said the papers will be ready by the end of the week. I'll need to start looking right away.

And I'll have to get the new place fixed up, with a bed for Mandy, and enough furniture and kitchen things for two, so I can show I'm ready to make a suitable home for us both. "Suitable"—whatever that means. As though pretty curtains and new dishes could satisfy a child's need for love and safety. But that's what they'll be looking for. I'll go over to Butcher's Fork in the next day or two, and start buying things. Thank God, the money will go further, now that I don't have to worry about legal costs. That, at least, is something to thank Cal for, bringing me to Ms. French.

She got through the day somehow—with her mind running on overdrive—and after sundown, when the guys went out for beer, Jamie was in no mood to join them. Instead, she picked up a copy of the *Desert Bee* and, with a paper-wrapped hamburger and a Coke balanced next to her on the car's front seat, she started hunting for a new place to live. With no success, as it turned out, but it was better than spending the evening at home, and it was definitely a step forward.

But she couldn't stop herself from watching for a sign from Cal— a phone call perhaps, or his blue pickup moving in a cloud of dust up her driveway. No matter how hard she tried, her mind insisted on being filled with Cal, replaying every word, every gesture that had passed between them, returning in maddening repetitions to their last night together.

* * *

By Thursday morning, she was back at work in an even more poisonous mood, veering uncontrollably between fury at Cal and the frustration of her helpless inability to forget him. By the time the sun was high, the day was hotter, and the dusty cloud around her was drier in her eyes and more grating in her throat, The harsh shards of anger were cutting though her like erratic razor blades, and she was a miserable muddle of blasted pride and murderous rage.

It showed in the way she worked the controls of the backhoe, viciously slamming the joysticks back and forth as she struggled with the impulse to smash something. She made the machine take great angry chunks out of the earth, and even Gordon noticed she was swinging the big boom too violently as she deposited the huge buckets of dry soil alongside the trench. He came up beside the yellow monster, shouting to be heard over the growling engine.

"Hey, Jamie! Take it easy! That's a hundred thousand bucks worth of equipment!"

Oh, go buzz off!

She didn't say it, of course. She had at least that much self-control. She knew that Gordon hadn't done anything to deserve such a harsh response. So she just lifted her hand instead, signaling that she'd heard and understood.

"Sorry about that, Gordon." she managed to yell at him over the machine's noise. "I'll watch it."

Gordon had seen, ever since she'd returned from Salt Lake City, that Jamie's mind was far away, and he'd already decided to give her a couple of days to settle down before he had a little talk with her. Might be she'd need a friendly ear or a little help with some problem. But Jamie made it through the rest of the day without causing Gordon any more concern and he stopped worrying about her.

It wasn't until she was on her way home that night that a sign of Cal Cameron's existence turned up. She had stopped to gas up at the Chevron station and there was the blue pickup, standing big as you please, at one of the pumps. Her heart jumped eagerly, but then she saw it wasn't Cal who was sitting in the cab. Ellie Jackman was waiting on the front seat, and Jamie realized the man filling the tank must be Cal's brother-in-law, Harvey Jackman.

Ellie had seen her get out of her car and called to her.

"Why, hi there, Jamie." She stuck her head out the window to call to her husband. "Harvey, look who's here. This here's Jamie Sundstrom, the girl Cal was talking about."

Harvey was a big man, maybe in his late thirties. Ruddy-faced and genial.

"Hey, Jamie. How're you doing?" He topped off his tank and replaced the nozzle in its holder, then came over to her as she was preparing to start the gas running. "Here, let me get that for you," he said, taking the hose out of her hand. "Fill her up?"

"Yes, thanks. It's nice to meet you, Harvey."

A thousand questions raced through her head but only pleasantries made their way through her mouth. Only when Harvey was screwing the cap back onto the gas tank did she finally bring herself to say what was really on her mind—what had been on her mind every minute since she and Cal had parted.

"I haven't seen Cal for a couple days. How is he?" She tried hard to sound casual.

"Far as I know, he's okay. Since you guys got back from Salt Lake, I haven't seen him much, either. He just saddled up his horse and said he'd be away for a few days. Yesterday, right about sunup, just after we finished the chores. Said he'd be gone a while—asked me to get his truck gassed up while he was away. Then he took off into the desert and I guess I won't be looking for him to come home till maybe the weekend some time." He used the bandana that was hanging from his back pocket to wipe his hands. "I wouldn't worry about him, though. Cal can take care of himself."

Jamie just nodded. She didn't trust herself to ask any more questions, but Cal's disappearance, with no explanation, not even to Harvey, only reinforced her certainty that she'd been dumped.

But why would Cal just take off into the desert? What would he be doing out there? Had he decided it was just time to move on?

But no. He left his truck behind. He'll have to be back, at least to get his truck.

Chapter Thirteen

Months before, when the cows were out on their winter range, something there on the desert floor had caught Cal's eye. He'd been busy that day, doctoring a sick heifer, so he'd made only a mental note and then forgot about it. Forgot about it, that is, until he was sitting in Elaine French's office, figuring what he could do about finding the evidence against Ray Nixon. That's when he remembered the burn marks in the dry soil.

The memory of the flat, blackened patches on the sand and some ideas about Jamie's ex-husband suddenly came together in Cal's mind, and with crystal clarity, he realized what the evidence against Ray was going to be. He knew it would take maybe a few days—and he also knew it would be premature to discuss it with Jamie at this stage. Anyway, the less she knew, the safer she'd be.

Now he packed a couple of days' food into his saddle bags, slung his bedroll over his horse's neck, and transferred one of the Winchesters from the gun rack in the truck to the scabbard on his saddle. A cowboy uses a gun as a tool first—to collect some dinner when the grub box is empty or to permanently discourage a predatory animal—and as a weapon only if it becomes necessary. The way Cal had this figured, he was not dealing with pussy cats. Wouldn't surprise him if he met up with some trouble out there on the range and he wanted to be carrying some firepower. He slipped a revolver—the .357 magnum that he always carried in the truck's side pocket—into a holster and belted it on over his jeans.

Twenty thousand acres of open country was a lot of territory to cover on horseback, and it wasn't until close to sundown on the second day that Cal found the marks in the sand he'd been looking for, like those he'd seen months earlier. The shadows of the sage were already long across the dusty ground, almost obscuring his discovery, but he knew he'd found the first link in the chain of evidence.

With one hand grasping the horn of the saddle and his other arm resting over it, he leaned forward, taking a good, long look at the hard, crystalline patch of white residue, about five inches across, just to the left of the horse's front hoof. A few feet away there was a second patch, and beyond that another. A quick glance told him the burn marks formed a square pattern, about forty feet in each direction, and that he was standing at its southeast corner.

"That's it!" he said under his breath. "I knew that's what it had to be!"

He sat up straight in the saddle and replaced his hat firmly, low on his forehead, shading his eyes against the huge, fierce sun that was dropping low over the western horizon. The silent terrain that surrounded him appeared to be devoid of any life other than the sparse foliage. There was no sign of the lizards and rattlesnakes and jack rabbits that were hidden in the dry cover, and even the sky, deeply, brilliantly blue, shimmering above the red and yellow desert, was empty and profoundly quiet. He'd be completely visible to a pair of distant binoculars, but he'd just have to take that chance; neither in the shallow draws nor beyond the scattered clumps of cedar, nor in the rocky rises that formed a nearby horizon, could he see any sign that he was being watched.

He dismounted and knelt next to the nearest patch, brushing his fingers against the hard mass. By the amount of wind-blown sand covering it, he judged the ash to be at least two weeks old, maybe three. As he expected, a long, nail-like spike was buried in the little white mound, confirming that burning road flares had made this pattern here in the empty, isolated reaches of the open range, hundreds of hard-to-reach miles from any unwelcome eyes.

He understood the significance of this square in the desert, about as big around as a swimming pool. It marked the spot where a small, low-flying plane had dropped off its packages of illegal cargo. It was common knowledge that this vast, untracked country was a favorite locale for operators flying in drugs from Mexico and South America. The drop coordinates would be radioed by an accomplice on the ground, who would light flares to guide the pilot to the site, then couriers with a van or pickup truck would collect the drugs. The country was so enormous and so sparsely populated, DEA agents couldn't possibly keep it all under constant surveillance, and it was easy to operate without detection. Within a few weeks, whatever track remained would have been removed by wind and weather and the plodding hoofs of ranging cattle.

He stood up and worked his shoulder muscles, at the same time following with his eyes around the perimeter of the square. At its far corner, the soil was worked over, and a large clump of rabbit brush was lying flat and broken, now brown against the reddish soil. He stepped his horse back, so it wouldn't mar the pattern, and led it around to the other side. It was clear that this was where the cargo had landed. A cluster of indentations remained, and footprints, two sets, showed there'd been considerable activity at this spot. An expert might be able to read the tread of those boot marks, but to Cal they looked like the ordinary imprint of any working boot in the county. There was probably not a pair for a hundred miles around that wasn't carrying this red-yellow dirt in its tread, and the same could be said of the tire tracks that led up to this drop-off spot. A vehicle had apparently been driven this far, turned, and backed up for loading. And here, too, there was nothing Cal could see that would identify the tread, except that the tires were obviously brand new and of a first-rate quality.

"That's okay," he muttered. "I'm on the right track."

With the reins loose in his hand, he knelt next to the broken shrub, examining it minutely. Crushed into the dried, flattened branches, brownish threads were caught. He picked them out with careful fingers.

"Looks to me like burlap." He folded the threads into a corner of his bandana and put it into his saddle bag.

He climbed back into the saddle and moved the horse up close to the tire tracks.

"With all this big country to use, they sure won't stick with one location. The next drop will be somewhere else."

The sun was too low for any more tracking, and anyway, his leg needed a rest. He'd travel a mile or two, just far enough to get clear of this drop site, and then make camp for the night. In the morning, he'd be able to track back to this spot and pick up the trail of those tires—see what it turned up.

Putting distance between himself and the burn pattern, Cal rode west toward where a distant, thick growth of pinyon promised a creek or waterhole where he could bed down for the night, and sure enough, when he reached the trees, there was a barely visible stream flowing thinly through them, providing water enough for him and his animal. He'd build no fire tonight, wanting nothing to signal his presence to hostile eyes, so he made a quick dinner of the remaining deer jerky and granola bars from his saddle bag and, as the day's last light left the sky, he unrolled his sleeping bag and settled down for a few hours' sleep under the emerging stars. By first light, he'd be able to head back and pick up that trail again.

A portion of his awareness had to remain on guard, even while he slept, and in any case sleep would not come easily. In addition to his physical pain—a day in the saddle was hard on his leg—it was also inevitable that here, under the cool beauty of the star-filled sky, the memory of that other night would come to torment him, tightening him helplessly in its silken grasp. He wasn't made of stone, after all, although a lifetime of hard work and solid discipline had taught him self-control, and he couldn't shut away the sensual images that flowed in his mind. He desperately wanted Jamie with him here, inside his sleeping bag, where he could hold her, warm against the cold desert night.

But she had pushed him away.

He groaned, and rolled onto his side, forcing shut the iron door of self-discipline.

And a far-away family of coyotes howled while Cal suffered through the desolate night.

By sunrise, he was back on the track of the vehicle and he followed for some ten miles until it reached a dirt trail traveling south through the desert. He dismounted and walked his horse about fifty yards along the dirt road, following the course of the tires. Their track, already two weeks old, quickly merged with the track of other vehicles, and he was satisfied that the truck had probably taken this dirt trail as far as the graded road that would eventually lead to Butcher's Fork.

"No point in staying with it now," he said to himself. "Today's Friday and I'd best be heading back. It'll be nightfall before I make it to the ranch. Harvey'll be expecting me, and now there's things for me to do in town."

He doubled back the way he'd come, heading west. If he followed along the base of the low, red-rock cliffs that rose to the south of him and just kept traveling west, that would bring him back to the ranch by suppertime. He'd eaten the last of his food the night before, so he'd just as soon not spend another night out in the desert.

He was making good time, even with the occasional stops at the waterholes to rest his horse and to check the irrigation pipes he and Harvey put in during the spring to secure a water flow from any underground springs they located. Everything seemed to be in good shape and he continued heading for home, relaxed in the saddle, planning his next moves.

Except for the occasional buzz and click of insects and the soft sound of the horse's hoofs against the dry earth, the desert was silent. The sun was blazing above him at the midafternoon mark, and a couple of hawks were circling each other off to his left. He squinted against the bright light, following their movements as they rose and dipped together, and as they dropped close to the rough cliff, Cal saw, through narrowed eyes, the long, low shape of an animal moving along the striations of rock, its tawny pelt camouflaged against the sunlit stone.

That cougar is hunting here on Harvey's range. Better discourage him away from the herd.

He slipped the Winchester from its scabbard.

It's too long a shot to bag him, but it wouldn't hurt to make him think twice about hanging around here.

He fired off a round without much hope of doing the animal any damage and the bullet pinged helplessly against the rock below. The cougar took off for the ledge-top and disappeared over the crest. Cal slipped the Winchester back into the scabbard.

I'll have to let Harvey know that cat's come this far south.

He flexed the stiffened knee a couple of times, rearranged his bones in the saddle and removed his hat, raking his fingers through his hair. He scanned the sky to the west, where big storm clouds were building up, moving fast over the distant mountain tops, heading straight for Sharperville. By Cal's reckoning, they'd arrive in an hour or so.

Best get back to home now.

He spurred his horse into an easy lope, and headed for the ranch.

Chapter Fourteen

The storm was fierce by the time it reached the construction site, black and noisy, throwing sheets of hailstones down on the crew and their equipment, calling its own early quitting time. Most of the guys headed for a beer at the Canyon Rim, but for Jamie, the extra hours were a chance to drive to the Big Buy in Butcher's Fork and she was excited by the prospect of finally getting to choose dish towels and sheets and pots and pans for herself and Mandy. Once in the store, she couldn't help letting herself picture the two of them together at last in a real home, making dinner, washing up, bathing Mandy before bed. It was risky, letting herself get caught up in the possibilities, for the pain would be awful if it didn't work out, but the idea was too delicious to resist. With a dish towel in her hand—white with big red strawberries printed all over—the fantasy came closer than it could have been at any time in these last two years. The imagined scene, her and her little girl, in a home of their own, just like any ordinary family, was irresistible, and she allowed herself to get lost in its sweetness.

And that, undoubtedly, was why she didn't notice that for the last few moments someone had been standing just behind her, a man who had watched her for a while before he finally spoke, enjoying the nasty shock he was about to give her.

"Well, well, well," he said at last. The voice was quiet, raspier than it used to be. "If it ain't my sweet little ex-wife. What the hell you doing here in Butcher's Fork?"

Jamie froze. She knew that sneering voice right away. A chill shivered along the back of her neck, there was a sick clutch in her stomach, and the dish towel fell from her fingers onto the floor. She didn't turn around to face him.

"Leave me alone, Ray. I have nothing to say to you."

"Now, now, sweetie-pie. Let's not get nasty."

He moved around to her side, bent down to retrieve the towel, and held it toward her. When she refused to acknowledge either the towel or him, he shrugged and dropped it onto a countertop, at the same time leaning one casual elbow back on the counter so he could look her over contemptuously.

"You ought to be nice to me, Jamie. I mean, didn't we have a few wonderful years together?" His snorting laugh made Jamie's skin crawl.

"Get away from me, Ray."

He had gotten beefier, his big frame thicker around the middle than it used to be. He was not older than Jamie, but his straight black hair was starting to recede.

"Hey, Jamie." He was having a good time, tormenting her. "That's no way to talk. After all, I am the father of your child, ain't I? Or was there maybe some question about that?"

She forgot all about towels and everything else. She wanted only to get out of there but didn't want to have to push past him. Not when the tears were beginning to burn in her eyes.

"You were never any kind of father to her, Ray." God damn him, he was making her cry, and he was making her say useless things. She could feel her throat constrict painfully, trying to control the tears. "Mandy deserves to have a *real* father, someone who loves her and takes care of her. And one of these days, I'm going to get her away from you!"

"Now, now, Jamie. You know what that judge said. He said *you* were the one wasn't fit to have her." Ray's smile was twisted, the meanness glinting in his eyes. "Said you weren't a suitable mother. Shit, how do I know? Maybe she really isn't even my kid, what with you screwing around in motel rooms and everything. It's right there in the legal record, ain't it? I think I got every right to get mad, ain't I? Ain't I? Ain't that what the judge said? Didn't he say you provoked me? Ain't that what he said, you provoked me?" He picked the towel off the counter and played with it idly. "You shouldn't provoke me. I don't like to be provoked. And you shouldn't be talking like that about getting the kid away from me, like you've got even a chance in hell of doing that." He leaned in close to her then, waiting while his words seeped in deep, giving their full impact time to churn down into her. Then he smiled and straightened up back against the counter again. "Anyway"—his eyes wandered casually around the store, as though he had abruptly lost interest in their conversation—"my mom likes having her. Gives her a chance to do the Lord's work, like she's always saying, seeing to the kid's spiritual welfare." Ray's laugh was short and ugly. "Hell, I heard enough of that spiritual shit all these years. Now the old bitch has Mandy to 'save.' I don't have to listen to that crap anymore."

It was more than Jamie could bear. She knew she should shut up, but she was too angry to stop herself. There'd been too much tension, for too long, too many things had been piling up on her and now the words poured out of her.

"Listen to me, you sonofabitch! It's been two years and I've had trouble enough. I want this over with. You know you don't really want Mandy. You know she wants to be with me."

This is useless. Why am I doing this? This is no place to fight with him. Save it for the courtroom.

Ray stood up straight and looked right into her eyes, letting her see his cruelty. His lip lifted, sneering at her, enjoying her pain.

"Hey, honey," he snarled. "As far as I'm concerned, you ain't never going to have trouble enough. Seems to me it was you tried to walk out on me. Seems to me—"

Jamie knew she'd gone too far and now she just needed to get out. With her hand against his chest, catching him off guard, she pushed him backward, forcing him out of her way. His big bulk fell back against a display of postcards, sending them toppling over the glass surface of the counter. All she wanted was to get to her car in the parking lot, her feelings a chaos of rage and humiliation.

How could I have been so stupid? Arguing with him like that. Giving him an opening to hurt me some more, just the kind of thing that bastard really loves.

She slammed through the store's front door, startling an elderly couple who were just approaching the store. She jerked open her car door and got in; she could pick up those damned towels some other time, some other place.

In the store, Ray disentangled himself from the clutching fingers of the display rack. He slapped the rack out of his way and, like Jamie, slammed through the front doors, giving the elderly couple their second jolt in a matter of seconds. He reached Jamie just as she was starting the motor. She was beyond tears now and looked up at him in a fury.

"I told you, Ray. Leave me alone."

But Ray put one hand on the car top and leaned in through the open window, close to her face.

"Something you should know, Jamie." His voice was terrifyingly quiet. "See, I've got this real good lawyer. *Real* good. And you want to know what he tells me? He tells me he can fix it so you *never* see Mandy again. You hear me? He says *never*! He says he can put together enough against you so no judge will ever let you near the kid. Not even a half-day every other week." He laughed briefly. "What's more, he says if we want, we can even have her put away in a foster home, and we can do it so fast your stupid little head will spin."

He stood up straight and stepped back, his face full of icy menace. "So don't mess with me, Jamie. You try to take me on, you'll find out. You're way out of your league." He turned and stalked to a big black van that was parked nearby.

Jamie's heart was pounding fiercely, driving the breath from her body. She stared helplessly after him and he turned once in her direction, just to give her an ugly smile. Then he got into the van and drove it out of the lot and down the road.

"Oh, Mandy!" Jamie whispered the words. "My baby."

She dropped her head forward on the steering wheel and her white-blond hair fell like a curtain about her face, hiding from passersby her desperate effort to control the terror that filled her.

"My sweet baby. What am I going to do?"

It was too much, on top of all the misery of these last days. Her habitual self-control went crashing around her and she was frozen by a horrible awareness of her helplessness. Ray was right. His kind of evil was out of her league. He'd been a move ahead of her every step of the way. Desperate to calm down her frantic emotions, she kept whispering the same words over and over.

"I've got to think. I've got to think."

She knew she was too distraught to concentrate properly. The car was already in motion, as though on its own, taking her back to Sharperville, and the wind blew at her face as she raced along, but it didn't clear her head.

She knew she needed help, but who was there to help her? Her mind turned toward Cal, of course, but Cal was gone for good.

She needed to think. She needed to go to the one place that was always good for her. She needed to get up into her private canyon. The air was still heavy and electric, but it had stopped raining, and she wouldn't care if the ground was wet. She'd get some coffee, get up into the canyon, take as much time as she needed, and try to think.

The Chevron station was just coming up on her left as she drove through Sharperville, and she pulled up under the GAS 'N' GOODIES sign. She wiped the tears from her face first and then took the thermos out of the lunch pail on the car seat next to her and went into the convenience store.

She was standing at the counter, waiting for the clerk to finish filling the thermos, when—of all people—Harvey Jackman joined her. He was carrying three bags of potato chips.

"Hey, Jamie. I guess this is getting to be our regular meeting place."

She could barely pull herself together in the face of his cheery smile, and her only response was a curt nod, barely acknowledging him. She didn't want to talk to any member of the Cal Cameron clan. Especially not tonight.

Of course, Harvey noted the red-rimmed eyes and the chilly manner. "Something wrong, Jamie?"

She brushed her hair back from her cheek, turning her head away from him. "I'm not much in the mood for talking tonight, Harvey." She paid for the coffee and took the thermos from the clerk. "I just ran into my ex over in Butcher's Fork. It's a real bummer."

Without another word, she walked out of the store, returned to her car, and drove away, leaving Harvey to stare thoughtfully after her.

Chapter Fifteen

Cal ran the water as hot as he could stand it and then let himself down slowly into the tub. He'd already iced the knee for a full twenty minutes and now, for another twenty, he kept a thin stream of scalding water trickling into the bath while he soaked and massaged his leg, easing the pain and, at the same time, softening up all the other accumulated muscle tensions. In the old days, he could have spent days in the saddle without needing any recovery time at all, but from now on, for the rest of his life, he'd have to take good care of that knee. The doctor had said it would get better, some, but the leg would never be as it had been before the injury. Cal was still fighting the bitterness in is heart.

"So that's how it turns out," he said to himself. "Cal Cameron isn't quite as special as thought he'd be, different from all the other rodeo riders. Turns out he isn't made out of three parts good luck and the rest all steel, like he thought he was. Turns out it's all over for him a lot sooner that he expected. And a hell of a lot sooner than he wanted."

Well, maybe not totally all over. Sometimes, like now when he was soaking in the hot water, and he felt a little loosened up, he'd get the idea that maybe he could bring it all back. Maybe, with the right exercise program, get a real good trainer, some real hard work, he might have another season in him. Maybe even two.

Then he'd remember what the doc in Vail said after the surgery, best man in the country. Sat there in that fancy office of his with all the wood panels and the diplomas on the wall and the pictures of his kids on the desk. "Cal," he told him, leaning back in his chair, "the real work ahead of you isn't the post-op stuff. I know you'll do the exercises and I know the pain won't stop you. You'll use the brace and you'll strengthen the knee on the passive-flex machine, eight hours every day, the first eight weeks, like the therapist showed you. It'll be months of real bad pain but I know you can take it. No, that's not the hard part."

Here, the doctor had paused and held his fancy letter-opener poised between the fingertips of both hands while he stared thoughtfully at his patient.

"For you, Cal," he said, finally, "the hard part is going to be the growing up. Your kid days are over, Cal. You'll be able to ride, but not in competition. I'm telling it to you straight and I hope you're hearing what I'm saying. You get some of that rough stock between your legs just once, and that mean sonofabitch makes his first turn in the air, and I promise you, you'll never walk right again."

Cal repeated those words to himself again, for the thousandth time.

You'll never walk right again.

"Ah, shit!" The ugly word seemed to echo off the tile walls, his private horror chamber, and he had to wait a long time till he felt the silence again.

Well, you're a grown man, Cameron, and a grown man doesn't cry. He just gets mad. But you asked for it. This is what you wanted. You always knew you'd get broken bones out of it. Isn't a rodeoer in the world isn't all broke up. And only if you were a hundred percent lucky it wouldn't get worse than that.

He flexed his arms, legs, shoulders, checking for pain, calibrating the stiffness and tension. He watched the water run in little rivers through the hair on his legs as he raised them experimentally out of the water. Most of his moving parts seemed to be back in normal operation, so he figured he'd soaked long enough.

Ellie must have dinner about ready. Come on, Cal. Time to join civilization.

He turned on the shower, stood up carefully in the tub, and lathered up thick swirls of suds over his whole body, all along the hard curves of his shoulders and arms and down his torso, massaging as he went and loosening the sand and dust that had worked in under his clothes. After three days out on the range, a man accumulates a lot of grit along with the smell of sweat and leather. He soaped up his thick black hair, rubbing at his scalp to clean out all the sand. A shaving mirror hung over the shower head, and while the water ran out of the tub, he lathered up and removed the stubble of the last three days.

Getting cleaned up makes a man feel better, and by the time he was rinsing the shaving cream from his face, Cal was even singing softly to himself while the hot shower stream washed away all the lather, the sand, and the pain in rivulets of sudsy water running down the muscles of his body.

So he was smooth and gleaming, smelling of soap and aftershave and dressed in clean jeans and a soft pale blue shirt when he came to the dinner table, hungry as a bear and feeling good. The whole family saw the change in his mood and figured the days on the range must have cleared up whatever had been bothering him. Dinner was lamb stew and fresh corn from Ellie's garden, and as soon as Harvey had said the blessing, he started to fill up the plates.

"Good to have you back, Cal," he said. "There's more fence down at the corral to take care of. And young A.J. here says he's waiting for you to teach him some roping." He passed the first plate to Ellie and then started to ladle stew onto Cal's plate. "There's something else. I ran into that cute girl of yours a couple times while you were away, and I guess she'll be glad to see you." He paused for a moment, stew ladle in mid-air. "Though, to tell you the truth," he added, "I saw her on my way home tonight, when I stopped to get gas. And that girl didn't look too glad about anything. Fact is, she looked to me like she'd been crying and she wouldn't even stop to pass the time of day." He handed Cal's plate to him. "Just grabbed her thermos of coffee and ran out."

Cal's face had darkened at Harvey's words. He felt as though a fist had hit him hard, square on his chest. "She didn't say anything at all, Harv?"

"Not really. Only that she'd just run into her ex over in Butcher's Fork. Said it was a real bummer. Must have been, too. She sure looked awful."

Cal was up instantly, almost knocking his chair over. It teetered slowly and he grabbed at it, setting it straight on its legs.

"I'm sorry, Ellie. Dinner looks great, but I'm going to have to take a rain check. Don't be mad. I'll make breakfast for us in the morning or something. But I've got to go now."

"But Cal, you must be starving. Just stop long enough to have *something.*" For almost thirty years Ellie had been trying make her kid brother behave, but she hadn't been successful since he was five. Now here he was, looking like fire and brimstone all of a sudden, not even waiting to eat. She knew it was useless to try to stop him.

He grabbed his fork, scooped up a quick mouthful of stew, and took a biscuit from the basket on the table.

"This'll do me," he said, his mouth full. He already had his hat off the peg on the wall.

Harvey was concerned. He hadn't had a chance yet to find out if Cal had checked the water pipes they'd laid out in the desert. And, while he didn't want to pry, he sure would like to know what the hell was up with him these last few days. Cal was acting like a man possessed.

"She didn't tell me where she was going," he called after Cal who was already out the door.

"That's okay, Harv. I know where she is," Cal called back as the screen door closed behind him.

To the east, the remnants of the afternoon storm still hung menacingly over the mountains, its streaks of lightning slashing at the peaks like an angry animal, retreating temporarily, but waiting to make its next attack, its rumbles of distant thunder snarling a warning. And to the west, more flashes of approaching lightning, in sudden washes of thin light, made a yet-distant announcement that the next wave of storm was on its way. Directly above, breaks in the cloud cover let the brilliant moonlight come and go, making the fields on either side of the highway glow wetly in the moving patches of light.

The tires of Cal's truck screamed along the road as he raced to the canyon where he was sure Jamie would be.

Something's happened. That sonofabitch must have done something to her. Harv said she'd been crying and wouldn't even talk to him. Just ran off like that. Only one place she'd go, up to that clearing in the canyon.

Up ahead was the clump of cedar trees where the dirt road turned off to Jamie's house and as he neared the trees, he saw that lightning had slashed one of the cedars in two, leaving one part bent downward, reaching out toward the road, and the other half still standing, naked, with great slivers of riven wood fanning out in jagged spikes. Cal had to fight off the spooked feeling they gave him.

She's all right. She's got to be all right.

He grasped at the reassuring straws to calm himself.

Been a couple of hours since that storm went through here. She must be out there somewhere, maybe scared and not being careful.

A distant light wavered momentarily in the sky. He didn't like the way he was feeling.

Maybe she didn't even go to the canyon. Maybe she's at home. She could be sleeping or something and the house could be set on fire and that father of hers wouldn't even know it.

A nightmare image flashed through his mind, of Jamie struggling to drag the unconscious man from the flames, screaming at him, helpless to save him. Helpless to save herself. Her hair, that beautiful hair, itself a bright light, flying about her face, her clothes catching fire—or she could be asleep upstairs while the smoke rose—a drunk like that is dangerous to live with, doesn't need any help from nature's random violence . . .

If anything's happened to her . . .

In the dark, the farm house was ahead of him. No smoke rising from it. No flames licking up the sides. In another sweep of the clouds, the moon showed through, revealing the house, quiet, ordinary, at no immediate risk. In the front room, the silvery, familiar light of the TV flickered. And her car wasn't there.

He looked up briefly, toward the roiling heavens. "Thank you," he whispered.

He realized his fingers had locked rigidly on the steering wheel; he lifted first one hand, then the other, stretching the muscles to relax them.

The heavy electric air filled once more with the pale aura of the distant lightning and Cal realized that if anything happened to Jamie, there'd be no pieces of him left to pick up. No knees, or arms, or legs, or head, or heart.

He hadn't known that until this moment. The anger of these last days, the humiliation, the frustration, all poured out of him and he was filled with a clarity of understanding.

The lightning flashed again, and in the glow that lit up the vast desert around him, Cal saw that he'd been wandering, like a lost kid, looking for the only thing in the whole world that really mattered.

He felt his heart twist inside of him and he prayed aloud.

"Please let her be all right."

Chapter Sixteen

The mug of coffee had long ago grown cold in her hand and still she sat staring into the valley far below, frozen into the helplessness that came of her combined fury and panic. She had already cycled through the inevitable fantasies—impossible, every one of them—of murdering Ray, of kidnapping Mandy—even of killing herself. Now she waited for rational thought to return. She was oblivious to the wind rising in the treetops, sending an ominous whisper through the aspens. She didn't see the enormous forks of lightning that slashed at the mountain tops across the valley. She had no thought for the approaching storm.

It was the sound of the truck turning off the road that broke into her isolation, and before she could think—who could be coming up here?—the truck's lights lit up the trees and the rocks around her. It was moving fast and it pulled into the space next to her Civic with a grinding of rubber against the earth. In almost the same instant the engine was cut, the lights doused, and she saw Cal coming toward her across the open space.

And in that moment, Jamie felt the earth shift on its axis. In a single moment, her terror-filled reality turned rational.

He's come back!

All her efforts to put him out of her life collapsed like a child's fortress of sand.

Why has he come? What does it mean?

"What are you doing here?" She couldn't help the challenge in her voice.

He was determined that this time he'd be careful; this time he wasn't going to scare her away. He sat down on the rock, careful not to get too close.

"Harvey told me he saw you. Said you'd been crying." He saw her raise her chin defiantly. "Why don't you tell me what happened." He kept the question casual—and as gentle as he could.

Her heart was racing but she only shrugged, trying to pretend it was no big deal. "It was Ray. He just came out of nowhere. I was over in Butcher's Fork, at the Big Buy. I wasn't prepared. Just all of a sudden, there he was." Hearing herself tell it, aloud, brought the memory back in all its ugliness and terror, and her brave pretense crumbled. She could feel her lip trembling and she looked up toward the treetops, trying to control the tears that were beginning to come. "He just came up behind me and he got me totally by surprise. Like one minute I was looking at dish towels, and the next minute there's this sneering big sonofabitch right next to me. Making fun of me. Laughing at me." She brushed her hair away from her forehead, trying to steady herself. "Laughing about what he was going to do to me."

"And just what does he think he's going to do to you?"

"He says he can take Mandy away from me." The words were strangled in her throat and now she couldn't stop the tears. "He said he can even have her put away—into a foster home. He said he can take her away from me for good. And oh, God, he would do it, too. I knew it, right then, I knew Ray would do it, just for the fun of it. Just for the sheer, goddamned, *fun* of it!" She dug her hand into her hair, clutching at it mindlessly. "I know how rotten that man can be and I feel so helpless. He kept laughing about what the judge had written about me and how the whole town thinks I'm no good because of what Orrin did. He made me feel like a stupid piece of dirt! I don't know what to do. It seems like every time I think I'm ready to take him on, turns out that bastard is a couple of steps ahead of me. I just don't know what I can do."

She felt hopelessly, helplessly muddled. On top of Ray's repeated assaults on her self-esteem, her life-long, lonely habit of independence had smashed up against her desperate need for help. Cal's arrival only added to her confusion.

"I'm in real trouble, Cal." The words, so hard to say, were choking her. She stared bleakly into the distance. "I feel like I'm all coming apart."

She was in some terrible, lonely place of her own and didn't see that Cal reached a hand toward her, and she also didn't see that he thought better of it and held back. She said nothing for a long time, and when she finally spoke, her words were barely a whisper.

"All my life, for as long as I can remember, I've known it was up to me to take care of myself. Other kids had families, maybe big brothers, or a grandfather, someone who kept an eye out for them, someone they could go to. When I was a kid, the only family I had was that tanked-up bastard who practically never even knows if it's day or night. The town drunk, that's who I have for a father. It's the same with that house down the road." She gestured toward the valley. "It used to be a nice place once, I've seen old photos of it. That decrepit farmhouse, the whole town calls it a disgrace to the community, that's my home. That's what I grew up with."

Still looking away from Cal, she brushed at her cheek, as though trying not to acknowledge the tears. "Listen to me. Like I don't have enough to worry about! But he's my *father*, for God's sake! I used to love him once, when I was a kid. I used to try to do things to make him be better. I'd try to cook for him, get a whole nice dinner ready, I thought if I made it look like the pictures I saw in the magazines, with soup and mashed potatoes and little pats of butter—it was all so useless. I tried so damned hard and I was just a kid, I didn't know you can't cure a drunk with mashed potatoes.

"And tonight, as I was coming up here, I saw that damned TV light in the front room and I knew he was home, and you know what I wished. I wished lightning would strike the place and burn it all up, with him in it. It's come to where I wish my own father was dead! And it really is a wonder it hasn't happened yet, him setting the place on fire. It wouldn't surprise me. And the damned thing is, what pisses me off most, I know I'd try to save him. Just like I used to try to make dinner for him, I'd still try to pull him out of the fire. Like he *deserves* to be saved! I *hate* feeling like this!"

"You and I both know," Cal said quietly, "that isn't what you want for your dad. He's got a stinking, rotten problem, and that problem has hurt you terribly, but no one deserves to die in a fire."

She sighed wearily. "I know. The drinking is his problem—not mine." She took a long, deep breath. "Cal, I don't have the strength to deal with this. There isn't a damned thing anyone can do to turn a drunk around. Only he can do that. And maybe he will, and maybe he won't. Much as it hurts, and much as it drives me crazy, that's the way it is. My problem is to live *my* life. And I've got Mandy to think about."

Suddenly, on a perverse impulse, as a comic thought zigzagged through her pain, she added, "And hey, so what if he is the town drunk? Every town has to have one. Like a mayor or a dog catcher."

Cal smiled. He knew that the silly joke meant she was settling her nerves. If there was no laughter at all, you really had reached rock bottom.

Her laugh was brief. "I shouldn't have said that. It's not funny."

"I know it's not funny. But you're right about having to live with it, just like everyone's got something rotten they have to live with."

"Not everyone. You don't." She was thinking of what she'd seen at the C-Bar—a happy home, loving parents, a successful life.

"What makes you think I don't have anything really rotten to live with?"

"Like what?"

"Never mind what. We can talk about my stuff some other time. You think I came racing up here tonight, didn't even get my dinner, just to talk about my problems?"

"Why did you come?"

He needed to let a cautious beat or two pass before he answered. He needed to let her keep some distance. There'd be time enough, later, to let her know that his heart would crack and never heal if she were hurt. That the thought of her pain was enough to make him tear down mountains. So he chose to keep it simple.

"I came because I have some information for you. Would have gotten to it after I ate some of Ellie's stew if I'd had a chance, but when Harv said he'd seen you and said he could see something was wrong, well, I just decided to get right on up here and tell you what I found."

"What you found?"

"I took a little ride out in the desert. It's a long story, but the bottom line is, I'm pretty sure I know what your ex-husband's been up to. It's drugs, Jamie. It's too soon to tie it to him, for sure, but I can feel it in my bones. And if I got it right, it's not any little two-bit stuff he's doing, either."

Then he gave her all the details. The burn marks in the sand. The tire tracks. The bits of burlap.

"Someone's using that desert to run drugs, Jamie, and from your description of him, I'd bet anything Ray's the one."

She chewed thoughtfully on her thumbnail. "It figures," she said. "He's got an auto dealership over in Butcher's Fork. Where would a young guy like him get the money for that? And what a great cover for hiding cash—all those big-ticket sales. And what a great excuse for traveling all over the state, delivering vehicles. Come to think of it"— she was getting excited now—"that explains what he was doing at the Big Buy today. I was in the housewares section, buying towels, and that's right over by the auto supply section. Where they sell road flares."

She shook her head, finding it hard to get a handle on this revised picture of her ex-husband. "I've known Ray since we were in kindergarten together. I thought I knew him pretty well. Hell, I was married to the guy, after all, and he is Mandy's father, for God's sake. I mean, I finally realized how slimy he'd become, but I never thought—I mean really, a big-time *criminal*?"

"But it's possible?"

She stared out into the distance. "Well, you know, Cal, I think it could be." She was seeing a number of things for the first time. "He was always sort of wild, in trouble in school, that kind of thing. I know that doesn't make him a criminal, and I always thought he'd get over it, you know, when he grew up, but Ray never mellowed out, the way the other boys did. It's as though his meanness just got more organized. Maybe it was that mother of his. He really hates that old witch and I wouldn't be surprised if all that phony righteousness of hers made him kind of crazy."

She snapped her fingers. "And another thing, tell me, what's Ray Nixon, in a little town like Sharperville, doing with a 'really good lawyer'? And that's not all. What *about* all this money he's flashing around. Big silver belt buckles and fancy boots, and I'll bet that ring on his finger is a real diamond. I don't care how good the auto business is, it's not that good. And what's more, I bet that's why he's stayed in that crappy trailer. With all that money, he could be living in a regular house. But the trailer's way out there, maybe a mile from town, where he can do what he's doing and folks won't notice."

She was talking faster now, putting things together. "Often he's away for days at a time. Why should an auto dealer need to be away so often? And what's Orrin Fletcher doing back in town? If that ex-con is around, you can bet he's hooked up somehow with Ray, and not in a good way."

She was connecting all the links. She remembered what Mandy had told her about the party at Ray's trailer. *Here, kid, sniff some of this stuff.* Of course!

"I think you're right, Cal. He's not just a small-time user, with Tina and their friends. I'll bet he's got a regular distribution going, flying the stuff up from Mexico and Central America."

Cal nodded. "That makes sense. The pieces fit. I'd seen burn marks like those in the sand months ago, but I didn't connect it up till we were in Elaine's office. I think she had a notion about what Ray's been doing and when she talked about getting evidence, that's when everything came together."

"Why didn't you say anything then?" The question hung there for a minute. In the excitement about Ray's activities, they'd both forgotten. Now they were each embarrassed.

Cal looked down at his hands. He waited a long time to answer

"I was mad," he said, finally. "I'm not used to being told to shove off—leastways, not by a woman. But I acted like a jerk. No excuse for that. I just wasn't thinking how hard it is for you."

She caught her breath. He was giving her a chance—for the first time since she was very little—to put a timid toe into the unfamiliar waters of trust.

But it was so hard. Did she dare?

"I acted like a jerk, too," she confessed softly. "We could have talked. We could have figured out what was going on."

With these words, she set aside, for the time being, all her other problems, set aside Mandy and Ray and drugs and Edna and everything else. "And afterwards, I was so miserable. I thought you were really gone. When Harvey said you'd left, I figured you'd just saddled up and ridden off into the sunset. I figured I'd never see you again. I thought, after that one night at the C-Bar, at that beautiful spot you took me to, your special, secret place—oh, Cal, you don't know. Everything I've ever wanted ... I saw it there in that house you'd grown up in—good parents, everything so perfect, so good—like life can really be like that. I could feel the love all around. Cal, you don't know how precious it is. And then, after what happened between us—all my fault—I figured you'd had enough of me and my problems. And I was so scared. It's all gotten too big for me, and I can't handle it on my own."

Cal recognized the pain of her vulnerability, acknowledged at last after so many years of punishing self-control. Involuntarily, helplessly, as though with a will of its own, his hand touched her face and, with careful fingertips, turned her gently to look at him.

And, although she stiffened at his touch, instantly wary, she understood his gentleness. She understood that he was trying not to frighten her. And perhaps, because she was exhausted by all she'd been through, because her defenses were exhausted, too, this time, she didn't resist. But she could hardly breathe as his hand stroked softly through her hair and all her nerves were on high alert. He moved closer to her and she knew she wanted him to kiss her, even as she was terrified that he would.

Behind him, the black treetops were being whipped by the wind, and his voice was barely more than a whisper, caught up in the harsher whisper of the trees that now were bending, fighting against the rising wind.

"Why, shoot, honey. Don't you know? Nobody can make it on their own. That's why the good Lord makes people *need* to be together."

He took her protectively into his arms, careful not to frighten her even as he drew her close against him, and suddenly there was the warmth of his body and the faint scents of leather and soap and of some scent of his own, something masculine and exciting. She could feel the smooth skin of his face against hers, and his heart was beating hard against her own.

"Did you hear what I said?"

He was so close now.

And then his mouth touched hers and his kiss was as gentle as a baby's.

What was it he had said? Something about being alone? But everything had slipped away, evanesced into the electric air that surrounded them. She knew only that in the midst of the threatening thunderstorm, his gentle kiss was like the quiet center of her own emotional storm, and against all her sad experience, his kiss was a safe haven.

She knew what Cal wanted and she knew that now she was going to let it happen. But she had long ago shut down the words of consent, lost them from her vocabulary. Instead, silently, she let her gaze answer the question she saw in his eyes. She was frightened, excited, and eager, all together, but his gentleness gave her courage, and she would not listen to the demons that were laughing at her, scolding her for giving in. She smiled—such a small smile—and nodded.

He understood, and he, too, smiled—a smile that was its own *thank you.*

"You're not alone, Jamie. I'm here. And I'm not going away."

And he kissed her again, and she allowed herself, timidly, as though this was the first kiss of her life, to return his kiss.

She knew what was about to happen, she knew she wanted it to happen, and she prayed that it would be all right.

But even as he began to undo the top buttons of her shirt, her hands reflexively, nervously, covered his.

He spoke so quietly. "Don't be afraid, Jamie." He opened the first buttons. "It's going to be all right."

She *was* afraid, but she took a deep breath. Then a second deep breath. She relaxed a little and, with a nod, let him know she wouldn't stop him.

He slipped the shirt back from her shoulders. He kissed the base of her throat. And she knew she would not stop him. He undid all the buttons and let her shirt fall to the ground, and she didn't stop him. She even surprised herself by reaching up and taking off his hat. She dropped it onto the ground and touched, with timid fingers the black waves of his hair that fell over his brow. His arms tightened around her. She slid her hands timidly across his shoulders, across the soft fabric of his shirt, across the hard muscle underneath. And then it was her own hands fingering the pearled snaps of his shirt, ready to pull them apart. Suddenly she couldn't get enough of him, she wanted his bare chest exposed. Then he was in her arms and she was in his and neither one of them knew the air had grown cold around them. Only as the first raindrops fell did they slowly realize that while they had been oblivious to all of nature except themselves, the storm had arrived with its lightning and thunder and they were in a downpour. The rain was pelting them hard and even as they grasped what was happening, small hailstones began to clatter against the rocks, bouncing slightly, raising little dusty puffs.

And suddenly it seemed terribly funny. It was nature's force and

not Jamie's fears that stopped them—and they were laughing, grabbing their clothes and running for their vehicles. Cal encircled Jamie's
body with his own, one hand holding her steady as they ran across the
quickly-muddying, suddenly slippery dirt, and propelling her at the
same time toward her car.

"We better get out of here."

As they ran, the lightning flashed repeatedly, brilliantly, turning
the road and the trees and the rocks around them arc-light bright. The
crashing thunder was now directly above them, violent in its intensity, and in the midst of another lightning strike, just as Cal's hand
grabbed at the door handle of Jamie's car to pull it open, just as everything turned brilliantly green-white, they were both stopped dead in
their tracks.

From somewhere in the rocks high above them, the air was dou-
bly split by the scream, lost instantly in the midst of the thunder, of
an animal in sudden pain. At the far-off sound, Cal's head turned
quickly and Jamie saw his face in the white light. He looked stricken,
as though the lightning blow had fallen on him also. His rain-soaked
face, his black hair plastered down, his half-bare body tensed, frozen
in mid-stride—in the airborne electric light, she saw his own terrible
pain, his own awful loss. She felt an unaccountable sorrow wash
through her, and she touched his face. He turned to let his mouth rest
against the palm of her hand momentarily. Then his face changed,
and he smiled at her.

"That damned lightning's going to fry us, too, if we don't get out
of here," he said, and together they struggled awkwardly into their
wet clothes.

And on a rock ledge, far out of sight above them, the stricken animal writhed in pain, its beautiful pelt scorched by the lightning
strike from shoulder to paw.

He followed her down the canyon in the pickup and when she arrived in her driveway, he pulled in behind her. He got out and ran
through the rain to her car and got in quickly next to her.

"Well, I don't see any smoke coming out of there," he said.
"Looks like we won't have to save his life just yet."

She looked toward the house.

"No, it looks like all's quiet in TV land."

"Would you like me to come in and meet him?"

"No. I couldn't bear that. Anyway, he's probably passed out, this time of night."

"I'm going to have to meet him some time, Jamie."

"Not yet. Not tonight."

"All right then." He leaned over and kissed her, lightly. "Will I see you tomorrow?" He kissed her again. "Seems to me we forgot about something back there." He gestured vaguely up the road behind them. "We need to make some plans."

She smiled at him. "Sure. Tomorrow night." She kissed him, a token kiss. A promise. Then they both got out of her car and she went into the house and he got into his truck and drove away into the drenching rain.

Chapter Seventeen

Saturday morning broke clean and quiet. The storm had moved on east and Sharperville's valley was returned to its ordinary, peaceful rhythms. The hawks and turkey buzzards patrolled the dark blue skies and the cattle grazed contentedly, their customary forage freshened by last night's rains. Jamie slept late—and well—and awoke as contented as the grazing cows, with secret, private smiles as last night replayed itself in her memory. But she could not remain contented for more than a few minutes. The harsh realities of her life were waiting for her, as full of unrelenting menace as an army of monsters. And her sense of a possible turn in the tide of her fortune was as fragile as the new growth that had sprung with last night's rain. But at least she felt sure that when tonight came, Cal would not have disappeared.

Gradually, as all the sleep cleared from her head, the day ahead of her took shape, her energies began to flow. It was to be a day of chores for Cal and for her, there were errands to take care of. Later on, they would meet and start making their plans.

In fifteen minutes she had showered and slipped into a pair of clean jeans and a fresh white shirt and gathered her hair quickly into a colorful ribbon at the back of her neck. She stepped barefoot into a pair of loafers and ran downstairs to make a fast cup of coffee before leaving. Her first errand of the morning was to take Mandy's gift— the sachet she'd bought in Salt Lake—over to the Nixons' house. It would normally be a day of Saturday errands for Edna Nixon, too, and Jamie wanted to be there before Edna left the house.

On her way out, she paused at the front door only long enough to look at her father, who was asleep on the couch. One arm dangled from the couch and his hand rested limply on the floor. His other hand was half-way tucked into the top of his pants, pants that were baggy and worn, frayed at the cuffs. Jamie looked at the sleeping man and felt only sorrow.

How thin he is.

She sighed as she turned to open the door.

And Cal's right. Of course I'd try to save him.

She closed the door quietly so as not to wake him.

By ten o'clock, she was waiting on the Nixons' porch, holding Mandy's gift in her hand. She poked at the pink bow, puffing it up, wondering what was keeping Edna. Someone must be at home. Their car was parked at the side of the house, and she could hear movement in the house, feet shuffling, doors opening and closing. She knocked again, harder this time.

At last the door opened, and Ervil was there, a pair of Edna's shoes in his hand. He peered at Jamie as though he wasn't sure who she was.

"Jamie?"

His eyes were narrowed at her, suspicious, as though trying to figure out a puzzle.

"Is Mandy here, Ervil? Or Edna? I know it's not my regular Saturday, but I have a little gift for Mandy," she held up the box, pretty in its fancy, flowery paper and bright ribbons, "and I wanted to leave it off for her."

"No, Edna's not here." Ervil's eyes looked funny, as though they suddenly got empty. "Edna's sick. Real bad sick. Doc Wallis had me take her up to the hospital in Salt Lake last night. I just got back." He looked like he wanted to put the shoes down but couldn't think where to put them, as though he couldn't remember where he was.

Jamie forced herself to say the proper thing. "I'm sorry to hear that, Ervil. I hope she'll be feeling better soon."

She wondered why she didn't have the nerve to speak her real thoughts. Why couldn't she say, maybe that means the good Lord has finally pointed His finger of judgment at the old witch.

"She's not going to be getting better." Ervil said blankly. "The docs up there in Salt Lake say she isn't going to make it. They say it's her heart. It's real bad." Ervil was looking around him, confused. "I gotta go back. I just came down to get some things for her."

"But where's Mandy?" Jamie was suddenly alarmed. "She's not

in Salt Lake, is she?" She tried to look past Ervil, into the house, seeing no sign of the child.

"No, she's here in Sharperville, I guess. I had Ray take her. Probably she's with him. I called him last night to come get her, but he wasn't home. That girl friend of his was there. Tina? She came and picked the kid up."

He turned away and went into the front parlor, with Jamie right on his heels. She was trying to get the distracted man to pay attention to her and the words were spilling frantically out of her.

"She's with Ray? No, Ervil, she can't stay with Ray! She *can't!*"

"Well, she's just going to have to. There's no one here can look after her, what with Edna sick and all." Ervil sat down on a straight-backed chair near the window and put the shoes on the table next to him as though that was the very spot he'd been looking for all the time. "She'll have to stay with Ray from now on. He's going to have to look after her. He's her father, ain't he? I just hope he sees properly to the child's spiritual life. That's what Edna would want." Ervil's chest heaved in a big, helpless sigh. "But there's no telling with that boy."

His eyes wandered aimlessly around the room and then finally focused on Jamie, as though he'd figured out at last who she was and what she was doing there. He gestured toward the beribboned box in her hand and added abstractedly, "You can leave that off if you want, but I don't know as how I'll be seeing the kid again."

"Never mind." Jamie had to get to Mandy right away, get her away from Ray. "I'll give it to her myself." She didn't even say goodbye as she let the front door slam shut behind her, leaving Ervil staring slackly into the empty room.

She had the Civic pulling up in front of Ray's trailer home in a matter of minutes. Sharperville's few short streets end abruptly in open rangeland and the trailer was set well off by itself, beyond the last of the streets, on three dusty acres, with only a rough dirt road leading up to it.

Jamie slammed to a stop and was out of the car instantly. In a moment she was knocking on the door, pounding on the door, yelling at the top of her voice.

"Ray! Damn it, *Ray!*"

She pulled violently at the handle, but the door was locked. She tried to see into the windows but there was no sign of anyone. Helplessly, she slammed her hand once, hard, against the locked door, and then ran back to her car. The rising waves of panic were taking over her rational self and she sat still for a minute, gripping the wheel, trying to get control of herself, of her feelings, of her thoughts.

Oh, God! Let her be all right. Please let her be all right.

Her hands were shaking as she started the engine. She turned the car around sharply, and in a moment was racing for the main road, heading for the Jackman ranch.

I need help. I need Cal!

She found him at the far end of the alfalfa field where he'd just finished repairing the fence. His tools were already loaded into the truck, and he was putting a coil of wire and a bucket of staples into the bed when her car pulled to a noisy stop on the dirt road.

He needed only one glance at her face. The color was drained away beneath her tan, and her blue eyes were frantic with fear and anger and frustration. He tossed the wire into the truck and took a few long strides toward her.

"Jamie, honey. What's happened?"

He tried to put his arms around her, but she was too distracted to let him. Instead, she walked to his truck, and slammed her hand against the tailgate, and then she strode back to him and then away again, this time to the fence, then back and around him. She was like an animal, looking for a way out of its cage.

"All right," she was saying as she paced frantically. Her tone carried a challenge. "All right. I'm coming to you for help. You said, I can come to you for help? All right, I'm in real trouble now and I'm coming to you. I need help. I need help real bad. You've got to help me, Cal." She stopped in front of him and her eyes filled with tears.

Cal didn't try to touch her. "What's happened?"

"It's Mandy. Ray's got her. Edna's sick, real sick, up in Salt Lake in a hospital and Ervil doesn't even know what he's doing, he's totally out of it. The doctors say Edna's going to die, so Ervil just handed Mandy over to Ray like she was a package or something. He doesn't even expect to take her back. Tina took her away last night and there's no one in the trailer and I haven't any idea where they are, where they've got her!"

Cal was sorting it out cautiously. "Well, darlin'," he said thoughtfully, "according to the law, Ray has the right to have Mandy with him."

That pushed her right to the edge, beyond caring what she said. "Yeah? Well, screw *that!*" She turned away from him and walked to the nearest fence post. She slammed it hard with her hand and then turned and came back to him. "You don't understand. I *promised* her! I told her I would see to it that she wouldn't have to be alone with Ray and Tina ever again." She was crying, but they tears were of rage; there were no tears in her voice. "I'll kidnap her if I have to, I mean it, Cal. I will."

Her tension had been strung too tight for her to bear and Cal's arms went around her protectively. "I know, honey," he said. "I understand. And you're not going to have to kidnap her. We're going to get her back."

"Okay. You just tell me how." She was tense as a drum in his arms.

"Well, for starters, we're going to do it legally. Mostly legally, anyway. Shoot, darlin', I don't want my girl winding up in the slammer."

His tone was easy, his kiss was feather-light on her hair, and his voice, so gentle and steady, helped her breathe again, a little more calmly.

Grudgingly, she began to settle down. "You better have a suggestion," she said. "Or I'm going to do something serious. I mean it, Cal."

"I know, sweetheart. I know. And I do have a plan. Thought we might talk about it tonight, but maybe it's best we don't, after all. The thing is, we don't want to risk having you too much involved."

"What do you mean 'not involved.' How can I *not* be—"

He stopped her with a calming gesture of his hand, stroking her hair back from her face. "You've got a court fight coming up and you've got to be absolutely clean. You leave this part to me. We're going to have to move fast and I know what I'll be looking for. But don't worry, Jamie. I'll be needing your help, so for sure there'll be plenty for you to do. You just hop into the truck while I get some stuff I need back here."

"You better know what you're doing."

"Trust me," he said, as he reached into the truck's bed and pulled out his toolbox. "It'll be okay."

She climbed into the cab and while she waited for him, she took a couple of deep breaths and had a quick little talk with herself.

You asked for his help. You came to him for help, you asked him to do something, so don't go trying to stop him, now that he's doing it.

Cal poked through a number of items in the toolbox and then muttered, "One of these should do." He removed a few small-size picks and dropped them into the pocket of his jeans. He checked his cell phone to be sure it was fully charged. Then he went around the front, hoisted his long frame onto the driver's seat, and started the engine.

"Okay," he said, backing the truck around on the dirt road and heading toward the state highway. "Show me where that trailer is."

"The very first street this side of town," she said. "Take a right on Eighth South and go way past all the houses. It's about a mile east of Main."

"Okay. Now, when we get there, if you don't see any sign that Ray has come back since you were there, I want you to leave me and drive away. Not too far. Stay right where you can see if he's coming back. If you see him, call my cell. Let it ring just once; I'll know that means he's on his way. Then, you just take off. Don't worry about me. I'll be long gone before he arrives. Otherwise, if he doesn't show, swing by and pick me up in exactly fifteen minutes. I won't need any more time than that."

"You're going into the trailer?"

"You betcha."

"That's breaking and entering!"

"Yup." He took his eyes off the road for a moment to smile at her. "Burglary, too, I guess. Don't worry, honey. I'll be real surprised if I don't find what I'm looking for."

Jamie took a deep breath and nodded once, knowing he'd say nothing more about it. At least, not for now. She turned away and stared out the window and started to chew on her thumbnail. It was probably a good thing she didn't see Cal take the big Smith and Wesson from the pocket in the door at his side and slip it into his belt at the small of his back. He lifted the tail of his shirt over the revolver to cover it. Then he looked over at her and he grinned. He reached over and took her hand from her mouth and brought it to his lips.

"It's going to be all right, Jamie," he said, kissing the rough fingernail gently. "Nothing's going to go wrong."

Cal waited till Jamie was out of sight. Then he pulled the tiny picks from his pocket and selected one. It took him only a moment to open the lock and let himself into the trailer home. He hadn't expected that Tina and Ray would be strong on housekeeping, so he wasn't surprised by the mess of papers and clothes and dirty dishes that littered the place. On the kitchen counter, he found the usual drug paraphernalia. Pipes, foil, a bottle of chlorine. A mess of steel wool, baking soda, glass vials. A scale. He took several pictures with his phone, making sure to get enough of the background to identify the location.

On the floor, shoved up against a cabinet in the corner of the kitchen, he found a crumpled bag made of a stiff, thick plastic. The blue logo stamped on its side was clearly visible and its interior was cloudy with a white dust which, Cal was sure, a laboratory analysis would show to be cocaine or heroin. He had no doubt that Ray had lifted a single kilo package of the drug for his private purposes, either business or pleasure. Skimming was a dangerous game, but Cal suspected that Ray was just dumb enough to try to play it.

A fast look over the rest of the place, over the unmade bed, the shoes and sweaters and pants spilling out of dresser drawers, cigarette-laden ashtrays, and Cal saw, on the table next to the bed, a couple of used syringes, more evidence that Ray was a user as well as a distributor. He had already noted a couple of cell phones and a beeper unit on the coffee table in the living room area. Those, together with the short-wave radio on the floor next to the front door, had confirmed his certainty, as soon as he entered the trailer, that Ray was using the electronic gear to signal ground coordinates to planes coming from Mexico.

As ugly as the disordered mess was, Cal was glad to see it. The clutter suited his purpose.

"Just as well. They'll never know anyone's been through this place."

He rifled quickly through the dresser drawers, finding only a couple of loaded pistols mixed in with Tina's panties and bras and another pistol in the drawer next to Ray's socks. A big Ruger .45 was in the nightstand along with a box of cartridges and few packs of detonator caps.

"Stupid sonofabitch."

He was moving fast but carefully. Learning to "take his time in a hurry" had been an essential part of his training, back when he was a little tyke on his dad's ranch. Without wasting any motion, Cal took some pics of the contents of the drawers, showing the firearms and the caps.

But it was in the corner of the closet, concealed under a stack of folded blankets, behind some scattered shoes, that Cal finally found what he needed. A ledger book, with entries showing Ray's record of his distributions, including dates, code names, quantities of drugs delivered, and the payoffs received.

And under the ledger, packs of hundred-dollar bills, still in their bank wrappers. Cal ran a thumb over the edge of one of the packs. Each of them held a hundred bills. A recent payoff, then, not yet removed to its more permanent hiding place. Most likely Ray planned to launder it through the car dealership to an off-shore numbered bank account, beyond the easy reach of prying regulators.

Still working quickly, he photographed the hiding place, then moved the blankets and took pictures of the ledger, closed and then opened to selected pages, and a careful close-up of the bills, fanned out to show the quantity.

He glanced at his watch. Only another minute before Jamie was due back. He checked to be sure there was no sign that he'd been there, and he picked his way through the cluttered trailer, back to the door. There had been no phone call and he'd had no need to use his Smith and Wesson.

He stood to one side of the window and checked that no one had approached the trailer. Outside, the field was quiet, dry in the hot mid-day sun, and in the distance, a tractor moved slowly, raising a shimmering cloud of dust.

Right on schedule, the truck appeared, trailing its own cloud of billowing, sandy dust, and Cal quickly let himself out of the trailer, being careful to lock the door behind him. Everything had gone perfectly.

"Good girl," he said as he climbed up to the passenger side of the truck. "Let's move it out of here."

"Are you okay?" Jamie headed back to Harvey's ranch as fast as she could go without risking the attention of a local trooper. "Did you find what you wanted? Did you have any problems?

"Yes, yes, and no." Cal laughed, answering her questions in order. "It was just like I figured. That ex-husband of yours is doing it big-time. My affidavit should be enough to get a court order, but I've got pictures to back it up." He slid down in the seat, his long legs braced up against the dash board and he leaned his head back against the seat. He pushed his hat forward almost over his eyes and grinned happily.

"Let's go make a phone call to Elaine French. We've got some good news for her."

Chapter Eighteen

They went back to the ranch to use the land line in Harvey's office.

"The van's not here," Cal said, looking over the row of vehicles parked in the smooth dirt driveway. "Ellie's probably got the kids with her over to Butcher's Fork." He paused on the kitchen steps and peered out toward the pasture.

"I don't see Harv, either. Looks like the whole family's gone."

She followed him through the kitchen where the table was already set for the next meal. There were kids' drawings on the refrigerator door and a bowl of fresh fruit on the countertop. The room was so clean and orderly it might have been waiting to be photographed. A pang of longing stopped her for a moment. For Jamie, this homey, ordinary kitchen glowed with the aura of normal family life, comfortable in its orderliness, its sense of children cared for, parents responsible and reliable.

This, she imagined, *is how it is in a normal, happy home. This is what I want for Mandy and me.*

She sighed, acknowledging the moment's bittersweet awareness of her dreams—and her losses. She kept it all to herself as she joined Cal.

"I'll show you were the phone is," he said, leading her down the hall, "and get you Elaine's number. Then I'll heat up some coffee for us. There's a pot left from breakfast. I'm the only one around here drinks coffee."

The room Harvey used as an office had a small desk, some file cabinets, and a big, comfortable old chair that was covered in dark brown leather.

"Here's Elaine's number," he said, scrolling through the contacts on his cell phone. "You start talking to her and I'll get us some coffee."

Elaine French sat back in the big leather chair, set a fresh yellow pad in front of her on the desk, and wrote the day's date in the upper margin.

"Okay, Jamie," she said into the speaker phone. "Tell me what's happening."

Jamie started with the news of Edna's illness, and a big satisfied smile brightened Elaine's face.

"This is super. Just super, Jamie. It's exactly what we need—just the kind of change in circumstances that can convince the judge to modify the original custody award." She ticked off the analysis: "One, Edna won't be taking care of Mandy anymore. And two, Ervil refuses to have the child there in his home. It's a beginning. It gives us a stronger case than we had before."

She didn't give an instant's sympathy to either Edna or Ervil. As far as she was concerned, they were on the side of the bad guys and now it looked like they were out of her way. Her mind raced ahead. Now, if Cal could dig up some information on Ray Nixon . . .

Jamie interrupted her train of thought. "There's lots more, Elaine. Hold on a minute and I'll let Cal tell you all about it. He's just getting us some coffee."

Elaine tapped her pen on the yellow pad in eager impatience.

This is great. I'll bet that darling cowboy has turned up something on that bunch. I knew I could count on him.

She heard Jamie say, "Here, you can talk to her," and then it was Cal on the line.

"How're you doing Elaine? I told Jamie you'd be in your office today, even if it is Saturday."

She didn't bother to tell him that it had been many years since anything gave her as much pleasure as she found in her work.

"Fact is," she said, "I'm just now preparing the petition to modify Jamie's divorce decree. What she just told me, about Mandy's grandmother being so sick. That's great. That's going to help a lot. And she said there's more. So what have you got for me, Cal?"

"We got plenty. We may even have enough to hang that ex-husband of Jamie's out to dry."

"Great! That's just great!" She flipped a switch on the phone console behind her on the credenza. I'm going to record this, Cal, if that's okay with you."

"Sure thing, Elaine. No problem. Now, here it is."

While Elaine made rapid notes on her legal pad, interrupting him occasionally to ask a question, Cal reviewed everything he had seen at the trailer.

"I got photos, too—just fifteen minutes ago—pictures of the ledgers, and all that drug stuff all over the place and the paraphernalia and what's probably the payoff money. And there's a bunch of guns in that trailer and loose ammo and everything. That's going to be enough to convince a judge that Mandy shouldn't be allowed to be with him, isn't it?"

Elaine laughed. "It should be enough after I get finished with him. And I'm not going to ask you how you got all this. I feel pretty sure Ray Nixon didn't invite you in to take a look at his place."

"Let's just say the front door was open and I sort of went in to wait for him, you know? Like one old friend to another."

"Some old friend."

"Well, I guess Ray and I have some mutual acquaintances." Cal glanced at Jamie and winked.

"However you got it, this is terrific stuff. If it all checks out, I think the custody change is going to be easy. We may even have enough here to get more than a custody change. We may be able to have that bastard put away!"

"Right. And there's more. Wait'll you hear what I found out in the desert." He gave her a full account of the evidence he'd found in the desert east of Sharperville. "The Feds ought to be interested in that. Experts would have no trouble connecting up those tire tracks to Ray's van."

Elaine grinned, looking over the notes on her pad.

Her energetic mind was already putting it all together.

"Cal, can you put me on speaker? I want to talk to you both."

Cal put the phone on speaker and in the staccato, highly concentrated style that was typical of Elaine French when she was going into action, she laid out her plan.

"First of all, I'll do a little digging to verify Edna Nixon's condition. That's protected information, of course, but I've got some friends up at the hospital." She smiled to herself. She had connections and contacts everywhere, and when she needed to have the rules bent a bit, she usually could get a little help from her friends. "I'll have to get it documented, but I think I can handle that. Shouldn't be a problem." She flipped over to a new page on the yellow pad and made some more notes. "Next, I'm going to locate the judge who's replaced Judge Joyner. Hold on a minute." She reached into the credenza behind her and pulled out a state Bar directory, flipping quickly through the pages. "Let's see. You're in the Sixth District. That's Judge Amos A. Prescott. I'll call him right now and tell him we need a temporary restraining order. Immediately. Let's hope he hasn't gone fishing for the weekend." Even as she was copying out the judge's address and office number into her notes, she added, "Don't worry. Even if he has gone fishing, I'll find him. I'll call you back as soon as I know when and where we can meet with him to get the order signed. Give me a number where I can reach you."

Cal gave her Harvey's number and she added it to her contacts. Then she looked at her watch and compared the time with the crystal-mounted gold clock on the bookcase across the room. "Let's see. It's almost noon. It'll take me about two, maybe three hours to get everything together here, talk to my people at the hospital, do the paperwork, and contact Judge Prescott. Depending on where he can meet us, I'd expect to need about four or five hours' driving time. So it'll be maybe seven, eight o'clock. Around sundown. I'll let you know as soon as we have it arranged."

"We'll be there," Jamie said. "Wherever you tell us to be, we'll meet you." She liked Elaine's take-charge style, but things were happening so quickly. "Just one thing, what does that mean—temporary restraining order?"

"It means we go directly to the judge, right now, wherever we can find him, without waiting for a formal court date, and convince him that Mandy is in danger of serious, immediate harm if she stays with Ray." That'll do for a simple explanation, she thought to herself. "We really do need to get her away from Ray as quickly as possible."

The harsh words came from Elaine so plainly, so unemotionally that Jamie felt as though she'd been dropped suddenly and painfully from a height, and she gasped, reacting involuntarily. Elaine couldn't see that Jamie was momentarily dazed, that she had made an abrupt stop in her slow pacing around the room and had leaned her head against the window, steadying herself, with her eyes closed. But Elaine did hear Jamie's gasp and she brought herself up short.

It wasn't the first time she'd been so preoccupied with her own rapid-fire thoughts and her typically super-charged level of activity she'd forgotten she was dealing with real people, people who had feelings, people who sometimes needed to be treated with consideration. She needed to remember not to just lay all this tough stuff on them—*boom-boom-boom*—without giving some thought to how it sounded from their side. After all, she reminded herself, Jamie is Mandy's *mother*. To Jamie, the idea of her daughter being in real danger was not simply a significant legal development. It was a crucial, life-and-death matter that touched her where she was most vulnerable, and she, Elaine, needed to remember that.

She slowed herself down a couple of calibrations on her activity dial.

"I'm sorry, Jamie. I didn't mean to say it so coldly. But that's precisely the point that we have to get across to the judge. Mandy *is* facing imminent and irreparable harm. Those are the words we have to use and I know that's tough for you to bear, but first of all, that's the truth, and second, for that very reason, it's what will convince the judge that he has to get Mandy away from that sonofabitch and back to you."

"I know. It's just, hearing you say it like that, just right out there." Jamie's hands were sweating and her stomach had gone sick. "I just can't help being scared."

"Of course. Perfectly natural. It would be crazy if you weren't scared. You're right to be scared and that's the whole point of the affidavits I'm going to prepare for both of you now."

"Okay." Jamie took a deep breath and steadied herself down. "What comes next?"

"Later, after we've convinced the judge to sign that order and Ray hands Mandy over to you, then the next step is to bring a full action to modify the decree, to make it permanent.

"And now, Cal," she continued, turning her attention to him, "there are a couple of things I want you to do, help me save some time."

"You betcha," he said. "Anything you say, ma'am."

"First of all, I want you to contact the local drug enforcement agents. There's a couple of DEA guys stationed downstate and I'll give you their names. Give them all the information you have. Tell them you're working with me, and if there's any problem, they should call me here at this number. Also, I'll give you the number of my cell phone, in case I've already left my office."

She waited while Cal took down all the names and numbers. Then she added, "And the other thing is, don't do anything with the pics you took. Text them to me and I can get them printed up here to have them available for trial. I think, by the time we're finished with Ray Nixon, he's not going to be interested in harassing Jamie anymore. Now, that's it, sweetie pie. I got to get going on this. Stay where you are. I'll be in touch soon."

That was all the goodbye they got.

She had too much to do to spend time on cordialities. There were calls to make. Papers to draft. Motions, affidavits, covering memorandums. And she'd have to change her outfit. On Saturdays, she usually wore casual clothes to the office—jeans and running shoes—but there was always a change of clothes on reserve in her closet, in case of an unexpected court appearance or, like today, a meeting with a judge. She checked quickly—pantsuit, blouse, pumps, handbag—everything there, ready for her. The weekend staff was in the office and she alerted the off-hours word processors to be ready for the affidavits and other papers she'd be drafting. Then she got busy on the telephone.

Cal hung up and went over to Jamie standing at the window, staring out across the field. She turned and looked at him as though he'd roused her from a sleep.

"She's some dynamo, isn't she?" Cal said.

Jamie wasn't listening. "Cal, I'm so scared. I'm so damned scared."

"Sure you are." He put an arm around her. "But we're going to get Mandy back. You'll see. It's going to be all right." He led her to the desk, and took his arm from her only long enough to dial the numbers Elaine had given him.

"I'm calling the drug enforcement people," he said. He held her close the whole time he talked on the phone.

* * *

In his cluttered office, the DEA agent swiveled his chair away from the stack of files he was working his way through, and grabbed the phone.

"Yeah?" It was no greeting, but Jerry Metzger didn't have much time to give away.

"My name is Cal Cameron. I'm calling from Sharperville and I have some information for you."

"Okay. What have you got?" Wearily, Metzger picked up a pen and started to take notes. He figured the call to be just another piece of routine citizen contact. Then he heard who made the referral.

"You're working with Elaine French?" He sat right up in his chair. When Cal was finished, the agent was already in motion.

Sometimes, Metzger was thinking exultantly, *it all comes together just right, like God decided to do you a favor and got everything organized just for your benefit.*

If they moved fast, this would tie right in with the simultaneous bust they had just finished setting up in several western cities. Six months they'd been putting it together and here was an important piece, just falling into place, like a gift from heaven.

"We'll get right on it," Metzger said brusquely. "We'll dispatch a team in there right away, Mr. Cameron. Give me a number where we can reach you. And you stay in touch with us, okay?"

"You bet," Cal said, and he had barely hung up the phone when Elaine was back on the line.

"We're in business!" she said. "I got hold of the judge. He's over in Garrison County this week, and he'll meet us in Flintlock. That's the county seat. You know where the courthouse is?"

"I don't, but maybe Jamie does. Don't worry, well find it."

"Good. Now, let me talk to Jamie." As soon as Jamie had taken the phone, Elaine said, "The courthouse in Flintlock. On Main Street. Be there at eight o'clock tonight. The judge will meet us at the front door and let us in. Any questions?"

"Is there anything I need to prepare? Anything I should bring?"

"Not a thing. I'm having the whole file faxed to Judge Prescott so he'll have had a chance to review it before tonight. And I'm preparing the affidavits and all the other papers now. You just show up on time. Go on home, if you need to change your clothes. I want you to look tidy and responsible. That's all we need. Be ready to answer any questions, tell only the truth, nothing more, and follow my lead. I'll do the rest."

And the phone went dead in Jamie's hand. She looked up at Cal. "Well, it's all set."

"That's right, darlin'. If all goes well, we'll have Mandy in your arms before morning."

Chapter Nineteen

The parking lot outside the Garrison County Courthouse was usually empty on a Saturday night, but Judge Amos Prescott's Land Rover was already there when Jamie and Cal pulled in at about a quarter to eight. They parked next to the big black SUV and Cal used the extra fifteen minutes to run across the street to a cafe to pick up a couple of cartons of coffee and some doughnuts. Earlier, when they passed through the town of Jimson, he'd insisted they stop for dinner at the town's combination motel and diner, but Jamie had only picked at her chicken salad, mostly just pushing it around on her plate.

Now, she was pacing back and forth in front of Cal who was leaning against the truck's front fender, drinking his coffee. She came to a stop in front of him.

"The last judge was such a jerk. How do we know this one won't be as bad?" She looked down and saw the doughnut he had put into her hand. She raised it, about to take a bite, and then forgot it just as quickly. "How do I know Elaine will be able to convince him? Maybe he'll believe what's in the record about me. Maybe he won't see any reason to take Mandy away from her father."

They'd been over this a hundred times already, through every mile of the drive from Sharperville, and Cal knew it was her nerves talking.

"Eat your doughnut, Jamie. You haven't had anything all day."

She looked at it and made a face. "I can't," she said. "It would make me sick. Here, you eat it." She handed it to Cal.

He gave up trying to get some food into her and scarfed it down himself.

"Where's Elaine?" She was fidgeting with the edge of her coffee cup, picking at the rim with her fingernails. "She said she'd be here by eight." She squinted down the broad, untrafficked expanse of Main Street.

On a Saturday night, the Main Street in Flintlock was pretty quiet. There was a movie theater in town, but it didn't do much business anymore. All the stores closed early, except for the big Kmart, but that was down at the other end of town, where Main Street curved around to join back up with the freeway, and it wasn't even visible from the courthouse parking lot.

Even as Cal was about to say that if Elaine said eight o'clock, she'd be there by eight o'clock, a dusty swirl appeared in the distance, coming off the freeway, and only moments later the silver Lexus was rolling toward them. It turned sharply into the parking lot and pulled up to a fast stop next to Cal's truck.

Elaine French, looking crisp in black patent pumps and black pantsuit with a white silk lining, got out of the car. She smoothed the jacket neatly in place over the white silk blouse and walked around to Jamie's side of the truck. She was carrying a black leather attaché case and she lifted the case for them to see.

"I have your affidavits here. We have a few minutes before our meeting. Read through these papers and if everything's okay, sign them." She opened the case, resting it on the hood of Cal's truck, and handed the documents to them. Then she removed her notary stamp and seal from the case. "As soon as you've signed them, I'll notarize them. Take your time. I'll wait here and check out the local scenery."

It had been two years since Jamie had been in a courthouse but this time it was different. First of all, this time she had a fighting team with her. They flanked her, Cal to her right and Elaine to her left, as they entered through the big glass doors at the front of the building. Second, the man who opened the door for them and introduced himself as Judge Prescott was not old and crabbed and tired, as Judge Joyner had been. This was a much younger man—not more than forty years old—and he had close-cropped reddish hair and a wiry mustache, which gave him a bristly, lively look. He was wearing casual clothes, jeans and a plaid shirt, and he led them down the carpeted hall to his chambers at a brisk pace. They passed the glass doors of the clerks' offices and a drinking fountain and wooden benches that had been varnished to a super shine. The judge stopped them in front of an unmarked door, just beyond a huge historical painting that depicted the early settlers' arrival in the area.

"Hold on just a minute," Judge Prescott said. "I've got to get my court reporter. The poor woman thought she could get away from me at least for the weekend, but when you called, I dragged her away from her rose garden. No one in this county grows roses like Betty Burnitz."

He opened the door and they had a brief glimpse of a lounge area, with more gray-patterned carpet and dark gray couch and a coffee urn. A fifty-ish woman with tightly curled, auburn-dyed hair, looked up at them. She was about to put her cup onto the low table in front of her.

"We're ready now, Betty. Bring your coffee if you like."

"That's okay, Judge," she said, leaving the cup behind. She followed them to chambers.

In the years to come, Jamie would not be able to describe the interior of the judge's chambers, except that she would remember the blue and gold state flag standing tall behind the judge, who had taken his place behind a very large desk, and the American flag near the window, where the drapes had been closed against the setting sun. The judge pointed to chairs across his desk for Elaine and Jamie. Cal took a seat near the window. They all waited a few minutes while Betty set up her computer. At her signal, Judge Prescott began.

"All right," he said. opening the file and crossing his hands over it. "We're ready to begin."

In a mechanical tone that reflected the many hundreds of times he had done this, he read off the case name and docket number, and Betty's fingers began their flight over the keyboard. Then he looked up at Elaine who was facing him across the desk.

"Okay, counselor. What have we got here?"

Elaine had the affidavits and other motion papers ready for him. She closed her case, put it on the floor and put the papers on his desk.

"We're moving for a temporary restraining order, Your Honor. Although custody was originally awarded to the plaintiff—that is, the father, in this case—the affidavits will show that the child is now threatened with immediate and irreparable injury if she is required to remain with her father."

Elaine's tone was modulated, direct, competent, experienced. She was comfortable with the language of the law. By contrast, Jamie was sure everyone in the room could hear the rapid thumping of her own heart and see her fingers, gone white at the knuckles, gripping the brass-studded leather arms of her chair. She felt the cold sweat of the worst case of nerves she had ever known.

For the record, Elaine told the judge what he already knew, that in this state the fundamental principle in custody matters was that the best interests of the child are always held to prevail over all other considerations. Then, in a less formal manner, she reviewed the high-lights of the evidence contained in the affidavits, emphasizing the dangers that Mandy was being exposed to. Then she moved on to the next element of the motion.

"In addition, Your Honor, as the affidavits state, there has been a material change in the circumstances of the parties since the decree was entered two years ago."

Jamie's hand started to tremble and she put it in her lap, hoping to keep it steady. Her eyes were locked on Judge Prescott's face, search-ing for a clue to what he was thinking, but except for his first quick glance at her as Elaine began her statements, she couldn't see that he paid her a lick of attention through the whole proceeding. He put a few questions to Elaine while he skimmed through the papers, and it seemed to Jamie that her lawyer and the judge were speaking a pri-vate, technical language.

Then he stopped skimming and, while they all sat silently he care-fully read Jamie's and Cal's affidavits concerning everything that had happened in the last few days, including what Mandy had told Jamie about Ray and Tina, and what Cal had found in Ray's trailer.

Finally, he stopped reading and looked at Cal for a long minute, while he pinched at his chin thoughtfully. At last, tilting himself way back in his big swivel arm chair, he spoke.

"I want to go off the record," he said, and immediately Betty stopped transcribing. Jamie felt her heart drop.

The judge continued to study Cal intently, looking him up and down, as though he was measuring him. He said, "Calvin Cameron. Cal Cameron." He repeated the words a couple of times, obviously trying to place the name. Cal was rotating his hat nervously in his hands and the judge had a sudden image of a handsome young man in the bright sunlight, raising his hat triumphantly to a cheering crowd.

"Didn't I see you maybe a couple of summers ago? Up in Cheyenne, at the big Frontier Days rodeo?"

"Yes, sir. That was probably me, sir."

"I remember. You had one hell of a day. As I recall, you went home a big winner that day."

"I guess I did, sir. Yes, sir." Cal was beginning to squirm in his chair, embarrassed. He was spinning the hat still more nervously.

"I've always had a lot of respect for rodeo cowboys," Judge Prescott said. "I did a little rodeo myself back in high school."

He said nothing more for a while, and the silence in the room became intense. He was apparently thinking long and hard.

"Young man," he said to Cal, peering intently at him. "I'm satisfied that the information contained in your affidavit is accurate and will be supported by the evidence. And I'm not going to make a fuss and ask how you got it. In a case like this, where the safety of a young child is concerned and where the possibility of serious harm is very genuine, I'm inclined to look the other way, so long as the evidence satisfies me. I presume you are prepared to face the consequences of a possible charge of trespass." He paused momentarily and chuckled. "Trespass, at the very least."

Cal only nodded and said, "Yes, sir. I am."

"Okay," Judge Prescott said. Without turning to look at his reporter, he said, "Let's go back on the record." Betty's fingers began to whirr again, and the judge turned to Elaine.

"Counsel, as far as I'm concerned, this evidence is adequate, pending a search pursuant to a duly executed warrant. It is my understanding that you will also subpoena the medical records for the civil action."

"Yes, Your Honor."

They talked some more technical talk and finally, while Jamie's heart raced excitedly, the judge unscrewed the top from his fountain pen.

"All right," he said, "I have no problem with this order."

He leaned forward again and put his signature on the precious piece of paper that Elaine had prepared for him.

"Here you are, Ms. Sundstrom." He passed the paper across the desk to Jamie, whose hand was still shaking as she took it from him. She hadn't spoken a word since they'd walked in, and she wondered if the whole proceeding could have been conducted without her.

"Thank you, Your Honor." She was surprised that any words at all came out of her nerve-choked throat. "Thank you."

For the first time, the judge smiled at her. "That's all there is to it, ma'am. Now, you go on home," he said, "and get your little girl."

Outside, in the parking lot, Elaine took the temporary restraining order out of Jamie's fingers, folded it and slipped it into an envelope that she took from her attaché case, and handed it back to Jamie.

Jamie was still looking a little stunned by how it had all turned out. She wanted to say thank you, but Elaine saw it coming and headed her off.

"It's nice, isn't it," she said, "when the legal system works the way it should?"

No one had a chance to say anything. She put a quick kiss on Jamie's cheek, another on Cal's, gave them each a hearty handshake, and was back in her big Lexus.

"Go get 'em, kids," she called out, waving happily at them, and she was away down Main Street, raising a cloud of dust as she went.

Cal watched her speed off toward the interstate and shook his head, laughing.

"Just like the Lone Ranger," he said. "Hi-ho Silver, and away."

"That's just what I was thinking," Jamie said as she climbed into his truck.

Chapter Twenty

He tried to get her to take a quick break for dinner as they returned through Jimson. "How about it, Jamie? You haven't had any solid food in you all day."

"I can't, Cal. I can't stop." The envelope with the restraining order was folded up inside her shirt pocket and she touched her fingertips to it repeatedly, as though it was a lucky charm. "I'm not hungry at all. I just want us to get back to Mandy as fast as we can. It's been a whole day Ray's had her, and I promised her, Cal. I promised her she wouldn't have to be with him. And now it's been since last night and God knows what he's done with her. I know she's scared and she's counting on me to come and get her. I can't stop to eat. I couldn't eat anything anyway. I'm too nervous."

"Well, we're just coming up on the Chevron station at the end of town, and I have to stop to fill up the tank. So why don't you run the gas and I'll hustle on inside and pick us up some candy bars and maybe some juice or something. Isn't good for you to be going all day without any food. Never know when you need your strength. Won't be but a minute."

As long as they needed gas, Jamie was willing to agree if it really didn't take but a minute, so while Cal paid for a handful of granola bars, a couple of packets of beef jerky, and some cartons of juice, she filled up the tank. They were out of there and on their way in ten minutes.

The sack of food was on the floor at her feet, and she pulled out a granola bar and showed him, for his approval, that she'd do the right thing and get some food into her. She peeled back the paper and took a bite. She kept it down, and she finished off some juice and stick of jerky.

While she ate, Cal kept the truck moving fast and steady along the wide open road that ran, unbending, like a painted line, inside the bright walls of his headlights. Only once did Cal have to swerve wide—to avoid a fawn that sprinted down the center of the road ahead of them, too confused to run into the shrubbery, while its mother ran desperately along the opposite side. The moon appeared and disappeared as a new front of clouds, wind-driven and moving rapidly, was building above them, threatening the next storm's arrival in a few hours. Cal switched on the radio to check the weather forecast, and then left it on, so music played a soft background as they talked, while the high country raced past them.

"Things have been moving so fast," Jamie said, "I haven't even thought, where am I going to stay with Mandy after I get her?"

"You don't want to take her to your place, I guess."

"No way. Not even for one night. She doesn't even know her grandfather, and I'm not going to have her meet him this way. But I just started looking for a place this week, and I didn't expect to be needing it all this soon."

"Well, shoot, honey. I don't even have to ask Ellie and Harv. I know you and Mandy can stay at their place. They've got a guest room, and I can bunk down anywhere at all, easy."

"Well, maybe for a couple of days, just till I get things worked out."

The shift in her life—all set in motion so quickly, much more quickly than she'd had time to plan for—began to present itself alarmingly, with demands and consequences she hadn't thought to sort out yet.

"Maybe for a couple of days anyway," she said again. "Maybe I could take a little more time, maybe Gordie would understand, and maybe Ellie would be willing to keep an eye on Mandy while I look for a place. It's just a couple of days."

"Why, sure she would. If I know my big sister, she'd just love to tuck another little one into her nest."

"Or maybe I can take Mandy with me. Might be fun for us to pick out our own new home together. Oh, God, Cal, I'm going to have Mandy with me." Jamie closed her eyes and rested her head back against the seat behind her. "Every day. Get to tuck her in again at night and read to her. Dress her in the morning and brush her hair." She opened her eyes and looked over at Cal. "That judge is going to make it permanent, isn't he?"

"I think you can count on it." Without taking his eyes from the road, he reached over to her and put his arm around her, pulling her close to him.

"Why don't you come over here," he said. "It's been a real tough day. You ought to just close your eyes and rest a little bit. Do you good."

"I couldn't. I'm too wound up."

But she did—she couldn't help herself—and she snuggled up against him anyway, and in a minute or two the whisper of the road beneath them and the comfort of his arm and the cool night air on her face all worked their nighttime magic, and she did indeed doze off.

It was well after ten o'clock when they reached Sharperville. In another minute, they'd turned east on Eighth South and were heading for the trailer.

Jamie took the restraining order from her pocket.

When he opens that door and he sees me, and Cal is standing there next to me so that sonofabitch can't pull anything funny on me, and when I show him that paper—

She was breathing fast now as Cal pulled the truck up into the dirt at the front of the trailer. The light at the kitchen end of the trailer was on and behind the curtains of the living room window the intermittent gray light of the television was visible.

"You're coming with me, aren't you, Cal?"

"You bet I am. We're just going to get her and leave. I'm not even turning off the motor."

They both got out of the truck and went to the door. Cal stood to one side, while Jamie knocked. She had the restraining order out of its envelope, unfolded and ready to show to Ray.

Here, she could say, *here, you sonofabitch, take a look at this.*

"What if he refuses?" she whispered.

"Don't worry, honey. If you have to, you just go back to the truck and call the deputy sheriff. Shouldn't be any fuss. And as long as I'm here, Ray's not going anywhere. Al Crosby's a smart fellow and a good deputy. He'll know how to make Ray listen to reason."

They waited another moment in the silence. She didn't like it, how quiet everything was. She knocked again. Someone moved inside and the light in the kitchen went out. She looked at Cal, suddenly alarmed.

The truck's headlights were behind him and Cal's face was shadowed, but she could see that his eyes had narrowed and that his expression had grown very serious. He set his hat forward, and then spoke to her, very quietly.

"Get into the truck, Jamie. Back it away from here and turn off the lights. Keep the motor running and wait for me."

She didn't ask any questions and she didn't argue with him. She turned and ran for the truck, getting in behind the wheel. Quickly, she folded up the judge's order, returned it to its envelope, and buttoned it into her shirt pocket. Then she backed the truck away, out of sight.

Cal didn't like the feel of this. He'd given a quick thought to getting his Smith and Wesson out of the truck, but if Mandy was in there, there couldn't be a gunfight. He flattened himself up against the front of the trailer, to the side of the door that would open away from him, and waited. He knew that Jamie's knock must have provoked some curiosity, and in a little while someone would stick a head out that door to investigate. With a little luck, this would be his chance to meet up with Ray Nixon. He could feel all his reflexes getting set. He'd just have to remember that if the little girl was there, he'd have to keep it quiet. Wouldn't do to scare her, and Jamie would never forgive him. But if Mandy wasn't there—

He kept his breathing slow, getting ready.

Just have to be careful not to kill the sonofabitch.

A minute passed and then, just as he'd expected, the door cracked and a man's lanky figure filled in the narrow opening. The television's light revealed his face.

Damn it! Wrong man!

Cal recognized Orrin Fletcher's ragged face. With his left hand, Cal pushed the door fully open and with his right, he slammed hard against Fletcher's chest, throwing him backward into the living room. Fletcher stumbled, landed awkwardly on the sofa, and sat there dumbly, like a man just looking up from his television program.

Cal, standing in the doorway, lifted his hand to one side and flicked on the light switch. He looked around quickly. No sign of the little girl.

The man on the sofa looked at him as though he couldn't believe his bad luck.

"Jeez, what are you doing? Following me around?"

"Maybe I should be. What are you doing here? And where's Nixon?" Cal watched him warily. The man didn't appear to be armed, but there were a lot of weapons around this place.

"I don't know nothing about where Ray is. I'm just waiting here for him." His voice had slid into a disgusting whine and Cal knew he was lying.

"Don't give me that crap, Fletcher. You know damned well where he is." Cal's voice was getting quieter, and he could feel a kind of slow, steady pulse growing stronger in him, like a bull pawing the ground, getting ready. He knew what was coming.

"Where's the little girl?" he asked. "Is she with him? Fletcher, don't mess with me. Is the little girl with him?"

"I told you, I don't know nothing." Fletcher's pale eyes moved back and forth as though he was trying to think through something that was too difficult for him.

Cal's mind was crystal clear. Like in the minute before you give the signal and the gate is opened and the ride begins. And your breathing and your timing and your reflexes all come together and you know exactly what you're doing. He reminded himself, be careful not to kill him.

Then he took two long strides toward the sofa and before Fletcher could move, Cal brought up his arm and backhanded him, throwing him back into the sofa. Fletcher's face twisted grotesquely, his mouth hung open, stupidly. He tried to come up off the sofa, and Cal hit him once more with the flat of his hand, hard, and then back again, a third blow. He saw the blood begin to run inside Fletcher's mouth and the quiet part of Cal's mind wondered how much would be enough to make up for what this stinking sonofabitch had done to Jamie.

"I told you, Fletcher. Don't mess with me." He grabbed the man's hair and twisted his head around so that he came off the sofa, one knee bent to the floor. "Where's the little girl?"

Fletcher was clawing at Cal's hand, trying to make him let go. "I don't know. Jeez, I don't know!"

Cal lifted him up from the floor, still holding him by the hair, and pulled his head back, his chin forward, a perfect target for Cal's fist, which drove solidly up against Fletcher's face, throwing him across the room. His body crashed into the door and he spun through it, stumbling into the dirt outside the trailer, with Cal right after him.

Nearby, sheltered by a thick stand of juniper, Jamie was waiting in the truck. She saw the two men spill out of the trailer and, in the light that came through the open door, she saw that it was Orrin Fletcher and not Ray, and she saw him hit the ground and she saw Cal, following hard behind him, pull him up and turn him around to face him. Cal hit the man again, once in the belly, doubling him up, and a second time in the face, throwing him into one of the cars that was parked there, the resounding metallic noise reaching Jamie in the truck.

Oh, God! Cal is going to kill him!

There was blood messing up Fletcher's face and splattering onto his shirt. Cal was straddling the slumping figure, with one hand holding him upright against the car and with the other smacking his face, back and forth, repeatedly, grimly timing the deliberate blows, putting his maximum strength into them. Gradually, as he continued to hit him, he let Fletcher slide slowly to the ground. Then, as he flattened out in the dirt, Fletcher rolled himself over, drawing up his knees and covering his head with his arms, trying to protect himself. Cal dropped to one knee beside him, pinning Fletcher's hands to the ground, the heel of his boot digging painfully into Fletcher's back. He spoke to him very quietly, his voice just barely above a whisper.

"That's just for openers, Fletcher. Now listen to me real close, you filthy piece of slime, before I kick your ribs into your dirty heart. I want to know where that no-good buddy of yours is and I want to know where his little girl is."

The heel of his boot dug in once, sharply. Cal was making sure he had Fletcher's full attention.

"All right! All right!"

The blood from Fletcher's face was running freely into the dry dirt, making an ugly mess beneath his head.

"A plane's coming in tonight, out in the desert. Ray went out to meet it. Him and his girlfriend. Tina." He squirmed futilely under Cal's boot. "They had the kid in the van when they left here. I don't know what they did with her."

"Where? Tell me, you sonofabitch!" Cal's rage made it hard for him to get the words out. Those freaking bastards had taken Mandy with them on this job! "Where's the goddamned drop?" He ground his foot angrily into Fletcher's back once more.

Fletcher gasped, unable to speak, and Cal eased up, letting him catch his breath.

"I got it written down," Fletchers said, when he could talk. "I got it on a piece of paper. In my pocket." He was still struggling to breathe. "Let me loose. Let me get up. I'll give it to you."

Cal backed off him, ready to kick him down again at the first wrong move. Fletcher raised himself painfully on all fours, his head hanging, the blood and dirt smeared on his face. He dropped back against the car, sitting heavily against the front tire, and reached with a couple of fingers into the pocket of his bloodied shirt, pulling out a torn piece of note paper. With his other hand, he wiped at his nose and mouth, looking at his hand as though he was confused by what had happened to him.

Cal took a step back into the light from the trailer and held up the ragged scrap of paper in order to read the numbers that had been penciled onto it.

"Are these the coordinates for the landing?"

Fletcher was testing a loosened tooth with his fingers. He didn't speak, but he nodded his head up and down.

"And this is the time written here, one-thirty? That's one-thirty this morning?"

"That's right." Fletcher only muttered his response. "I'm supposed to be meeting him in a couple of hours."

That's not giving us much time.

"After the pick-up, where is he storing the stuff?"

Fletcher was looking more and more like a trapped animal every moment, dropping his head, snarling his answers sullenly.

"He rents one of those self-storage units. It's a place just north of Butcher's Fork."

Cal kept his guard sharp. He knew that this animal, although trapped, could still be dangerous.

"Who's he distributing to?"

"Jeez, how would *I* know? You think he'd tell *me*?" He saw Cal's fist clench and he added quickly, "Some guy up north, in one of those ski towns, I think, is one of them. They all use code names, anyway. Honest, I'm not lying. I don't know any more than that."

Cal looked down the road and saw the truck waiting about fifty yards away. He raised his arm and motioned to Jamie to drive down to him.

"I don't have any more time for you, Fletcher. You're coming with me."

Jamie brought the truck up close and leaned her head out of the open window.

"Jesus, Cal, you scared the hell out of me. I thought you were going to kill him."

"I wouldn't have killed him. He just needed a little convincing."

"Convincing? What about?" Oh, God, she thought, the knife-edge of panic beginning to screech up her spine. "Where's Mandy?"

"I'll tell you in a minute. First, back the truck around so I can get at the tailgate. And toss me that lariat that's hanging down behind the front seat."

Jamie twisted around and found the coiled rope that was suspended from the bottom of the gun rack. She pitched it over to him, and then, while she backed the truck around, Cal flipped Fletcher flat into the dirt and tied his hands and feet, much as he would have roped a calf, only there'd be no getting out of these knots. When he had the man safely trussed, he stood up and quickly unlatched the tailgate. Fletcher could have been a big bag of feed, the way Cal pitched him onto the bed of the truck. He slammed the tailgate shut and came around to the driver's side. He opened the door and Jamie scooted over to make room for him.

"There's a map in the glove compartment," he said. "Let me see it." While Jamie dug around for the map, Cal pulled a couple of papers from his shirt pocket. When he'd found the one with Jerry Metzger's number on it, he took his cell phone from the dashboard and dialed the number the drug agent had given him.

The familiar voice barked at him through the phone.

"Yeah?"

Cal motioned to Jamie to open up the map, and she spread it out in front of him, across the steering wheel.

"This is Cal Cameron. Is this Metzger?

"Yeah, Cameron. What's up?"

"I think we've got something for you here. A plane's coming in tonight at one-thirty. I can give you the coordinates."

"That's great, Cameron. Let me have it."

Cal read off the numbers from the paper he'd taken from Fletcher.

"There'll be a black van meeting it." With his finger, he located the exact spot on the map, about fifteen miles from the previous drop site. "I'm heading out there right now. Should take me about an hour to get there. Listen, Metzger," Cal flashed a smile at Jamie, "I'm in a blue and white pickup, and I've got someone with me. Try not to shoot us up, okay? The bad guys are in the black van. And there's something else, Metzger." Cal paused.

He wasn't smiling now and her reached out and took Jamie's hand. "They may have a little girl with them."

Jamie had been looking at the map, but at his words, her head came up sharply, her eyes wide with alarm. Cal nodded grimly at her.

"Four years old. It's Nixon's kid, but I don't think they're going to be watching out for her. Your guys had better be real careful."

"A kid? How did *that* happen?"

"It's a long story. It's her mama who's with me." He pulled her close to him, protectively. He couldn't bear the look in her eyes.

Someone had better be keeping an eye on Jamie, too. If anything happens to Mandy, Jamie'll do the killing herself, for sure.

"Just be careful," he continued. "If you people get there before we do, just watch what you're doing. And Metzger, there's something else. Take a look at your map." Cal's finger traced around the drop area until he found what he wanted. "There's a graded road, leads into the desert from the state highway, about four miles south of Sharperville. It runs about six, seven miles and then becomes a dirt cattle trail. Right there, I'm going to drop off one of Nixon's buddies. An ex con named Orrin Fletcher. He's tied up like steer for branding and he's not going anywhere, but I'll put him off to the side so no one runs over him—though they'd probably be doing the world a favor if they did. You might have to wait till daylight to find him, but I expect he'll be making a racket so as you can hear him. It gets plenty cold out there at night, and we'll be getting some rain here pretty soon, so he'll be real happy to have you locate him."

"Okay," said Metzger. "I've got it. We'll get our agents on it right now. And something else, Cameron. You carry a CB in that truck of yours?"

"Yeah, I have one."

"Good. I'm giving you a restricted frequency you can use to contact me later."

Cal wrote down the information.

"And Cameron?"

"Yeah?"

"You watch yourself, you hear."

"You bet." Cal switched off the phone and put it back on the dashboard. He marked a circle on the map and then handed it to Jamie.

"We've got to move fast." He pointed to the circle he'd drawn. "That's where we're headed."

Chapter Twenty-one

Mandy was too little to understand, and she was scared. Ray and Tina had pushed her into the black van and slid the door shut, with a loud bang, like they were mad at her. When Tina got into the front seat, she was complaining.

"I don't see why we have to take the kid with us." She lit a cigarette, nervously, and dropped the match onto the floor of the van.

Ray had enough to think about without listening to Tina bitching at him.

"For Crissake, Tina, use your head. I couldn't exactly leave her at the trailer, could I? We're not going to be getting back till late tomorrow. And you yourself told me there wasn't going to be anyone at my mom's place, that she's up in Salt Lake and my dad went there with her."

"Well, you could have found *someone*." She turned her head away from him, looking petulantly out of her window.

"Sure. I can just hear it. 'Hey, would you mind looking after my kid for a couple of days while I run out into the desert to pick up a load of cocaine.' Jeez, you sure can be stupid when you want to, you know that, Tina?"

Tina had a smart response for that one, and they went back and forth for a while, both of them really edgy and each of them taking it out on the other. Mandy tried not to listen because their anger scared her. That wasn't the only thing that scared her. She didn't know what cocaine was, but she knew it was something bad. And she knew her Grandma was in Salt Lake again, only this time she was going to die. Grandpa had told her. And he told her she couldn't live in their house anymore and he had called Tina to come and take her away.

She made herself as small as she could in the corner of the seat, and put her thumb in her mouth. Mommy said she wouldn't have to be with Tina and Daddy anymore. Her mommy *promised.* If Mommy knew, she would come and get her. If Mommy knew—

She was afraid to cry, afraid to make Tina and her father even madder at her. Through the window, she could see the sky, beginning to get dark now, with just a little bit of light still left to show a big cloud collecting up there, looking black against the tops of the mountains. Those clouds looked scary, too, and Mandy closed her eyes, keeping them shut for the longest time, while the van rolled along, its occupants silent now, thinking their own thoughts.

Keeping her eyes closed against all the scary things, she settled gradually into the steady rocking of the van as it traveled south along the highway, and soon she was fast asleep, unaware, even when the van turned onto the rough side road and then, eventually, onto the dirt trail that went directly into the desert. She slept so soundly, she never heard the thunder over the mountains, or the wash of the brief rainstorm over the vehicle, as the predicted storm crossed the desert.

It was almost an hour later that Mandy awoke to an unsettling stillness. The van was no longer moving, its front doors were open, and Ray and Tina were gone. She could see that the windows were wet, but the rain had stopped and she had occasional glimpses of a cool moon through the rapidly moving clouds.

She didn't like being here in the dark. How was Mommy going to find her if she was so far away from home, in the big car, in the dark? She could hear voices somewhere nearby, and when she looked up over the front seat, she could see her father and Tina up ahead, walking around, smoking, looking at the ground. If they came back, if they drove her even farther away from home, her Mommy might *never* find her.

To one side of the van, she could see a long way across the big desert space, and on the other side, not so far away, the hills rose up steeply, deeply cleft by winding canyons, thick with trees and spiny brush.

She remembered seeing a tree like that, with the little leaves, like pale green pennies, shaking on their skinny branches. She remembered a road, running up between the big rocks. There might be scary things out there in the big, black darkness, lizards and snakes and even lions. But it was even more scary with Daddy and Tina in the car.

She crawled over the front seat and climbed down out of the van.

She made no sound, and neither Ray nor Tina heard her move quietly away. In the still-damp ground, her baby footsteps were silent, and the clayey soil grabbed at her little red tennis shoes. As she started the slippery climb up the hill, into the canyon, her foot slid backward into a wet clump of stumpy juniper. One little shoe slipped off her foot and wedged into the scratchy growth. She pulled herself upwards, too scared by the dark to rummage for the shoe. And minutes later, the second shoe was lost, too, left behind somewhere in the shadows. It frightened her to be barefoot, like a baby, and she felt like she was going to wet her pants. Grandma would be mad that she lost her shoes. But Grandma was going to die. Grandpa had told her.

Mandy started to cry, but very softly, trying not to.

Her Mommy wouldn't care if she lost her shoes. Her Mommy wouldn't care at all! She just needed to get up to the big rock way up in the canyon where she thought they'd last been together. Her Mommy had told her, just like the mama cow and her calf. Her Mommy would come and get her.

When Ray and Tina returned to the van, they never looked into the seat behind them. They closed the doors, Ray started the motor, and he drove away to the rendezvous point in the desert.

And Mandy continued to find her way up the canyon, her path lit occasionally by patches of moonlight.

Chapter Twenty-two

Jamie kept the truck's lights off and the engine running, ready to move as soon as the black van showed up for its one-thirty rendezvous. Beside her, in the passenger seat, Cal was loading one of the Winchesters with cartridges from a box on the dashboard in front of him. Next to that was the radio, set to the frequency Metzger had given him, and he had quickly shown Jamie how to use it so she'd be able to handle the communication with the feds while he handled the firearms. Metzger had said a helicopter was on its way, but the timing was going to be dicey.

"Whatever you do," he warned them, "don't give the bad guys a chance to alert their contacts by mobile phone or radio. We've had this bust in the works for months and we're set to jump people in three states tonight. You two better not mess us up."

Metzger was hoping he hadn't gotten too greedy, trying to net a couple of small fish along with the real sharks. But the information was good and this bust fit right in with the bigger operation.

"You better know what you're doing," he added. "You and the little girl's mother are the only ones on the scene and we have to rely on you, at least until our people get there. So just be careful, you two."

Cal had looked over at Jamie who was clutching the steering wheel tightly, her fingers white with tension.

She isn't thinking about Ray anymore. Or about Tina. She's just going to get her daughter, no matter what. It'll be up to me to do this.

"Don't worry, Metzger," he said. "We'll watch it." He'd signed off and replaced the radio on the dashboard.

So they'd waited, for over an hour now, screened by a shadowed clump of scrub oak, positioned on a rise that overlooked the desert where the plane was due to land. Thick clouds filled the sky, keeping the light of the full moon from the sand and the sage. Only occasionally, as though a shutter were being opened, did the clouds break apart and allow the rough terrain to become clearly visible. And then . . . "I see them!" Jamie exclaimed softly.

In a momentary burst of moonlight there was the dull gleam of the black van, moving without lights, approaching from the west.

Jamie's voice was quiet, intense, her eyes fixed on the vehicle in the distance.

"Right." Cal followed the line of her gaze and spotted the van moving slowly along the rough desert floor. He placed a restraining hand on her arm. "Don't move yet. Let them get to where they're going."

Jamie didn't need to be told. She concentrated on the vehicle, watching it move over the rocky terrain, waiting for it to come to rest. She watched and she tried to think clearly despite the pounding of her heart and the flood of adrenaline through her body. She was in the grip of a need that was so powerful it was almost physical, a need to close the distance between herself and Mandy. It took all the strength she had to control the irrational impulse to race down into that valley, to throw herself at the van and hope somehow to gather up her little girl out of it. Foolish, she knew. Foolish but almost irresistible.

When the van stopped, Jamie leaned forward over the steering wheel.

"Now," she whispered to Cal. She put the truck into gear but kept her foot on the brake.

In the distance, she saw Ray get out and reach behind the seat to take out a handful of stick-like flares, and watched as he drove them into the sand, every ten or twelve feet, pacing out a long rectangle, with Tina driving behind him, leaning through the half-opened door, torching each flare in turn. It had been too dark for Jamie to have seen it earlier, but in the flares' light she could see that the makeshift runway had already been roughly cleared and now that it was ready for the plane's arrival, Tina brought the van around into position, about fifty feet away from the burning flares, ready to meet the plane.

"Okay, Jamie," Cal said quietly, looking at his watch. "Those flares won't burn for very long. That plane will have to land in a few minutes. Start driving in slowly and come around behind them."

Jamie took her foot off the brake, letting the truck's own weight carry it quietly down the slope. Keeping as much as she could within the sheltering hollows, and steering for the cover of thick clumps of scrubby trees, she touched her foot to the gas, just enough to keep the truck moving, keeping their advance as quiet as she could. She made a wide arc around the end of the runway, keeping an eye on Tina and Ray who were facing south, away from her. With the engine of their souped-up van running, they never heard her approach.

"Hold it there," Cal said quietly, at about a couple hundred yards' distance from the runway. With luck, if the clouds continued to cover the moon, the darkness would conceal them for as long as they needed, and Jamie held the truck there, ready to move quickly, as soon as she got the signal.

The flares would have only seven or eight more minutes' burning time, but as Jamie and Cal watched from the truck, they could see, silhouetted against the silvery clouds, the plane approaching from the south. It was showing no lights, except for the interior cockpit lights, and it came in quickly, touching down and rolling up close to where Ray and Tina were waiting. As soon as the plane came to a stop, the pilot climbed out and joined Ray and Tina on the ground.

Jamie eased up on the brake and the truck rolled forward, a few feet at a time, while the three people below, blanketed by the noise of the plane's engine, unloaded the cargo onto the ground. She set the truck into position, now only two hundred feet from the plane, and Cal took aim through the open window.

"Hold it steady right there, darlin', and stay down." Cal sighted carefully. "There's going to be plenty of action in a minute. Be ready to move fast."

In quick succession, Cal fired twice and the plane's front tire exploded, the landing gear collapsed, and the plane dropped, disabled, to the ground. In the confusion of noise and billowing dust, the three people froze momentarily, looking into the dark, trying to find the origin of the shots.

Jamie turned on the headlights, illuminating the little group.

Ray tried to back out of the glare while he grabbed at his phone that was snapped to his belt. The pilot jumped to the plane's wing, with a big pistol in his hand. Tina was running for the van.

Jamie had the truck in motion and Cal had his door open. He yelled back at her as he dropped out onto the ground.

"Go get her, Jamie!"

Speeding now over the rough terrain, Jamie circled the truck around Tina, getting between her and the van, herding her as though she was a frantic cow, back toward the plane, as the woman ran about wildly, trying to avoid being run down by the onrushing Ford.

On the ground, Cal knelt, quickly sighted and squeezed the trigger. The phone was blown away out of Ray's hand, the force of the impact throwing his hand up over his head and spinning him off his feet. The second shot pinged off the plane's door, throwing sparks into the pilot's face, and he crouched down in a hurry. Cal fired once more, this time directly at the pilot who was again reaching into the cockpit for his pistol. The shot slammed him, spread-eagled against the plane. He fell to the ground, rolling over, clutching his right shoulder as blood ran down between his fingers.

Ray, on the ground, was trying to think fast, trying to figure out what was happening. The truck's headlights were moving toward them, pinning Tina in place like a moth on a board, and like a black cut-out against those lights Ray saw a tall man who was walking slowly toward him. The man was carrying a rifle and Ray knew the man was coming for him. He saw the man stop about twenty feet away, then lean forward and lay his rifle on the ground. Then, still slowly, purposefully, the stranger kept coming, his face illuminated by the burning flares. Ray saw what was in the man's eyes and he knew he was in for a fight. He came up from the ground swinging.

Cal blocked the first blow easily, but Ray was a big man who sensed he might be fighting for his life. He drove his fist against Cal's face, feeling hard bone against his knuckles. That was the last blow he landed.

When he'd started for him, Cal's anger was still rational. He was seeking revenge—for Jamie's sake. But something happened to him in the first instant of contact between them, something that was powerfully intensified when Ray's fist crashed against his face, something born of his anger and the night's darkness and the fiery backdrop of the burning flares, something that had been gathering itself in him for many months, something awful and evil.

Cal's rage exploded, ignited by a fury that went far beyond Ray Nixon. In the light of the flares, sparking and sputtering behind them, the writhing figure before him became every blackhearted devil that had ever raised its head against him, and Cal struck back with his fists, blow after repeated blow And as he fought, there seemed to him to appear in the twisting glow, in a procession, every one-ton animal that had ever fought him or thrown him or tried to stomp him, and especially—oh, most especially—the one, finally, that had ground him up against a stinking piece of steel and taken his youth away from him. And he saw, in the flames and in the shadow, as though in a strobe-lit parade, every golden day of his own glory, now gone forever, and he saw every careless, jaunty afternoon in the sun, carelessly enjoyed, too soon lost.

All Cal's self-restraint was gone and his rage fed on itself. In a fury that seemed to flow from him in a deadly slow motion he slammed his fists over and over again into Ray's face and body. When Ray slipped to the ground, Cal lifted him so he could hit him again. The violence was unnecessary—a simple arrest would have been enough—but Cal was beyond knowing that; he was driven by demons that he had to destroy and Ray was their substitute, a handy big brute of a man against whom, at first for Jamie's sake, and for Mandy's, and then for his own, Cal continued to fight. He beat against him until the flares had burned down to the ground, and only then, as they hissed and sputtered out in the sand, was he finally released from his own fury and only then did he let Ray go.

He stood over him, breathing painfully, his rages and his demons finally wrung out of him. It was all over, and he stood at the center of the steady light from the truck, and only then did he see that it had been only a man he'd been fighting so mercilessly, and only then did he think to look and see if he had killed him.

But Ray was not dead. The dumb sonofabitch was only collapsed and bleeding on the sand. Cal stared at him for a while, unaware that his own face was wet with blood and tears. His breathing felt strangled and it made his chest hurt. He took his bandana from his back pocket and wiped it across his mouth. Slowly, he caught his breath. On the ground, Ray was gasping, too beaten to move. Cal grabbed him by the back of his collar and dragged him, stumbling, back to the plane, where he dumped him onto the ground, next to the pilot, who was gripping his bleeding shoulder and moaning. Cal wiped his hands on his jeans, as though they'd gotten into something dirty.

"In my great-grandfather's day," Cal said to them, "they hanged your kind from the nearest tree."

Then he turned his back on them and, as he went to pick up his rifle, he shot a lightning-quick glance over at Jamie to be sure she was okay.

What he saw made his breath come more easily and he had to smile. She had positioned the truck between the van and the immobilized little group in front of the plane. Through the driver's-side window, she was holding the big Smith and Wesson on them, and nobody was moving. Cal knew she hadn't a clue how to operate that big revolver, but she sure looked ready to kill. Her hand was steady and eye was cold, and if he'd been the one looking into that deadly barrel, he wouldn't have been inclined to fool around with her.

He walked to the truck and, standing next to the window where Jamie was bracing the revolver, he turned toward the three people on the ground.

"Get your faces in the dirt," he yelled at them, "all of you! Put your hands behind you, where I can see them, on your head!" Then to Jamie, loud enough so he could be sure they heard him, "Hand me that radio, honey, and if any one of them moves, shoot to kill."

He knew she'd be no more able to shoot to kill than she could fly, and he winked at her, giving her a little smile, as she passed the radio to him through the window.

But Jamie was in no mood to be flippant. She was very scared and she was desperate to get this over with so she could get Mandy out of the van. And she'd seen what Cal had done to Ray, and she knew that wasn't all for her sake alone. She knew she'd seen him fight his demons, and it scared her to see how fierce Cal's demons were.

But she did her best to hold the revolver steady, and she waited silently while Cal radioed to Metzger on the special frequency.

"Hey, Metzger. Where *are* you people? Jamie and I are holding the bad guys here for you. You expect us to hang around all night?"

He grinned mischievously at Jamie. He was feeling a whole lot better now.

"Stop showing off, Cameron." Jerry Metzger's hard voice rasped back at him over the radio. "You cowboys think you're a bunch of freakin' heroes. You just keep those people under control and our chopper will be down in a minute. Then we'll show you how it's supposed to be done." Even as he spoke, Cal heard the roar of the helicopter's engine and saw its lights, moving quickly toward them.

"Okay, Metzger. I see you now. We'll keep them on ice for you here."

"And hey, Cameron"—Cal could hear the good humor in the agent's voice—"in case I forget to tell you later, you two did a real good job.

Thanks a bunch." The radio went silent and Cal handed it back to Jamie. Even as Jamie took it from him, the helicopter descended, whipping up the sand fiercely around them all. She handed the revolver to Cal, and he slipped it into his belt.

Now she was free to do what she'd been waiting for through all the excitement, and she opened the door, jumped out and raced for the van.

She slid the van's door open, expecting to find Mandy, frightened and cowering inside. Instead, there was no one. No one! She climbed into the vehicle and crouched helplessly at its center, looking around and around again, as though maybe if she looked one more time, Mandy would miraculously appear. As though maybe she'd made a mistake and not looked carefully enough. When her mind finally let it get through to her that Mandy wasn't there, she got out of the van fast and ran back to Cal just as the DEA chopper was setting itself onto the churned-up ground.

"Cal! Cal!" She grabbed his arm, demanding his attention. "Mandy's not there! She's not in the van!"

Agents were jumping from the helicopter, their guns drawn, and Cal was able to relax his guard on the three prisoners. In the midst of the engine's roar and the yelling of the agents and the whipping sands being blown by the helicopter's rotors, he had trouble making out what she was saying, but he saw in her face how frightened she was. He put an arm around her and put his mouth close to her ear.

"Take it easy, honey," he shouted. "What's happened?"

"I'm telling you, Cal! Mandy isn't in the van! She's gone!"

Jamie's eyes flashed wildly out to the black desert around them, invisible beyond their small, illuminated area. She pulled out of Cal's arm and ran to Ray.

"Where is she, Ray? What have you done with her?"

She paid no attention to the agent who was frisking Ray and handcuffing him. She grabbed her ex-husband by his jacket and turned him to face her.

"What happened to her?" She was screaming at him

He stared blankly at her, obviously confused by her presence here at this desert rendezvous, and equally baffled by her questions. Ray was badly beaten, bloody, in serious pain, and plenty of trouble. He had enough to think about without focusing on Jamie and questions about Mandy.

"Jesus, how the hell should I know? She was sleeping in the van." He looked over at Tina, who was also being handcuffed. "What happened to the kid, Tina? She was sleeping in the van, wasn't she?"

"How should I know?" Tina's responded sullenly, also concerned with her own problems as the agents prepared to take her away. "She's *your* kid. I *told* you we shouldn't have brought her."

They were being led away, and Ray called back to Jamie, over his shoulder.

"I don't know what happened to the kid. We stopped once, about five miles back. Maybe she got out then."

Cal couldn't believe their callousness.

Stupid sons of bitches!

He saw Jamie's face, a white mask of panic. How much more of this nightmare could she take? As he put an arm around her, one of the agents approached him.

"Are you Cameron?" Cal nodded at him and the man held out a hand. "I'm Metzger," he said.

Cal saw a forty-ish man with thinning hair, the pouches of fatigue beneath his eyes emphasized by the helicopter's light flashing brilliantly over their heads.

"Glad to meet you, Metzger."

"This was a close one," Metzger said, "but we pulled it off, the whole operation. The others are being picked up right this minute. Even as we speak." His words were triumphant but the worn, cynical expression on his face made them almost sarcastic. It didn't mean much to win one battle in this never-ending war. "We got a bunch of the big guys. In Park City. And in Vegas. A couple of other places. This here was a small piece of a much bigger operation. We're going to need you folks to come in and make a statement, give us some information."

Before Cal could answer, Jamie interrupted him.

"No. Not now. My little girl is missing. We've got to find her. We have to go."

"That's right," Cal said, backing her up. "What you could do for us, Mr. Metzger, on your way back, you could call the deputy sheriff in Sharperville. His name's Al Crosby. If we don't pick up the little girl's trail ourselves, we'll need a search-and-rescue team to start looking for her when daylight comes. He can start alerting the volunteers."

Briefly, Jerry Metzger focused his attention on Jamie. Sometimes he had to be reminded that there were other problems in the world besides breaking up the drug business.

"Sure thing. You've already done plenty to help us. I'll radio Crosby for you."

As he walked back to the helicopter, he called back to Jamie.

"I hope you find your little girl. It's a big desert out there."

The helicopter lifted up, twisting to the south, and Metzger was gone, leaving a couple of agents to guard the van and the plane until they could be examined for use as evidence. Later, flatbeds would take them away and soon the only sign of what had happened here in the desert would be the burn marks left in the sand.

In the sudden, dark emptiness, Jamie pressed close to Cal, trembling, feeling what was left of her control slipping away from her, as though her very breath and blood were draining out of her body. She was so frightened; she needed help so badly.

Cal's strong arms around her should have been a reassurance and a comfort, but she could only stare wild-eyed, out into the night, cold now with the wind coming up. Far away, a pack of coyotes howled and Jerry Metzger's last words repeated themselves coldly in the dark.

"It's a big desert out there."

Chapter Twenty-three

With the flare-fires burned down and the helicopter lights gone and the desert's evanescent shimmer not yet visible, Jamie looked out into the eyes of a pitiless, terrible reality. Somewhere in its silent spaces, the desert was hiding Mandy from her, making no promise to keep her safe or even to return her at all. Jamie's mind seemed to have frozen and suddenly she was hollow—empty inside.

She took a few aimless steps, trying to think. "We could build a fire. If we make a big fire, she might see it."

She paced away from Cal, as though to look for firewood that might be strewn about, but she was seeing nothing. She circled back to him, distracted, and as he put his arms around her again, she burrowed briefly within their protection.

Oh, God. Help me. Please help me. I can't think. I can't think. I don't know what to do.

Even her skin felt numb and nerveless.

"No, wait," she said She pulled out of his arms one more time, walked away a little and then came back. "Ray said they stopped about five miles back. If we drive straight back the way he came, and make the fire there, we'd have a better chance of her seeing us."

"Good thinking," Cal said. "A fire's a good idea. That might just—"

She hadn't heard him; she was already climbing into the truck. She had no thought for what was in his mind.

Poor kid, Cal was thinking. *She's going to eat herself up. And a fire may not be much help. Hell, Mandy may not even be able to see a fire. Most likely she's hidden herself away somewhere, scared and exhausted, probably fallen asleep by now, under some brush or behind the rocks.*

Still, Jamie's going to go nuts if she doesn't take some kind of action and it couldn't hurt to build a fire. Who knows? It's a remote chance, but Mandy might see it.

Assuming she's still okay, of course. Hell, anything can happen to a little girl lost out in the desert at night. There are animals out there. Plenty of rattlesnakes. Wolves, even. Or, she could have taken a bad fall in the rocks. She could be caught in a crevice, maybe with a couple of bones broken.

She could be unconscious, or she could have gotten herself into some place that's too hard to find, or she's just too scared to call out.

In the lights of the truck he checked the rifle's breech to be sure it was empty.

I don't even want to think what might yet happen before we get to her, and there isn't a damned thing we can do until morning. Jamie's going to be a basket case by then. I guess building a fire's a good idea, help her feel she's got some control. Help her keep the panic down. Help her get through this.

Cal looked up into the scudding clouds and sent a few silent words into the sky.

Don't let this get really bad, okay? Let the little girl be safe. And please let Jamie come through it all right. Please?

Then he walked to the truck's door and reached in to set the rifle into the rack behind the seat.

"Why don't you drive, honey," he said. "This gimpy leg of mine could use a little rest."

He'd have used any excuse at all to give her something to do, and she didn't even answer him; she slipped right behind the steering wheel and had the truck in gear by the time he'd come around the front to the passenger side and hoisted himself up beside her. She'd turned it in a tight arc and was moving even before he had the door closed.

"I was thinking," she said, "maybe we could call the deputy." She was peering into the band of light that ran ahead of them like a broad line of pale, glowing yellow laid over the sage and reddish sand. Her stomach felt like a huge fist had grabbed it. "If Al Crosby got the message from Metzger, he might already have some information for us. Maybe Mandy's been found already. Maybe he could check at the Nixons' place, or even at the trailer. She could be waiting for us right now. Someone could even have taken her to my dad's."

She was grasping at any straw and they both knew it.

She stopped the truck when the odometer showed they'd traveled five miles. She left the headlights on, got out of the truck, stood inside the lights' glare and called out into the night. Several times, as loudly as she could.

"Mandy. I'm here, honey! Mandy! Mandy Nixon!"

Her words rolled, like tumbleweed, wind-driven, across the emptiness, bumping against the clumpy growth and rolling up the cliff faces and into the canyons and crevices.

"I'm here, Mandy! It's Mommy! Mommy's here! Do you hear me? Mandy!"

Only silence came back. She called several times more, turning in all directions, and then waited, but only the soft ruffle of the canyon winds, stirred by the storm remnants, returned to her across the dry earth.

"Mandy."

This time she whispered the name, as though on gentler wings, not more than a shiver in the wind, her call might more readily reach the little girl.

And still, of course, there was no sound.

But the effort had done her good. Now that she had confronted the stillness and heard her voice disappear into it, she was more able to accept its incontrovertible truth: her ordeal was only beginning. What lay ahead might yet be very bad, and she would have to be ready. The fear remained—there was no way she could lose that—but the blind panic had subsided and her heart was now beating more slowly, no longer pounding in her throat. Her thoughts focused more steadily.

"Let's get that fire started," she said abruptly, for the first time wondering where Cal was.

"Right," he said.

And there he was, with an armful of wind-drift pinyon he'd already gathered. He dropped it some thirty feet away from the truck, mounded it into a rough pyramid, and set it ablaze. While he did that, Jamie collected more, enough for a bonfire, enough to make a beacon that would burn at least until first light.

He brought a sleeping bag from the truck's storage box, and a tarp, blankets, a couple of warm shirts and a handful of granola bars.

"We can start tracking her as soon as we get a little light. In about three hours," he said, looking at his watch. "The ground's damp from the rain, so she'll have left good prints. In the meantime, you need to get a little rest and have some dinner."

He handed her a granola bar.

"I know. I know, Cal. We should both get some rest.—"

He'd brought a long-handled shovel from the bed of the truck and she stopped to watch what he was doing. With a few quick moves, he flattened out the base of a low hillock, forming it deftly into a back rest. While she stripped the paper from the granola, he spread the tarp on the ground and laid the sleeping bag over that, its head against the makeshift headboard, and rolled up a blanket to form a pillow, which he tucked snugly in against the angle. Then he held the shirt for her and she slipped her arms into it. She rolled up the sleeves—they were much too long for her—and buttoned it up warmly.

"She must be so cold," Jamie said. "I'm sure she's not dressed for the night. What's she going to do?"

"She'll find some little space to hunker down in. That's what animals do, and that's what even a little kid'll do when she's cold. It's instinctive. And it's not like it's winter. She's not in any danger from the cold. She'll pull herself in out of the wind, and she'll go sound asleep."

He sat down on the sleeping bag and held up a hand for her. She took his hand and sat down too, and he put his arm around her. It was wonderful, how snugly they fit into the space he'd made.

"But she'll be so frightened," she said.

"She'll be okay, honey. She knows you're coming for her."

"Does she, Cal? Does she really? Are you sure?"

Even as she put those helpless questions to him, Jamie knew she was relying on him to have a power—an almost magical power—to make it all be so. And once again, Jamie realized how scared she was. She was in real trouble, a trouble so serious she could no longer be alone with it. Her head had gone all muddled. She would have to lean on someone else. And Cal's head was clear and his arm was around her and he was letting her lean on him.

And in that moment, a connection was made. In that moment, a lifetime of aloneness came to an end and Jamie knew, whatever might happen, this man had entered her life forever and made a difference. She trusted him—and that had never before happened. Her pain and terror were fully exposed before him—and that, too, had never before happened. She was flooded by an emotional force so powerful it was a physical wave throughout her body: he brought safety with him. He'd put himself in the way of serious danger, for her sake, and he'd known how to handle it. What was it Elaine French had said? A cowboy in love was like a knight in shining armor—ready to slay dragons.

She glanced sideways at him.

A cowboy in love . . .

He'd taken his hat off and put it on the ground next to him and he ran his hand through his hair, as a child might, messing it up, making the dark curls fall forward in a tangle over his forehead. The firelight muted the sharp line of his jaw and softened the deepening creases around his mouth; in its glow his face became a fine mix of moving dark shadow and golden places.

He looks different.

The change was subtle, perhaps only an effect of the breathing, warming firelight, but it seemed to her that a dark place in him had been opened and something had been dragged out of him, leaving him exposed and vulnerable. Her heart twisted in her, aching for what must have happened to him. After the turmoil of the last hour, only now did she think of the unreasoning, animal violence of his ferocious attack on Ray. Only now did she wonder what it could have meant.

"Cal, I saw what happened back there."

His hand paused.

"You mean with Ray?"

"Yes."

He took a deep breath, but didn't say anything.

"What was that all about?" she asked.

Still he was silent, frowning into the fire.

"It looked like maybe you were trying to kill him," she said. "But it wasn't that, was it? It wasn't even Ray, was it?"

"At first it was."

"I don't understand."

His answer came slowly. "I don't know how to explain it."

He was silent for a long time. In all the excitement, there hadn't been time for him to think about it, but now he realized that something important had happened back there. He was trying to figure it out, trying to find the words, but it hadn't sorted itself out yet.

"When I saw him there," he said finally, "near the plane, I knew he had to be stopped. I saw he had the phone in his hand, but he was close enough, so it was an easy shot. And then suddenly all I could think was I wanted to get my hands on him. I didn't want to use the gun. I just wanted to get my hands on him. And then he hit me once. I remember that. He hit me once and then it was like everything changed. I was hitting him but it stopped being Ray that I was hitting. It's like Ray was just an excuse."

He turned toward her, pulled her close in his arms and his thick shirt was warm against her face. He rubbed his cheek against her hair, as though its silkiness was a comfort to him.

"Oh, Jamie," he said. "It didn't have anything to do with Ray. You're right about that. It's something else, has nothing to do with you and Ray—except it's all about the bad things that happen to people. Who knows how long I've been fighting that battle. At least a year. Maybe it started even before that. But this whole last year, ever since the accident, ever since I wrecked my knee, it's been a goddamned hell. Like my life was already over, only I was still walking around, fooling the whole world. I mean, dammit, here I am, I'm strong and except for the goddamned knee I'm healthy and I know there's lots of folks would think that's a real good deal. But Jesus! This isn't the way it's supposed to be!"

He was holding her tightly, his hand against her head, pressing her to his chest, his face against her hair. She couldn't see that his eyes were closed in pain, but she could feel that he was holding on to her for comfort. She stayed quiet and let him cling to her.

Like we're both hanging on for dear life.

"And then," he spoke softly almost to himself alone, "there was something about the dark, and the fires all around that damned plane, and the feeling of Ray just crumpling up as I hit him, and he seemed to change into all the goddamned devils I've been fighting all these months, like they'd all gotten stuffed into one evil person and this was my chance to wipe them all out. And I just couldn't stop. I didn't want to stop. It felt so good!"

He paused and then took a long, slow, deep breath. "It *still* feels so good! Like I just got split open and cleaned out. Like finally it's all over. It's been hurting like hell for so long, but now I'm okay." He kissed the top of her head. "Now I'm really okay."

"You mean Ray Nixon was finally good for something? In his whole rotten life, he finally was useful to someone?" She couldn't help chuckling.

Cal laughed, too. "Yeah. He made a real good punching bag. Pity you couldn't get in a few licks yourself. Would have done you good."

"Well, then I owe you for doing it for me. And you sure were doing it better than anything I could have done. It was all I could manage to hold that gun on them while you were doing it. I can tell you, I was plenty scared I was going to have to use it and you know I didn't have a clue—" She stopped abruptly and looked up at him. "You knew that, didn't you?"

"I sure did, honey." He got a kick out of remembering the sight of her with that Smith and Wesson about as big as she was. "But you looked so fierce, I knew there wasn't anyone going to try you out."

"Well, I didn't feel fierce. All I could think was that we had to get Mandy back." It brought her up short to speak Mandy's name aloud, and she could feel the quiver in her chest. She waited until it quieted. "And I sure don't feel fierce now. Now I just feel scared. I forget it for a few minutes, like when we're talking, and then I think about her, and I get scared all over again, like I've got dragons all around me."

"There isn't anyone, I guess, doesn't have a team of dragons always coming at them."

"Well, then, thank God for the dragon-slayers." She pressed more closely against his chest.

"Well, they're not in shining armor, not anymore. But fair damsels can still get some help even in these modern times." He stroked her hair tenderly and kissed her cheek. "You've helped me, Jamie, maybe even in ways we don't really understand yet." He kissed her again, and then smiled. "So now, let's just line up those dragons of yours and start knocking them off, one after the other."

"Well, next to the big one, the one that's got Mandy, the others don't seem quite so fierce as they did a few days ago. Before you came along." In the dark, she was blushing. Those last words were a huge admission, and she was glad her face could not be seen.

"As for the other ones," she said, thinking, sorting them out, "well, Ray has been taken care of. Then, there's the people in town who've had it in for me, I don't care about them so much now. I can leave, if I want, as long as I have Mandy with me. I could take her anywhere I want. Salt Lake City. California. There's nothing to keep me in Sharperville. Not even my dad."

Cal took her hand in his and kissed her fingertips.

"He's got his own dragons to slay," she said. "But I can walk away from that one; it's not after me anymore. And there's another one I never admitted to anyone before. I don't want to live so shabby anymore. I want to have a real home, with nice things in it. I want to make enough money to have pretty clothes. I want to do some kind of work where I don't have to wear a hard hat and boots. I want to have pretty hands. I want to wear nail polish and have pretty hands."

Cal laughed out loud. "Sweetheart," he said, "you've been so damned brave for so long. It's about time you had someone doing some of the dirty work for you so you can start tending to those hands of yours and make them just as pretty as you please." He stroked her hair and she pressed against his chest.

God, how good he feels.

"All we have to do is find Mandy," she said.

"That's right, sweetheart."

"That's the only really bad dragon now. I won't be able to stand it if anything happens to her. That's something I wouldn't be able to survive."

"Don't worry, sweetheart. In just a couple of hours from now we're going to be able to start tracking her. As soon as it's light, we'll pick up the tread from the van and find out where it stopped." He pulled the blanket up around her shoulders. "But until then, I want to see you get some rest. An hour or two would do you a lot of good. You're going to need your strength for tomorrow."

He didn't need to say it more clearly than that; she understood. What lay ahead might be much worse than anything that had come before.

"Okay," she said, and closed her eyes.

And he watched the firelight create moving shadows over her face and he stroked her hair until finally she fell into the nervous sleep of exhaustion and prolonged anxiety. She slept, but he saw that her dreams were troubled and painful.

And then he let himself doze, too, for an hour or so, holding her still in her arms.

And so they slept, while the fire burned, and the night's blackness slowly came to its end.

And because they both slept, they didn't see the dark form, big and shadowy, that had been drawn to the light and the warmth of their fire. They didn't see the cougar's tawny coat glistening silver as he materialized out of the shadows, and passed around them. They didn't see the black-tufted ears or the golden eyes, reflecting back the fire's light, blinking once, and then again, as it paused for few silent moments to observe them. And they didn't see the wound it carried, the burn of the lightning strike, or hear it scuffing the ground with its dragging foreleg as it padded painfully past them, moving south of them, into the canyon, making a track of its own.

Chapter Twenty-four

The thin, early song of the birds was just rising in the cool air when Cal kissed her cheek.

"I hate to get you up, sweetheart," he said, "but it's time to get going."

He had been careful to make no move to wake her until the first light of morning paled the eastern sky, but as his lips touched her, she was instantly awake, her blue eyes filled with the terrible dreams that had been with her in sleep.

She was on her feet immediately and in only minutes, Cal had covered the remaining embers of the fire, everything was packed back into the truck, and they were ready to start.

It wasn't difficult to pick up the trail of Ray's big van. The distinctive tread of its outsized tires had marked the damp ground clearly and they quickly found the place—not far from where they had built their fire in the night—where hours earlier Ray and Tina had stopped to walk around. Their shoeprints were clear and sharp in the red soil, and even the butts of their cigarettes were still on the ground, discolored by the rain but otherwise undisturbed.

"Cal! Look!" Jamie called to him to come and see what she had found, and Cal joined Jamie kneeling on the ground. "Look, here. These are Mandy's prints! I've found her prints!"

She was pointing to the flat depressions in the ground, the marks left by a child's short steps leading away from the place where the van had stopped. Cal was at her side in a moment, kneeling down to examine the outlines of the little shoes.

"The prints are so flat," Cal said, "and they don't show hardly any tread at all. Do you know what she'd have been wearing?"

Jamie touched her fingers to the shallow mark. The tangible evidence of Mandy's presence was a reassurance even as it wrenched her heart.

"She's been wearing her tennis shoes all summer." Jamie let her eyes follow the line of steps, leading toward the hills. "She couldn't be dressed very warmly. Maybe just jeans or shorts, and little T-shirt." She stood up, needing to hurry up, needing to follow those steps immediately. She could hardly breathe.

Cal stood up too, his gaze also led southwards by the trail of baby steps.

"Looks like she was headed for the canyon. If she didn't get that far, if she stayed down on the flat, we'll be able to use the truck to follow her."

He turned and headed for the vehicle, but Jamie stopped him with one hand on his arm.

"And if not, Cal? If she didn't stay on the flat? What if she did get up into the canyon?"

"Then we'll just have to leave the truck and track her on foot."

Don't say anything to Jamie yet. One thing at a time. If the kid got into those rocks, it's going to be a lot harder to find her. There wasn't much moon last night—just occasional after the rain—and she'd have become completely disoriented moving in the dark. There are steep drops off those rocks, and deep crevices, plenty big enough for a little girl to fall into. Best not to talk to Jamie about that yet.

He scanned the terrain quickly, and then looked up to the sky, which was crystal clear. All signs of yesterday's storm had vanished. The sun, just starting to show over the far-away hills to the east, had not yet climbed high enough for the unrelenting heat to bake the desert dry, and the air was still fresh with the early morning chill.

They got into the truck and Cal drove slowly, holding the door open with one hand and leaning far out as he drove, keeping an eye on the trail made by the little tennis shoes, moving the truck slowly. On her side, Jamie peered ahead of them, watching intently for any sign.

They were nearing the rise of the cliffs when Jamie spoke suddenly.

"Look! Up ahead, on your side."

Almost hidden at the base of a clump of sage, directly in the path of the little footsteps, something small and bright red was caught in the stiff brush. Cal pulled the truck up to it and swung his long legs out. Jamie was even more quickly out of the truck and was already holding the object cupped in the palm of her hand when Cal reached her.

"It's her tennis shoe, Cal. It's one of her red shoes."

It rested in her hand like a piece of long-hidden treasure, as significant to her as if it were a talisman, rich with meaning and magical power. As though she'd found her own lost little sneaker—watched for these many years—it was like a sign—from another place and another time. But there was no other place or time for Jamie now; the little red shoe was real and palpable evidence that Mandy had passed through this place and there was no time to explore mystical connections. Jamie's eyes followed the direction of the little footsteps as they approached the bouldered cliffs ahead and disappeared into the brush and rocky passes.

She's alone up there, somewhere all alone. She's lost her shoe and she's scared and she's waiting for me to find her.

Meanwhile, Cal strode quickly to where a growth of aspen trees bordered the entrance to the broad canyon that cut through the sharply rising cliff. At the base of the aspens and up along the canyon sides, the scrub oak grew thickly and a few junipers could be seen, thinning out as the canyon rose more steeply above him. Cal knelt beside a clump of stunted, dry juniper, and dug his hand around its base, were he had spotted the mate to the shoe Jamie held in her hand. It was lying, jammed up against the woody trunk, and a little skid mark above it showed Cal that the child had slipped in the wet soil, losing her second shoe up against the stubby tree. Broken twigs, about a foot above the ground, told him where she had grabbed the branches trying to steady herself.

He picked up the shoe and then took a few steps further, the print of Mandy's tiny toes making a clear trail for him to follow. He looked ahead, far enough to confirm that the truck would not be able to climb much further along this course, when suddenly, he saw something that made his pulse jump. He took another couple of steps forward and dropped to one knee.

Oh, Christ!

One careful look and he knew just how bad it was. Another track had joined the print of the little foot. At least five inches across, it was the unmistakable footprint of a mountain lion. By the size of the print and by the length of the cat's stride, Cal judged it to be a fully-grown male, its body alone easily five feet long. The shallowness of the track told him the print had been made several hours after Mandy had passed by, when the soil had had a chance to dry out a bit.

But the cougar's footprint told him something else, something much worse. Cal ran his fingers along the inside of the left front print, and then moved ahead to confirm, in the next stride, what he had seen in the first. He followed the track for a distance of abut twenty feet, making sure.

Now we've got some real trouble.

He stared at the print, trying to decide whether he should tell Jamie.

She's had to be so brave. How much more of this is she going to be able to take?

But it was too late for him to make that decision. Jamie had already come up the slope and was standing beside him. He looked up, shading his eyes against the sunlight that now was strong and flat at the horizon, and he realized she had also seen what he had discovered. Her eyes were riveted on that print and he knew there could be no hiding it from her.

"What does it mean, Cal?"

She knelt beside him, touching her fingers to the little print Mandy had left and then moving her hand over the track of the big cat.

"It's not good, Jamie. That's the track of a mountain lion. And it looks to me like he's following her."

Jamie made no sound, but he saw her fingertips whiten as they dug against the ground.

"That's not all," he said. "This cat's been hurt." He pointed to the inside of the front print. "You can see here where it's favoring that left front leg." He showed her the scuffed edges of the print. "That paw is being dragged. You can see how shallow the print is and the whole stride on the left side is shorter and weaker than normal. And he's compensating on the right side—the opposite print, on that side is much deeper than it would usually be. No telling what got him— could have been a fight with another male, or maybe he tangled with a mother bear. Or some rancher took a shot at him. Whatever it was, he's been hurt badly."

He stood up. He didn't need to spell it out for her. The cat had been injured and that made him dangerous. A cougar wouldn't normally try to attack a human child, but if it couldn't hunt its usual prey, it would settle for whatever it could find. And this cat was following Mandy.

Jamie's eyes now fixed on the canyon winding up ahead of them, her fingers tracing the inside of Mandy' footprint, as though it might speak to her. Cal bent down and put his hands on her arms, lifting her to her feet.

"We don't have time to stand here. Jamie. The truck isn't going to be able to make it into this canyon. I'm going to have to track them on foot, and you're going to have to wait down here for me."

In a few strides, he was back at the Ford and was lifting the Winchester from the rack. He loaded some ammo into the rifle quickly and he dropped a handful of additional cartridges into his pocket.

Jamie was already back at his side.

"No, Cal, I'm not waiting in the truck."

"Jamie, I've got to move fast and I've got to move quiet."

"I'm not staying behind! Mandy's waiting for me to come and get her! I'm going with you and we don't have time to stand here and argue!"

"That cat is dangerous, Jamie. It's been hurt and it's probably in pain, and it's going to be mean. Don't you understand, I don't want you anywhere near it?"

"Don't *you* understand? That animal is after my baby! I'm *not* waiting here!"

And she turned from him and was already climbing the slope, following the tiny footprints.

He was momentarily weak with love for her.

Sweet Jesus, please don't let anything hurt either one of them.

"All right," he said, catching her up quickly. "Let's go."

Together, they entered the canyon and picked up the double trail of the child and the cougar.

She had no experience tracking, so she had to let him go ahead, but she stayed close behind. Once they were into the canyon, he moved slowly, staying low and holding his rifle ready, and she matched her pace to his, keeping her steps as silent as she could on the dry earth. He paused every few steps to look ahead, beyond the tracks in the soil, to scan the rocks and ledges that rose above the twisting, narrowing trail, and Jamie paused when he did, searching desperately, on every twig and in every niche of rock, for even the tiniest sign the child might have left behind—any twisted branch, gripped by a little hand, or a few threads of fabric caught against a rough stone.

The sun, now fully risen and hot, baked the red earth beneath their feet as they made their silent way. The canyon breeze was stilled and the usually-fluttering leaves of the quaking aspens no longer moved, suspended breathlessly on their thin branches. Overhead, a raven rose from its perch in the boulders and circled away, down to the desert floor, now far below them. Mandy's trail became harder and harder to follow as it continued farther up the canyon where the ground became rockier, and there were fewer low bushes to show the marks of her passage through them.

Even as Jamie was instinct-driven to close the distance between herself and her little girl, she simultaneously became, in the primal way of all mothers when their children are in danger, one person with her child, again a child herself, existing in Mandy's place, as though it were she herself who was the lost child. She felt what Mandy must have suffered, alone in the dark and the cold, trying to figure out what to do and not having the grown-up skills she needed.

Please, God. She breathed the words silently. *She's just a little girl.*

Her feet slipped a little and she dug her fingers into the earth to catch herself. Cal paused, looking back, and she signaled to him that she was all right.

"Go ahead," she mouthed the words silently, gesturing to show she was steady.

He turned and continued on.

What would she have done without Cal? She let her eyes leave the trail for a moment, just to watch the way he moved through the brush. He was so careful and patient. The rifle weighted him forward, like a casual extension of his arm, as natural to his hand as a length of rope or the horn of his saddle.

What would she have done without him? Without a protector standing by, someone who would take care of her for *her* sake, she would herself have been helplessly exposed, for in the face of her child's danger, she was entirely without any capacity to protect herself. So she followed behind him and concentrated only on the small signs, as Cal pointed them out to her, the occasional mark of a little foot where it touched a bit of damp ground as the child struggled through the tumbled stones, the mark of baby hands grasping at the small branches, leaving them snapped and bruised. There was encouragement in these tiny signs.

But there was terror in the parallel track of the cat, moving right along with Mandy's trail, and she couldn't bear to look at those marks. She kept her eyes on the brush and stayed close behind Cal as they picked their way silently up the canyon, following a trail that grew fainter as it climbed higher.

The trail was very sparse indeed when up ahead the craggy face of the canyon wall bent away from them. As they rounded it, a broad plateau opened up, rimmed in the distance by great flat-topped boulders lying up against the far rise of the mountain. Blue spruce and lodgepole pine were growing up here, and the aspen were bright against them. To the east, the mountain dropped away and the desert shimmered far below.

Jamie knew, the moment she came around the bend and saw the open space and the great table-like rocks strewn across it, this was the place where Mandy would have stopped to wait for her. Although Cal had advanced a few steps, looking for the next sign on the ground, Jamie paused where she was and scanned the great boulders that lay ahead of them.

"Cal!" she whispered urgently. She came up quickly behind him, her hand reaching out to touch his arm. Her heart raced. "Cal, I see her!"

At the far side of the broad plateau, where the flat rocks lay like huge, ancient lizards baking in the sun, there was one on which a little barefoot girl was sitting, playing with a small branch of aspen she'd gathered on her long trek up to this barren, dry place. The sunlight glinted off her white-blond hair and her bright red T-shirt was like a flag signaling to the searchers that their hunt was over.

Oh, God! She's alive!

Jamie forgot everything. She was about to stand up, to run to Mandy, to call to her, when Cal's arm thrust back at her, his hand almost striking her as he forced her down. He was silent, but she saw that he was not looking at Mandy. His face was turned up to ledges of rock that rose in great tiers behind the child, and Jamie saw what he saw. She went ice-cold, her heart constricting painfully.

The cougar was immobile. He lay, like a statue, not more than ten feet from Mandy, watching her from the ledge above her.

Jamie froze, not daring to make a move, not daring even to breathe.

Next to her, Cal dropped to his right knee.

The lion's head came up and he looked toward them across the broad sunlit plateau. The black-tufted ears came up, and the long tail switched slightly, a deliberate, slow motion, back and forth, back and forth. As though he had all the time in the world, he raised himself slowly.

Cal raised the Winchester's stock into his shoulder and bent his eye to the scope. In the crosshairs, he saw that the animal, a hundred yards away, was looking right at them. Cal adjusted his aim.

He had a perfect shot. His finger on the trigger began to tighten—

"No!" Jamie's hand was on his, stopping him. "No, Cal, don't shoot! Don't shoot him!"

"What are you doing? Get your hand away!"

Even as he tried to reposition to take the shot, the lion began to move.

"Don't you see, Cal? He's not going to hurt her! He's leaving!"

Through the gun's sight, Cal saw the lion turn away, his whole left side, exposed, presenting an easy target. Slowly, almost deliberately, with a single last look at Mandy, the lion moved to the far edge of the rock. His injured left shoulder twitched spasmodically but there was nothing damaged in those powerful hind legs and in one move he leapt to the ledge above him. Cal again adjusted his aim again and again Jamie stopped him.

"Cal! Don't hurt him! Please! Don't hurt him!"

Cal turned momentarily toward her, saw something in her eyes that spoke to him. He took a deep breath and put a brake on his frustration. "I don't understand." His expression was a mix of confusion and irritation. "I don't understand. But all right, Jamie. I won't hurt him. But you'd better have a good reason. And at least I hope you won't mind if I do just scare him on his way. I don't like him being that close to Mandy."

Once more, he aimed, and this time she didn't interfere. His shot pinged off the rock just beneath the lion.

Cal stood up, ready to fire again if necessary, but the lion had disappeared among the boulders. Jamie now was running across the plateau, whispering under her breath as she ran.

"Thank you, God! Thank you, thank you."

In a moment, she had reached Mandy who, at the sound of the gunshot, had looked up and seen her Mommy. She was already climbing down from the rock, her little bare feet reaching with difficulty to the dry earth below. As Jamie gathered her up close, Mandy's vivid blue eyes were wide, looking excitedly into Jamie's.

"I was scared, Mommy. Daddy and Tina left me alone in the car and they were fighting and I was scared. The door was open and I got out and they didn't see me. And I climbed all the way back here to this place, so you could find me. Just like you said, like the mommy cow and her baby, how they go back to where they were together. And it was so cold and it was dark but I found the place, didn't I, Mommy? Isn't this the place?"

It was good enough. What difference would it make if for all her life Mandy would not know? One canyon is as good as another, as long as she'd been found!

"Yes, sweetie. Oh, yes! This is the perfect place."

"I walked right here, and I didn't move at all, the whole night, so you could find me."

"Yes, sweetie, yes. You were such a good girl. You did just what Mommy told you."

Jamie knelt beside her and kissed Mandy's hair and pressed her cheek against her little girl's hair. It was all over and Mandy was safely in her arms, not only for now, but for always.

Mandy wrapped her arms around Jamie's neck, and laid her head down on her Mommy's shoulder. Then she raised it again, for she had seen a tall man, wearing a cowboy hat and holding a great big gun. The man was coming toward them and his face looked very serious.

Cal was mystified by Jamie's behavior and he wanted an explanation. He'd had a sure shot at that animal, and a wounded lion was dangerous. He couldn't see any reason why he shouldn't have finished him off. But it was true, the animal hadn't seemed to be interested in attacking Mandy and when he moved off, it was almost thoughtfully, as though he knew something Cal didn't understand.

What could Jamie have been thinking? And what could that cougar have been thinking?

But there were Jamie and Mandy waiting there, kneeling together in the sunlight, their bright heads touching. And he felt his heart turn over and he knew, no matter what, he would love these two forever.

When he reached them, he knelt down beside them. He loved how the little girl's hair was a mirror image of her mother's and how her eyes held the same vivid blue brightness.

"Well, *you* sure came a long way," he said to her.

And then, to Jamie, he said quietly, "What were you thinking?"

And just as quietly, she answered him.

"I just understood, Cal. I saw it all so clearly. That cougar was not preying on Mandy. He wasn't hunting her. He wasn't going to hurt her. I just knew it. I knew he was following her because"—she hesitated because she knew it would sound crazy—"he was following her because . . ."

"Because what?"

"Because he was *protecting* her!"

"Jamie! That's crazy."

"I know. But I just know it. He's the same one, all these years. And you saw. He never did hurt her. He was there, watching her, watching over her, staying with her, the whole time. Just the way he's always stayed with me. You don't have to believe me. I just know it."

Cal studied her face, her beautiful, open, sincere face. A long, long, thoughtful look. And then he grinned at her.

"Sweetheart, I can see you and I are going to argue about this for all the years to come."

Jamie smiled back at him—a wicked, intimate little smile.

"I know," she said.

"I'm just glad it all worked out and no one got hurt."

"I know," she said.

They kissed briefly, and exchanged a long, long look.

Then Cal turned to Mandy, who'd been watching them intently.

"You left your tennis shoes down below," he said to her, "and I've got them in my truck. It's kind of a long walk. How about if I carry you?"

Mandy looked him over thoughtfully, for a long time. Then she held out her arms to him.

"Okay," she said, and Cal shifted his rifle to his left hand and hoisted Mandy onto his right shoulder where she laid her head down. And she slept all the way to the bottom of the canyon. She didn't even wake up when they arrived at the truck and Jamie climbed in and Cal put the exhausted child into her mother's arms.

"Okay, darlin'," he said as he got in behind the wheel and started the engine. "Let's take our little girl home."

ABOUT THE AUTHOR

Joan Myra Bronston grew up in New York City, married her college sweetheart, and went with him to Germany for a year while he was in the Army, where she worked as a telex operator and mail clerk. They then moved to Austria where Joan spent five years teaching at an international school. She is the mother of three wonderful girls and the grandmother of a super-wonderful grandson. Joan was also a secretary, social investigator, and psychiatric researcher, before entering law school and eventually becoming a corporate attorney. In addition to her years in Europe, Joan has lived in Pittsburgh, Chicago, and, for eighteen years, Salt Lake City. At last, she has closed the circle and returned to her first and most beloved—New York City. Visit her website at jmbronston.com, find her on Facebook, and follow her on Twitter @JMBronston.

She's just
getting started...

Her
Winning
Ways

J.M. Bronston

Summer on the Cape

J.M. Bronston

www.ingramcontent.com/pod-product-compliance
Lightning Source LLC
Chambersburg PA
CBHW020443270626
47155CB00022B/1352